The Bell Earth Witch

By Sam Wicker

First Edition

Printed in the United States of America

Paperback ISBN: 978-1-965770-04-7
Ebook ISBNs: 978-1-965770-02-3

Cover design by: Carder Wicker Writing
Published by Carder Wicker Writing

To the small town I grew up in. I both loved and hated you, still do. I wouldn't be who I am without you, but I grew outside of you, too. Here is the evidence of how much I know you, but the little I'm willing to share of you.

Chapter One

"Dammit, Bel!" She rubbed the back of her head where the racoon had used her hair to swing from her chair to her nightstand. He was shaking strands of green and blue off his front paws from his new perch. Happy he was human-hair-free at last, he slammed a paw on top of her screeching alarm clock until it stopped.

Nita growled at her familiar as soon as his first chatter hit her ears.

The thick bark-bound book still rested on her thighs, open to her great-grandfather's notes on splicing witch hazel with sassafras. He'd planned on making a super herb out of the two trees. A powerful aid for purifying blood for spells and contracts. It would cleanse disease from the body quicker, too. He had spliced one tree, still surviving to this day. It was far from his dream of being able to produce enough for the witch community.

Her soul itched for a new project, so why not one already started? One to make her ancestors proud. To distract her from worrying too much.

She closed the book with a gentle nudge and a wide yawn. Running calloused fingers over the smooth bark of the Ironwood cover, she slowed over his initials, H.B.B. under his carved rendition of the tree of life. It had been nigh fifty years since he had touched the grimoire, but she still sensed his power when she handled it. She stretched as she stood and placed the thick book back on the homemade wood slab shelf, crowded with books and knickknacks. Nita had inherited three grimoires, but her grandfather's was her favorite as she took the most after him.

Nita wandered downstairs to her kitchen, the smell of coffee leading her by the nose. She poured herself a cup and gave Belsauros, who had followed her, still chattering, a saucerful of the pungent black liquid. She took a sip before glaring at her raccoon. "You had the bed all to yourself last night. Stop it."

Bel showed his sharp teeth to her, Nita returned the favor.

After a quick breakfast of her last pair of strawberry toaster strudels and another cup of coffee, she started her usual routine. She thanked the old walnut house for still standing. Things seemed well within her little world. Her plants were prospering inside. The ancient Bell home was running the water through the pipes and the power through the wiring, with no flickering or sputtering. The land and her business were thriving under her care.

The greenhouse herbs and the garden thrived, too.

She wiped a red strawberry off on her jeans before popping it into her mouth. Carrying her new harvest into the greenhouse, she hosed everything down before drying most of it and packing it away in her old truck. The tailgate groaned and squeaked the whole way closed on the Silverado. Her business was Bell's Herbs & Spices. Another thing she had inherited from her family, but they never took it to the legal level.

Her great-grandparents had done very well with a corn-based liquid in jugs back in their day, the complete opposite side of the line where she wanted to be on lawful issues.

Nita still made some of it. Per her tax information that she turned in every quarter, the burning water was for 'medicinal' purposes only. And it was, for the most part.

She waited for Bel to climb into the cab before she got in herself. The old truck was a tank, and the only vehicle she ever felt safe in. It could go through rivers, not dried ones. Her brother had tested that theory a few times and failed most of them. Her fingers traced over his graduation tassel still hanging from the rear-view mirror and wished for him to be beside her.

Not having the heart to take it off, she found it brought her hope he might return to her sooner rather than later.

Camden returning would be a relief after she beat the life out of him and begged the earth to bring him back so she could do it again. She needed someone other than Belsauros to keep her company. Christy, her bestie, was great, but there were just some things her friend didn't understand about her world, and never would. In addition, Camden usually handled the public, another reason she desperately missed him.

Going into town each week filled her with dread. After driving for thirty minutes, she backed up to the back. People could hear her Silverado's loud noises from a mile away, but Clifford Greene claimed he was deaf in one ear and blind in the other. His place, Greene's Diner and Produce Barn, was a faded old barn covered in ancient tools of agriculture. On the inside, it was the best produce and home-made goodies shop in the tri-state area. Nita jerked her tailgate open from its usual stubborn position as the old man limped out of the double doors with a stainless steel cart rumble-rolling down the concrete ramp behind him.

"Hey Nita, girl," Clifford huffed as he pulled the cart flush with her truck. "Where's that rascal at?"

Nita smiled and pointed to the ground right before the raccoon stopped his tuck-and-roll to pull at the old man's jeans. "How ya doin' Mr. Greene?" she asked loudly so he could hear her.

Clifford Greene chuckled, showing a set of spotless, but loose, dentures. He grunted as he bent to give his favorite customer an ear of boiled and buttered corn he pulled from the now empty cart. "Can't complain, girl. Whatcha got fer me this week?"

"Strawberries, sage, watercress, my Peppered Citrus spices and Black Cherry powders." She pulled a jar out from a box, "And this is for your leg. Rub it on every mornin' and right before bed. Don't be shy 'bout it either, let it work in good."

Clifford's weathered face shifted into a thankful expression, taking the jar from her and reaching back to pull out his wallet from his faded overalls.

"No, go tell that wife of yours I want some pie and a big dollop of her homemade whipped cream," she said as she waved him off. She began loading the cart.

He chuckled, "Stubborn. Just like yer pa." He gave her a wink before hobbling back up into the shop.

Nita shook her head, "If he only knew, hm Bel?" She glanced at her raccoon slurping away at the juicy corn cob with whimpers of pleasure.

She liked Mr. Greene well enough. His family was a lot like hers. The market was now on the side of the main road going into town and passed down for several generations. It started from a traveling trading wagon to the squat wide building it was now. The old barn fooled tourists, but it was as state-of-the-art inside as a supermarket produce section. If not more so.

Greene's also held a diner; where his wife and four daughters created delicious, healthy dishes. And diabetic, coma-inducing desserts.

After loading everything onto the cart, priding herself on making a single trip this time, she pushed. It didn't budge. Nita gritted her teeth and threw her weight into the handcart, and realized one trip would not happen. She puffed the hair out of her eyes as she glanced around. She drew the symbols she needed on the cart's edge, humming softly to align her inner tone with the earth's. With her strength thrown into the trolley, it rumbled halfway up the ramp. Leaning against the cart as it dared demean her efforts by rolling back to her truck, she gathered herself for another push.

"Thought I recognized that ass."

The cart nearly won.

Sam Wicker

She heard Bel growl and glanced back and down the concrete slant. He was hovering over his decimated ear of corn as if he was a mother bear guarding her cub. She tilted her head, a strand of green falling in front of her eye as she spotted who had spoken leaning against her tailgate.

If she let the cart go, it would slam into him and cut him in half against her truck.

"Mason." She growled, still debating if the mess was worth it or not.

"Nita." He murmured, eyeing her growling familiar at his ankles with narrowed eyes, "See ya still got the rabid pest."

"Yeah, and you're still hella ugly." Nita clicked her tongue at Bel, trying to persuade him to back down. It wasn't worth her furred friend getting a disease.

"Lemme help with the buggy." Mason, all quarterback shaped and equal attitude, strode forward while giving the raccoon a wide berth.

"I got it." Pushing the cart again, she found anger was a powerful force.

Something brushed against her backside and her boot heel came up behind her in a mule kick. Mason grunted, stumbled, and held his crotch as he doubled over at the edge of the incline. She hissed as she moved the trolley into Greene's as her blood tried to boil its way out of her skin. As soon as it was on the flat of the processing floor beyond the double doors and plastic hangings, Nita whirled back around.

"Listen, you piece of shit, you touch me again, ever, and I'll gut you like the pig you are. Understand?" Her finger was in his face, and she wished it was something deadlier.

He gave her a crooked little smile as he half straightened, leaning against the smooth wood railing bracketing the concrete. "Piece of shit or pig, make up your mind, witch."

She stared him down. "I wish I was one so I could turn you into a frog and feed you to your chickens." He was the last person who deserved to know her truths.

He laughed and pushed off the railing to tower over her. He'd always been taller than her, even in school. His musk washed over her, Barbasol, Skoal, and Dial soap, and her stomach grew slick. She shifted away. And quickly regretted that move, too.

He stepped back into her face, taking advantage of her show of weakness, "One day, little witch, I'll prove to this town how you have everyone under your spell and you'll be done for."

"So you're just immune to my charms? Must be more shit than pig then. Can't charm feces." Nita spat back.

His wide hand was in her hair and the painful tug had her neck stretching, bared to him. When had he gotten so fast? He'd always been so big, all brawn.

"You've got somethin'. Even now I wanna have ya." His breath flowed hot over her jaw.

The slick in her stomach turned and rolled with his words. She swallowed the burning bile down before it could hit her tongue, "Too bad I still don't like shit on me. Why don't you go find another piece of shit and have a shit ton of babies?"

The growling along the ground prowled around, and she knew Bel was just waiting for her to allow him to attack. She couldn't let that happen, though. Not here.

"Mace! There you are. I thought you were gonna wait in the-Mason Dallas! Let her go right now!" an all too welcome voice screeched in anger.

She fell back on her heels and swallowed again as he loosened his hold on her. Nita observed with a shudder as he trailed his meaty fingers through the loose strands of her hair, a smirk still on his face. She nodded as Christy asked if she was okay. "Yeah, just having a little chat."

"Mason, if you had any brains left, you'd learn to leave everyone alone." Christy shoved the man with both of her hands on his chest. The brute barely budged.

"Didn't seem to mind me pawin' at you a few times, Jump." Mason sneered.

Nita and Christy shuddered together, but it was Christy's cheeks that pinked on the apples.

"It's fine, Chris. Come on, Miz Greene has me some pie waitin'." She watched as her bestie, Christy Jump, tried to square off with a boar while she was nothing but a willow slip. "Come on, I'll buy you a smoothie. Don't you have a shoot today?"

Mason made the first move.

Nita gave him a single finger salute and hated that he answered with a smirk and wink at her. She grabbed Christy's hand and put it on her elbow, walking with her to the front of the store and then into the Diner. "So, why are you riding with Mason?"

"My car's gone berserk again." Christy's voice drowned in a heavy sigh.

"Told ya not to pick anything pure electrical. Shoulda got a hybrid. All the copper and iron 'round here…" Nita rolled her eyes, hating that her bestie had to put up with Mason so much. But Christy also didn't mind as much as she pretended to. For some odd reason, her bestie kind of liked the neanderthal that was Mason Dallas.

"Yeah, yeah, I know. But it's just so cute!" She tilted her head back, sighing at the ceiling, and her blond hair fell off her shoulders in waves down her back before she straightened up to smile at Nita. "Wanna come with me to the shoot?"

"To Atlanta?!" Nita guffawed, "How 'bout no?"

"Come on! Save me from Mason!" Christy's voice held a whine well.

"He's gotta drive that way anyway!" Nita shook her head. If there was anything that she hated more than Mason, it was Atlanta.

She sat with her best friend at one of the small two-seater tables in the diner. A few other patrons nodded in Southern greeting to them, then continued their conversations or meals. Greene's Diner was well lit with rustic lanterns hanging from the dark wood ceiling and placed on carved dark stained stands along with walls. Flickering electric candle bulbs still gave the ambiance of being back in the old days, while providing smokeless and bright lighting. The booths were soft faux dark brown leather with polished maple tables. In the middle, between the booths and the counters, were wooden chairs with comfortable brown checkered cushions around smaller tables.

"Yeah, but that's him. I could ride with you. My bestest-estest friend ever." She smiled and batted her eyelashes.

"No." Nita would love to save her friend from having a two-hour ride with Mason, but her truck wouldn't make it. Nor would she. Overpopulated and full of concrete, Atlanta was a hellish place. She noted Christy's sigh and then looked around the diner.

Mrs. Greene and her girls decorated for each season or holiday. Each table had a single rose in a white vase with Happy Mother's Day written on it. The main entrance had banner with the same wish lettered in multi colored triangles swooped across the door's top glass. Vinyl flower bouquets decorate the door and corners of the showcases. The narrow glass display by the register held a few Mother's Day cakes with beautiful flowers and butterflies by the careful hand of Mrs. Greene herself. A few cupcakes and cookies with various floral shapes and designs filled the rest of the space. Next to that one was the regular fare of muffins, slices of cakes, pies, cookies, and other pastries. Next to it were fresh-baked breads that completed the diner's carbohydrate and sugar heaven. In the kitchen, open to the customers' view through a small rectangular window behind the counter, the scents of grilling meats wafted in to mingle in their noses with the yeasty scents.

"Here you go, Nita. Christy, you want the usual?" Mrs. Greene said with a warm smile that made wrinkles appear at all the corners of her alabaster face.

Nita grinned at Mrs. Greene as the lady bustled over to their table with her pie piled high with whipped cream. Without waiting for Christy to order, she dug in. The tartness of the lime hit her tongue before the sweet whipped cream smoothed it away. "New recipe?"

Mrs. Greene nodded with a small smile. "Trying out something. Sugar free, 'cept for the whip. Whaddya think?"

"It's good for it being sugar free!" Nita gushed.

"Thank you, little Nita." Mrs. Greene leaned over and kissed Nita's temple. "You been eatin'? Sleepin' okay?"

"Yes and yes, ma'am."

"Good." Mrs. Greene waved at one of her daughters, Abigail, who ran back to start on Christy's smoothie. She borrowed a chair from next to them and lowered herself into it at the girls' table; her hands wrung a clean dish towel she always had on her person. "Nita... dear... I don't quite know how to say this..."

An icy hand slid around Nita's heart. She rested her fork on her pie. "Say what?"

"Just spit it out, ma'am." Christy added, patting the old woman's ivory hands.

"Jasper's back, girls."

Nita wanted to find out exactly where he was that instant. Her blood boiled again, even after she had calmed down some. Bel climbed up into her lap and stuck a paw in the whipped cream to lick it off with loud smacks of his lips. "Is Camden with him?"

His words played through her mind. The last time she saw Jasper Price, he was getting out of his new truck, and her brother wasn't anywhere in sight. He told her Camden wanted to stay out west, Yellowstone, where they had been camping for the past week. 'He'll be back next week,' Jasper told her with that affable grin of his while he toyed with her braid. 'I like this new color on you.'

"No. No, he's not Nita." The elder woman smoothed the towel, only to wring it again.

She pulled the pie plate to Belsauros, letting his paws grab the pie and whipped topping in large handfuls before he stuffed them into his mouth. "Where's he staying?"

"I don't know, girl. I haven't seen him. Just heard he was back."

"Thanks, Mrs. Greene." Nita said, her lips trembling in an effort to smile.

"Now, calm down now." Mrs. Greene patted her arm, then squeezed her hand and held it in her own. "We don't understand what went on. Maybe Camden will call. Or maybe Jasper dropped him off at your house."

"When did he get back?" She asked, her whole body filling with too many emotions and she felt like she was about to shatter.

"Real early this morning. Hal saw him drive through town at four this morning."

"I gotta go." Nita said as she stood.

"Wait!" Christy grabbed her drink from Abigail, "I'm coming with you."

"You have a shoot." As if on cue, a horn blasted and all three women and a majority of the other patrons looked out the window to glare at the large red dually.

"Please, Nita, let him come to you." Christy said, putting a steady hand on her friend's shoulder.

"To hell with that."

Without even knowing what it was, Nita slapped down a bill before swiftly making her way back to her old truck. She ignored Christy and Mrs. Greene's calling out to her. Bel gripped tightly in her arms and he squirmed to loosen her hold. She didn't until she sat him in the truck. Gravel spit out from under her tires as the engine roared, and she hit the highway with a squeal of rubber on asphalt.

In a handful of minutes she was downtown, pulling into a parking spot in front of a white two-storey building. The bottom was a tool shop. She barrelled into the alley and up the groaning metal stairs to the door of the second-floor apartment. After banging on the baby blue entrance, she dropped her hand to her side. It throbbed along her knuckles, her skin tight from the abuse. She waited a few seconds, then banged again.

After a couple of minutes, she kicked the door, cursed, and leaned against the railing. Her foot throbbed too, and she swore she stubbed her toes even through her boots. "Damn him. Damn him to hell."

"Miss?"

She glared down at the man standing at the foot of the stairs.

"Um…he's…he's not in. Left a couple of hours ago…" The man looked anywhere but at her.

"Where to?" She winced at the bite in her voice as the guy stepped back, holding his hands up, palms facing her.

"No, miss."

"Fine. If he comes back, tell him Nita's looking for him. And if he don't wanna find an early grave, he better come find me."

"Yes, miss."

Chapter Two

"Hello, my mighty friend," Nita whispered, pressing her palms and forehead against the rough, sinewy bark. Her body thrummed. Her soul and mind eased. The ancient magic pulled away her unease and anger and left her with peace. The leaves of the old ironwood tree rustled, calming and comforting her with softness and love.

"You always know how to make things better." She stood still for a while, breathing in and out and relishing the vitality and comfort it brought her. "Jasper is back. Camden is not. Where is he? Where is my brother?"

The old ironwood rumbled deep within its core. She sensed the power stretching, searching. She knew the lines of magic had shared nothing with the old tree and it was desperately scouring their land again.

A depressed sensation seeped into her, flowing from the points she touched the tree and ground to her heart.

"He will come back. You still have me." A warmth radiated, still tinged with the sorrow.

The ironwood had witnessed many births, deaths, joys, and sorrows. It shared hopes and dreams with her family. It held true, a steady constant, a force she leaned on and gave more to when she could. Now she needed its strength.

Jasper hadn't come by. Nor had he called. She had waited the entire night, sleepless. When she caught a few minutes of sleep, she dreamt of Camden in a darkened space, void of all things good, only evil to keep him company.

Her face still felt swollen and bruised from the tears she cried upon waking. After completing her morning chores, she found herself at the tree again. Needing its comfort.

A little tremor tickled her fingertips.

She groaned inwardly and said, "No rest for the wicked, hm?"

The tree's leaves shook, and she felt the warmth as if the old thing had smiled. "You have such a dry sense of humor. I'll be back soon." She hummed to the tree for a moment, her voice meeting the tone of its magic. And she hummed in the same tone on her way back.

The dead leaves from the previous fall and winter crunched under her bare feet. When she broke out of the tree line, soft mossy grass soothed and squeezed up between her toes as she walked. Until she met the freshly tilled soil she had worked that morning. It vibrated gently from the coming stranger.

She ran to the greenhouse as the car crested the hill, before it wound its way down the half moon of the drive that circled to her house. She tugged on her boots, ran her fingers through her hair to smooth it, and stepped out to meet them.

A young couple, possibly around her age, slipped free of the little silver coup.

Nita plastered a smile on her face, "Welcome, how can I help you?"

"Is this Bell's Herbs and Spices?" He asked, his voice a light tenor and holding the smile he had on his pale face.

"Yes, sir. I'm Nita Bell." She held out her hand. He had a firm handshake, as did his wife, who had a lovely little amethyst wedding ring on her slender finger.

"I'm Derek and this is my wife, Eve. We're here…well…Honey?" His pale cheeks turned pink and his hand that had just shook hers raised to the back of his neck.

"We're trying to get pregnant." Eve said with a roll of her doe brown eyes, "I'm a…I was told that you might help us."

"Did the Smiths send you?" Nita asked, remembering that Mrs. Smith had called earlier that month to inform her of a couple that might find her.

"Oh, yes!" Eve smiled, "Small town, right?"

Nita tried a laugh and managed one that wasn't creepy or a bark. It was a win in her book, even if it was weak, "Yup. Come right this way. Don't mind the raccoon, he's safe."

"Aw!" Eve exclaimed, automatically dropping into a crouch to reach for Belsauros.

"Honey, she said safe, not to pet!" Derek whispered loudly as he tugged her back up.

"It's fine. He likes the attention." Nita swallowed to clear a frog in her throat, "Now… what exactly is the problem? I assume you have been to a physician?"

"Yes. I was told to bring you our bloodwork, allergies, and ancestry? Is that right?" Eve asked as she pulled a file out of her monster of a blue leather bag.

"Yes, that's correct." Nita took the folder and led them to her greenhouse. Just outside, she had set up a small patio set under a large overhang. She motioned to the chairs, "Can I get you anything to drink before I dive in?"

"No, thanks." Derek said as he sat down on the edge of his chair.

Eve smiled, her fingers clutching the strap of her bag over her cream colored t-shirt sporting a logo Nita didn't recognize, "Do you have any water?"

"Only the best water." Nita gave that fake smile again as she ducked into the greenhouse and took a jug out of her mini fridge and three clean glasses. She poured each of them full.

"Oh, I didn't want..." Derek held up his hands, waving them gently behind the glass in front of him.

"I know, it's a southern hospitality thing." Nita allowed herself the small dig at his accent. Very northern, while Eve's was a light drawl of southern lady.

She sat and flipped through their files, looking for specific points of interest that her nutritionist and one of the local doctors had taught her to look for. Not seeing any of the normal red flags, she handed the folder back to Eve. "Thank you."

"This is great water. What brand is it?" Eve turned the jug on the table, looking for a label.

"It's from my well."

"It's well water?! Isn't that...unsanitary?" Derek nearly choked on the sip he'd finally taken.

Nita laughed at the absurdity, "No, no. We are up to code on everything. Proper filters and all that. Plus, this stream comes down from those mountains...untouched because they are forest service property."

"That's nice." The wife nodded, taking a longer draught of the water and licking her pink lips.

"From what I've seen, I should have no problem helping you. I must ask, though, which one of you is sterile?" Nita flicked her gaze between them, noting the reddening of Derek's cheeks again. Each couple was different, and this one had the male being shy.

"I am," Eve said with a frown. "Not that I'm sterile, I just...my eggs don't produce often."

"I see. I will need two days to make a special blend according to your body chemistry and needs." Nita leaned forward, as did Eve and Derek. "This is not a miracle cure. It won't help overnight. It may not happen for months. Like any medication, this takes time to settle into your system to work properly. Understood?"

"Yes, of course!"

"Good. Can you come back here in two days' time? That will be a Thursday." Nita felt a little more relaxed at Eve's enthusiasm.

"Yes, yes, of course." Eve smiled.

"I will have a supplement for you as well. I noticed your iron is low." Nita said to Derek.

"Thank you." He looked at his wife, then back at Nita, "How much?"

"Bring me Mrs. Greene's cookie of the day and eighty dollars. You will receive enough for six months for both of you. After that, if there is no baby, I will provide another six months' worth for half the price and make it more potent."

"That's...that's not bad." Derek's eyes were wide while his eyebrows tried to hide in his blond hairline.

"Thank you, see you on Thursday." Nita shook their hands again as they stood.

She waited until their car had disappeared back over the hill before she turned to Bel. She held out her hand. Bel dropped four strands of each of their hair in her palm. "That's a brilliant fat devil."

Bel chittered at her.

The little pansy reached over and flipped on the radio once Nita, and Bel entered the greenhouse. She smiled as smooth jazz filled the air. Humming again, she set her singing to work mode, her inner tone thrumming with those of the plants in the greenhouse and the earth beneath her feet. She kicked off her boots, feeling the magic of the land tickle her toes.

Picking up two mortar and pestles, she set them on her workbench. Her fingers dipped into the earth at her feet, and then into a small pail of water by her bench, she drew a series of runes and shapes along each tool while humming softly. Her vocals gathered the magic from her land and her body while the runes wrested it into her tools. Bits of the sounds and magic danced along each plant until it found what it needed, the magic tones rested, resonating with the plant.

Those plants began a tone, becoming one with hers.

Once Belsauros gently gathered what was needed from each humming plant, the magic danced to the next one.

Nita began her spell. Humming as she ground the herbs she needed, and soaked the others in a small teacup full of fresh water at her side. The hairs she placed in the cup and the water began vibrating within.

For an hour, Nita worked unhindered. Until a miniscule vibration in her toes told her that something else was coming. She began humming softer until her tones waned to silence. The magic seeped back into the earth and into her body. She put the teacup and tools away on a wide wooden table in her 'office' space. She wrote a note on where in the song she left off, before putting her boots on and stepping outside in time to see the next car crest on the hilltop.

She smiled as she recognized the car.

The lady that stepped out was in her mid-fifties, with short salt and pepper hair and a roundness to her that softened her features. "Mrs. Hawkins, how are you doing today?"

"Fine, just fine, Nita." Mrs. Hawkins toddled over. "I'm a day early, but I've got to take little Victor into Ellijay tomorrow."

"It's quite alright, I always have a supply of your needs. How is he doing?" Nita asked, holding out a hand to help Mrs. Hawkins steady herself over the soft earth and grasses next to her greenhouse.

"He's much better, thank you. That little rascal climbed up another tree and nearly fell to break his other arm! Boys! How he clumb up it with one arm in a cast is beyond me."

Nita laughed, "Boys will always scare their mothers and grandmothers." She ducked inside her greenhouse, leaving the door open for her to follow. "How is retired life?"

"Can't figure out how I had time to teach!" Mrs. Hawkins laughed, leaning against the frame of the door. "I need to see if they'll take me back."

Nita shook her head and grinned, "They would, so you better think hard on that." She grabbed a few tins and a bottle of powders to place them in a cloth bag. "Here you are."

"How much is it again, Nita?" Mrs. Hawkins asked as she dug around in her multi-colored patchwork skirt.

"Thirty-five, ma'am." Nita answered, glad that she had never charged her old teacher much.

"You're a lifesaver." Mrs. Hawkins handed her two twenties. "Keep the change." She turned and walked toward the door, then stopped to look back, "Any news on Camden, yet?"

"No, ma'am." Nita felt her heart sink as her former teacher's face fell into a frown.

"I'm sorry dear. He'll turn up soon. Just you wait." The elder woman patted the old greenhouse, as if reassuring it, too.

"I hope so. Thank you, Mrs. Hawkins."

"Keep your chin up. I'll see you next month, if not in town, before then." Mrs. Hawkins picked her way slowly across the path back to her vehicle.

"Yes, ma'am." Nita noted the stiffness in the lady's shuffling gait. "I need to make her more. Seems like she's needing to use more," she told herself, the best way for her to remember when she had nothing to write on.

Nita sighed and sat on her bench. "What do ya say, Bel? Ready to check on everything, then go rest?"

Sam Wicker

When Bel climbed up into her lap, and then onto her back and shoulders, she smiled. He nuzzled into her neck and cheek.
"Yeah, I think so too."

Chapter Three

"She slipped into the cool waters. Letting herself sink, she let the water hold her weightless. She breached the surface, taking a deep breath before floating on her back. Leaves rustled in the light breeze, playing through the tree branches overhead. "

"What are you talking about?" Jasper couldn't help but ask. It wasn't often Wade talked much. Gus was usually the mouth.

"Oh, hun, she's there again. Jasper!" Gus trotted over to the edge of the balcony, waving his hands.

"Yeah?" Jasper stood, sliding the hammer home in his belt before walking over to the men. Both had salt and pepper looks going on. Gus was slimmer, shorter by a handful of inches from his partner Wade. Wade was built like a track runner, all long limbs and quick reflexes even at his middle of the road age. "What's up?"

"Do you see that little beauty?" Gus asked as he practically bounced on the balls of his feet in his white fuzzy slippers.

Jasper leaned on the railing he had just finished building the day before. "What tree am I supposed to be looking in now?"

"Oh no, my little hot carpenter bun, that little pond in the creek down there."

He followed Gus' finger down the mountain to the creek. Green hair webbed out around her like a wide halo and his breath caught in his lungs. His neck, face and ears heated, and a warmth spread in his gut. Reeling himself in, he looked away, "That's... I'll go talk to her." *And probably get killed.*

"Please don't. Seems like she's done that for years. Has ever since we built this house. I don't want to ruin her lifestyle. I just would like to know that angel's name. She's inspired plenty of his words of late." Gus gushed.

Jasper cleared his throat to hide his groan, "It's Nita, Nita Bell."

"Oh! that's right. Her property borders ours. Bell's Herbs, I think?" Gus flapped his hands, blue eyes wide and face bright.

"That's the one."

"You've met?" Wade spoke up for the first time since Nita made her nymph-like appearance.

"Yeah. Small town." Jasper tried to pawn it off as simply as he could. If the men only knew half of the story between him and Nita he'd never have peace.

"Think it's a bit more than that. You've been three different shades, boy." Wade's neatly trimmed brows rose toward his widow's peak hairline.

"What straight man wouldn't!" Gus chuckled with a grin and wink at Jasper. "Small town? How well do you know her, hm?"

"I… her brother's my best friend. Camden, the one missing?" It would not get easier, not at all.

"Oh," both men sobered.

"Jasper, you've been here or home sleeping since you've gotten back. You haven't talked to her yet, have you?" Gus' hands were still on the move, fluttering together in wringing worry.

"I need to finish this, then I'll drop by and talk to her." He turned back to his work.

"No, I think you should go now." Gus placed his hands on his narrow silk covered hips.

Jasper laughed sarcastically, "Not while she's naked. Nope."

"He's red again. I think he's done it before." Wade had a twist to his lips before he covered them with a sip from his coffee mug.

Jasper tried not to remember the last time he had snuck up on Nita bathing in the creek. He rubbed the back of his neck, cursing softly as he felt the heat of his embarrassment on his palm. These guys always needled out his secrets. He turned, starting back to work on the last of the banister he needed to bolt down at the corner of the new staircase leading to the third floor.

It was some of his finest work. Even if he had taken a longer break from it than he had expected. Taking two weeks' vacation to go with Camden camping in Yellowstone, then another week to find his best friend when he didn't answer any messages. He was still getting daily calls from the cops out there, updating him on their search. Luckily, the men on the deck with him were understanding, and pushed for him to stay in the National Park.

He couldn't do that to Nita. He couldn't leave her alone. Even if he still couldn't bring himself to face her.

His landlord badgered him about it, too. Nita had scared that man out of his wits. Jasper just wished he had been a fly on the wall to see it that day.

Listening to the men talk behind him as if he wasn't there, between hammering and drilling, he wished for a young, carefree Nita. Not a Nita haunted by a missing brother, and alone. A Nita that had to stand tough, like that old ironwood, and not cry or ask for help like she needed.

Nita had always been the tree, while Camden had been the wind.

Jasper was always in-between, translating them from one to the other, and often failing.

"I wonder how it feels to be in love with your best friend's sister. I mean, did Camden know?" Gus crooned behind him.

"No."

A gasp and another sound like the fluttering of hands again, "So you are in love?! Fascinating!"

Jasper almost drilled his thumb under the bit. "Dammit, Gus, I'm working."

"And? You should drive down to that little angel and tell her your feelings. Also, updating her on her brother." Gus put his hand on top of the drill.

"She's going to kill me. You know that, right?" Jasper glared at the hand, then up into Gus' blue eyes.

"Tell her about bathing first. She'll at least wonder if she's going to have witnesses. Maybe you can get away then." Wade offered with another twist to his lips.

Jasper tested his work. Then pulled himself up by the finished banister. All he needed to do was a bit of decorating, as the men wanted to hang baskets of flowers off the deck rail and a few of the supports, and clean up. He'd wind some fake vines through the supports on the stairs, even though the couple hadn't thought of doing that yet. Then he could start on their other projects and his next clients. He figured he could take another trip out to Yellowstone in two weeks, and still be able to pay his bills.

Polish and stain. He'd need to do that soon, too. He'd have to consult old man Greene's knee and almanac to see if the weather would hold out. Or Nita, if she'd talk to him.

"You can shower here." Gus grinned.

"Will you promise not to steal my clothes this time?" Jasper brought his shoulders down from his ears and began unbuckling his tool belt.

"Yes, yes. Now I know you're all straight and narrow, I'll be on my best behavior." Gus waved a hand, even as his bottom lip protruded.

Jasper took off his cap, scratching at an itch on the top of his head, before sliding it back on. He needed a haircut. The strands wanted to push his cap back off the top of his head and always tickled his ears.

"Maybe we should dress him." Wade gave another winning suggestion.

"We should!" Gus crowed, kissing Wade and then marching toward Jasper. "Come! We shall dress you.

Wade's clothes should fit perfectly! Maybe a little tight on the chest and biceps, but that will be beneficial!"

"Huh? Wait…no…wha-?" Jasper tried to dig in his heels, but Wade moved to help his husband. With the two men pushing and steering him toward the master bath, Jasper found that he no longer had his belt around his waist and his shirt was halfway off by the time they made it to the bedroom. "Oi! Just stop right here! Hellfire, what are you two goin' on about now?" He couldn't understand when they started chattering like squirrels. Jasper swore they had their own language.

He tugged his shirt off, cursing as his cap flipped off with it and disappeared into the folds. Jasper brushed the sweaty brown, almost dirty blonde strands back from his eyes and glared at the men. The heat seeped back into his neck and ears as Gus fanned himself, leaning against Wade. "Stop it."

"Just take the ego boost. From what little we've gathered about this Nita, you might need it." Wade said, motioning to Jasper's pants and boots.

"Oh! scents! and don't you dare shave that scruff! Surely she likes the whole man-sexual thing like any sane woman would!" Gus padded into the bathroom. The water in the shower started full blast a second later. "She's an herbalist! What does she like? Oh wait, lavender! Nevermind."

Jasper shook his head, glaring a moment at Wade, "You know that's not going to work."

"Let him pretend." Wade's simple grin spread with a lift of his narrow shoulder.

He strode into the bath, shoved Gus out, and took a shower in the most lavish bathroom he'd ever been in. The country boy didn't have to turn to rinse because of five shower heads. He was a touch jealous of the money the two made, but they paid him well. Too well. And they were good people.

If a little too grabby. At times, a bit too eager to see his bare skin too.

During his rinse, Gus waltzed back in and offered him a towel. Jasper had long forgotten how to be bashful around these men, and during his days as a basketball player in school. He let Gus dry and style his hair after he dried his skin and wrapped the towel around himself.

His cap was nowhere to be seen.

"You didn't burn it, did you?" Jasper's brows twitched as he narrowed his eyes at Gus.

"Nope. Just well hidden." Gus' grin was too wide to be innocent.

Jasper kept himself from sighing and wondered how many times he had sighed because of the gay couple. "Could really use it. Not like this styling stuff is gonna matter once I'm on the road, with the windows down…"

"You have an AC in that thing." Gus admonished.

"It's such a pretty day." He continued as if he was talking about the prettiest thing in all the world or the sweetest ice cream.

"Air conditioning. I'll turn it on for you once you crank it up. Show you how it works, Mister cave dweller." Gus' hands were back on his hips.

He couldn't help but chuckle, "Alright, Gus. Let's see what you've done to me. The hell? It's a mess!"

"Mussed! So she'll want to run her fingers through it!" Making his point, Gus worked his fingers through the strands again.

He eyed the gay man, "Look, I know you write romance novels, but this ain't one of 'em."

"It's gonna be. Now, remember everything and give me a full report." The silk pajama'd one stood at attention, comb smacking the palm of his hand like a whip.

He shook his head and pushed away a few strands of his stupid hair as it fell in front of his eyes, only to have Gus swat his hand. "What?"

"Let her do it!"

"She's not here!"

"Don't make me beat you." Gus waggled a comb at him. "Now, go get dressed. It's laid out for you on the bed."

He steeled himself, expecting some kind of floral shirt nonsense. He raised a brow at the light red and black checkered flannel and boot cut jeans. They brushed his boots off and had them waiting for him at the base of the bed, too. He looked at Wade, who was sitting in his reading chair in the room's corner.

Wade shrugged with a slow grin.

Jasper got dressed and was rolling up the sleeves when Gus came back in.

"Yes, I like it. It's you, but not you. A cleaner you. A lumber sexual you."

"Yup, that doesn't make this awkward at all." Happy now that the sleeves weren't showing off that the shirt was too small for him. He gave a wave as he started to the door, "Thanks dads, don't wait up."

Gus wailed, "Aww, our little boy is all grown up and making us promises he can't keep already!"

Finishing up Eve's medicine, Nita stood from the bench and took the time to stretch. Her grandmother had been a stickler for stretching after each segment of work. There had to be something to it, because until her last days, her grandmother could still move around fairly well for being in her eighties.

She dug her toes into the rich dirt and smiled as Bel stretched with her. Nita leaned down, brushing the ground with her fingertips. She stopped, studying the tingling warning her land sent her. The Bell witch stepped out of the greenhouse, watching the headlights bounce off the trees between her and the truck in the gray shadow of the mountain sunset.

She shaded her eyes, and as the truck rolled to a stop, the driver cut the lights. A new, shining silver Silverado sat beside her rusting blue one. Her land thrummed still, little shoots of electrical shocks tickling the bottom of her feet like excited little wires. A signal her land welcomed whoever it was home.

Before he slid out of the door, her heart dropped and fluttered at the same time.

"Hey, Bellbean."

Her body tightened, his voice tickling over her like the tendrils of magic in her land. She clamped down on them, the feelings. "You have no right to call me that anymore."

Her feet carried her to him, and before she knew it, she shoved him. His body slammed into the side of his truck. She stared into those wide chocolate eyes. "Where is he?"

"I don't know, Bel- Nita." His hand raised toward her, paused, and dropped to his side.

She glared at that hand, then looked back into his eyes. She folded her arms under her breasts as she stepped away, trying to keep the magic encased, to keep her heart from leaping toward him. "Why don't you know? What did you do to him?"

"I didn't do anything to him! I-"

"Why did you leave him alone?!" Her fists knocked into his chest as she interrupted him.

His hands covered hers, holding them. She could feel his heartbeat against her wrists. "He wanted to stay. I had to work. Nita..."

"I don't need an excuse, Jasper." The anger swarmed with the thrill of his gentle touch of calloused hands and soft flannel.

His teeth clicked shut, then he started again, "He told me he would be fine. I thought he would be fine. It's…it's Cam. He shoulda been fine."

She felt his body tremble under her hands as he dropped his head. Strands of his hair fluttered and tickled her nose as she stepped into him. His breathing turned ragged, and his hands loosened over hers.

Sadness arced from her toes to her lungs, making her breath hitch. The earth translated his movements to her and her heart broke. Nita pressed her forehead to his. He smelled good. She breathed him in, deep. He was as home to her as her land. He'd been part of her life for so long.

"I'm so sorry." His words growled through his emotions.

Anger roiled through her. The need to blame someone, him, reared, and she leapt back. No longer enveloped by his scent, she seethed, even as his red-rimmed eyes sought hers out. "You left him alone."

"I know."

"You- you left me alone." The rage slipped to depression in a quick drop of her heart.

He slumped against his truck, deflated. "I know."

Her claws wanted to rip his face apart. She wanted to tear that shirt off of him. She wanted to beat dents into his brand new truck. Nita wanted to see if he tasted as good as he smelled.

Magic snaked up inside her like a shock of ice, and she held it in her. She screamed the tone it wanted, letting the anger and pain out that way instead of through beating him and his. She whirled on her heels and half marched, half slid on the magicked earth under her feet to her house.

"Nita wait!"

She cut his voice off by slamming the door behind her. The boards creaked under her weight, under the desperation she carried. She crouched by the kitchen island, willing the ties of the earth to slow and ease. Willing her emotions back down so the lines would feed off it.

The door swung open, and she whirled, standing her ground.

Jasper caught her fist with his jaw, "Damn…woman, stop!" He shook his head after catching himself against the entrance. "Wait…don't…" He dodged another punch by catching it in his palm. "I need to tell you something."

"Better be a lot of things!" She tried jerking her hand free. Then tried another punch with her free hand. She blinked, he'd used her move against her as she faced the island. Her body curled into his, her back to his chest. His breath on her temple, and the anger seeped into the earth as if it'd never existed in the first place.

"Just be still. Give me a moment." His voice was soft, the sadness still drowned his words. Then he rambled, words flowing like water in her creek. "Camden and I went out there on vacation. He always wanted to go. To see or feel how the earth felt. He planned it, I didn't know. I thought we were all going together, the three of us, but he loaded up my truck with our gear and you were nowhere around. He said you wanted to work." He struggled for words. "I just… I just figured you didn't want to be stuck in a truck with us for that long."

Nita nodded. She had thought of that, too. It would've been hell. That, and Camden threatened he would read Jasper her high school journal if she came along. He had stolen it, and she had yet to find where he hid it.

"So we went. I drove most of it because I don't trust him with a new anything." He paused, a half chuckle broken by his earlier grief. "When we got there, we explored. Did the normal touristy thing. He took a ton of pictures. He talked about weird stuff."

"Like what?" She asked when he paused. Her body was too aware of him holding her captive against the granite of her kitchen island.

His chest and belly pressed into her further, before his breath released hot against her cheek. He had recently brushed his teeth. Warmth encased her.

"Moving there. Living there. He said it felt so alive. He did. The land did. Everything."

Something tore in her heart, "He ran away?"

"No. Yes? The park rangers and police say there's no proof of a struggle where he was camped last. It's all in evidence, they won't let me bring anything home, yet."

She turned, his grip loosened on her, "You've been talking to the cops?"

"Yeah, Nita! I mean, what else could I do? You couldn't get a hold of him on his cell, neither could I. No one had seen him in days. Weeks."

"I called them to report him missing when you came back without him and I couldn't reach him for two days. They said they were already looking for him."

"They told me that. They've been trying to call you…"

"Oh…" Nita felt her world crumble around her.

He grunted in disappointment, rolling his head back to look up at the ceiling, "We really need to figure out how to have a better signal out here. Or you a phone that isn't a brick."

"My phone's just fine!" Nita at least had a thing to blame now. She felt the anger dissipate even more.

Jasper released her, pulling his phone out of his back pocket. He tapped it a few times and voicemails started playing. He played through a handful of them, each from park rangers and police on Camden's missing case. "Now you know what I do."

"You didn't kill him?"

Jasper stepped back, "What?"

"You didn't kill him, did you?" She asked, looking from one brown eye to the other. His eyes were wide on hers, the color draining from his tanned face.

"Are you joking? You're joking, right?" He stepped toward her, his hand coming up to cup her face, "Nita… please…"

His touch was so familiar. His eyes begging, his mouth ajar. Her emotions and magic were all over the place. She wasn't sure if it was him or her, but she fit her lips to his. Jasper's hair was soft in-between her fingers, like silk threads.

"Nita…" he whispered against her lips.

She pressed another kiss onto him. The desire from her teens threading through her. All those years of wanting to do what she was doing now. She pushed her body against his. His arms wrapped around her, warm and hard.

Then his tongue was against hers and she tasted the mint she had smelled before.

Her lungs burned, and she pulled back, resting her forehead against his chest.

His breathing sounded as ragged as hers. She waited on his revulsion. He didn't pull away. Jasper kept holding her.

"So… you kiss the guy you think killed your brother?" Amusement laced his words.

She shook her head, "I'm… I feel like I'm going crazy."

"You sound it."

"Ass."

His chuckle was low and deep, "There's my Bellbean." His voice was a whisper, his lips against the top of her head, pressing a kiss on her hair.

Chapter Four

Nita jerked awake, sitting up with a growl. Something was odd. She listened, sitting completely still in her bed. Her head throbbed, and she stared at her pajamas, still on the end of the bed. The clothing she wore yesterday was still on her person.

She tried to remember last night. She still felt his arms around her. With a lick of her lips, she no longer tasted him; only the bad breath that happened each night and into the morning. What had awakened her?

She took a deep breath in. The smell of eggs and bacon stirred her stomach into a grumbling beast. How had she ended up in her bed? Hadn't they sat at the kitchen counter and talked last night?

Wait…

She slid out of bed, padding over to her door while missing the board that creaked the loudest. Nita pulled her door open a crack. She could hear the sizzle of a frying pan as the radio paused between songs. David Bowie's Dancing In The Street came on, drowning out the sounds of breakfast making.

Who would make her breakfast? No, who would make breakfast other than herself? And burning toast. The acrid smell wafted up to her before she shut the door back with a soft click.

Jasper.

Had he spent the night?

She eyed her bed. Not with her, he didn't. That was good. She hadn't done something stupid like that. He would mark her as one of his conquests and move on. She shook her head, then cringed as she caught sight of herself in the mirror. Her hair was everywhere.

She rushed across the hall and jumped into the shower. After a bit of a shock from the cold water, the old house decided she could use a scalding shower instead.

Muttering to herself, she washed, dried off, and opened the door.

"Hey."

She slammed the door in his face and grabbed her towel back off her hook. She wrapped it around herself, crouching into a ball and covering her face in her hands. How had she forgotten he was here and just walked right out into him, all naked?

"H-hey...um... I uh... you smell great?" His voice was strained through the door.

She heard him curse under his breath, call himself a stupid child, and then clear his throat.

"There's breakfast."

His voice cracked on the last syllable, and she groaned.

"I'm sorry!" Nita said around her heart in her throat.

"F-for what?" He sounded surprised.

"For being naked?" She pressed the backs of her hands to her face, trying to cool her cheeks down. Then pressed her forehead against the cool porcelain of the sink edge.

"I like you naked."

A long pause hung in the air between them.

"I mean! It's great. I didn't mind at all. In fact, you can eat naked. If you want." In a lower voice, he said, "Jesus Christ, Jasper, what the hell are you saying? Idiot." After another pause he added, "I'll... I'll go downstairs now..."

"'Kay," she said, feeling her skin burning, and it wasn't at all from the shower. She listened to his footfalls, then the groan of the third step from the bottom, and whimpered. "Just... just swallow me whole, old house. Please, for once in your life, just swallow me whole when I ask!"

The pipes made a shaking sound in the old walls and she swore the house was laughing at her. She stood, pressing her ear against the door. Once, a long time ago, the boys tricked her into thinking they went downstairs, and they hadn't. She'd almost peed her pants from their tickle tackle.

She peeked out, and not seeing him, ran back across the hall to her room to get dressed. Nita debated on whether she should go downstairs. She was about to crawl back into bed when she heard a yell, a curse, then another grumbling curse from downstairs.

Nita ran down the stairs before she realized she had left her room. At the entryway from the hall to the kitchen, she stopped. Stared.

Her raccoon was growling while grabbing a piece of bacon that Jasper had gripped in his teeth. One hand had a hold of Belsauros' right back leg, while the other kept swatting clawed paws from his face. He stood over a fallen chair, weaving a little for balance while fighting off the fat fur ball.

"Itsch mine! Off! leggo!" Jasper growled around the bacon in his teeth.

Nita sighed, plucking Belsauros from Jasper's grip and holding the raccoon to her chest. Her face burned when Jasper looked at her. His face grew red, too. Was he embarrassed about fighting with Bel?

Bel ate the half of bacon he had stolen from Jasper quickly.

"He's not used to sharing." Nita said weakly from behind Belsauros' thick fur.

"Apparently." Jasper muttered, rubbing the back of his neck. He bent to pick up the chair, "I uh… so… did you have a nice shower?" He grimaced and shook his head, his face tomato hued.

"Yeah." She sat. Finding herself across from him at the table, she cursed her luck. They stared at each other for a moment as Bel reached for her plate and stole a burnt piece of toast. He sniffed it, then flung it at Jasper.

"Hey! Go pick that up!" Jasper snapped his fingers in Bel's face and then pointed to the toast that landed on the floor after he had dodged it.

Bel huffed.

Nita sat him on the floor, "Don't do that to him."

"He needs discipline." Jasper snapped his fingers again, trying to get the raccoon to do as he was told.

"He does not! He's used to just me!" Nita ran her hand down Bel's back.

"Bel's been around long enough to be used to me, too." Jasper returned to eating, eying Belsauros.

She gritted her teeth, "Don't tell me how to raise my animals." The burning in her face changed, still there, but not as hot.

"I'm not! He wasted food!" He defended himself, pointing back to the toast on the floor with his empty fork. "It's burned!"

"Yeah, it ain't perfect, but I tried, dammit! How was I supposed to do anything with your running around naked upstairs?" Jasper said, and his eyes widened as they swung to her from the fur ball at her side.

"I wasn't running around naked upstairs! What made you come up, anyway? Hm? Wanted to see me naked so you could make fun of me like you used to?" The heat returned, blistering hot. Her heart thrummed in her chest, and she wondered what was getting into her. Little sniping contests between them like this always happened. It was normal. Why was today different?

"Huh? No, I was gonna ask... I couldn't... the coffee pot won't turn on." A blush on Jasper was like a balm to her.

"It's on a timer." Nita drawled, "For daybreak."

"How am I supposed to know that with this house acting all weird? Hell, half the time I was cooking, the gas flickered off and on! And the toaster cut itself off three times while the bread was in it! You should have these things fixed by now, Nita. You can't live like this."

"I have and I will. Who are you to tell me what to do again? You've not been around that much!" Nita felt her hair bristle like Bel's fur when he was angry. She wished she had his teeth so it would be scary if she growled. Why was she doing all this without coffee?

"I work!" Jasper said with less venom than when he told her to fix her place up.

"No shit. So do I." Nita spat back.

"What the hell are you even yelling at me for?"

"You're the one that started yelling." Nita bit out as the coffee pot began percolating.

Jasper took a deep breath in, then released it, eying the coffee pot. "Look… I-"

"Now what? Another excuse?" Nita didn't know where that came from, and she hated her tongue for spilling it before her brain could think over whether the words were worth saying or not.

He stared at her, his jaw tight, "If you'd let me finish talking, you'd know by now."

A chill crawled half up her spine at the slow calm in his words. She swallowed, trying to force the feeling to go away. The coffee couldn't be done soon enough.

"I make plans, and sometimes they fall through. I don't make excuses. I tell you what happened, and that's that." He paused, watching her, "You've known me for so long and you still think I want to tell you how to live? I just… I'm just worried about you. This house could go haywire and burn down. Or it could burn you with that gas acting like it does. Something." He stood, going over to fill a coffee mug full and bringing it over to her. He set it down in front of her.

"I'm not a child." Nita said, still picking up the coffee cup and taking a good long drought out of it. At least the warmth spread, not staying in her face.

"Oh, no." He laughed, running a hand over his face, then both through his hair, holding it back from his face by resting his hands on top of his head. "You've never been a child and you are definitely all woman now. I-" he cleared his throat, his face going red again, "I should keep my mouth shut."

He blinked, "Shit. I forgot to tell you. I came here last night to warn you."

"Warn me?" Nita asked after she drank down half the coffee left in her mug.

"Yeah, the er... swimmin' hole? There's a gay couple that live above it. Can't really see it from the hole, but they can sure see you." Jasper said as he sat back down across from her, his voice softer.

Her face was determined to burn off. "They can?"

"Yeah, asked me who you were yesterday. Gus is a writer, and he's used your look, I guess, as inspiration." Jasper lifted a shoulder, "Thought I should tell ya."

"So, you'd rather tell me about you and two gay guys watching me swim naked than about my missing brother?" Again, her mouth ran away with her before her brain could catch up.

When he said nothing, Nita squeezed her eyes shut and shook her head. "Tell me something, Jasper, why is that more important to you than Camden? Than my sanity? Than me not being alone to burn down the house because I'm so inept?" She wasn't sure when she had gotten in his face.

"It isn't! I thought the rangers and cops had been in touch with you. Hell, maybe Camden's called and your shitty little phone didn't have a signal." Jasper said, not backing down from her.

She'd thought of that before. Having him say it to her face made her heart hurt. "I have a landline still..."

"Nita..." he said with a heavy breath, resting his hands on her shoulders, "When are you within range of that?"

"All the time. Except-"

Jasper interrupted her to say, "When you're tilling. When you're gathering seeds from the trees. When you're naked in the water for all the damn world to see!"

"There's one house! One! And you said they're gay!" Nita shot back, trying to shrug out from under his hands.

"What if they weren't? What if it was someone like me who has thoughts?!"

"What thoughts?! Throwing rocks at me or making me fall into a mud hole?"

He stared at her for a moment, "I did that to you?"

She nodded.

"I did. I did, didn't I?" he laughed, "Boys are stupid, Nita. We don't know how to flirt."

"Flirt?" When had hurting someone been turned into flirting in this world? She wished she could go back in time to correct it.

"Hell, I have half my brain trying to keep my hands off you. And the other half is trying to figure out how to make you mine." Jasper's face drained of blood and tan. "That's not what I wanted to say. No. Let's see, I meant to say that I-I'm...I gotta get to work."

He was around the table and counter in what seemed like three strides, and she hadn't realized he had moved. "Oh, hell no."

She ran after him, cursing as the screen door slammed in her face before she yanked it open. The morning dew cooled and dampened her bare feet as she stretched out her stride into a run. "Don't you dare!"

He ran track in high school when he wasn't playing basketball. He thanked all that was holy that he still had the skills. Nita had always been quick. Especially barefoot. His truck fender was cool under his hand as he used it to spin toward his door.

Something caught his foot, and he ate dirt. He pushed up, spitting it out. In mid spit, he felt hands pushing him to his back. He kicked out, trying to find his feet under him.

Her body slammed into his. The sky was turning to a soft gray-blue with some little clouds. The fog had yet to be burned completely away from the ground. Then all he could see was thick green and black hair making a curtain around them, shutting them from the world. Her hands pressed his shoulders down.

She wriggled.

He held her hips, trying to get her still before his body reacted in a way he was certain she would hate. A piece of dirt or grass still stuck to his tongue, so he turned his head, to try to half spit and blow it off. He jerked back when her hand cupped his chin and nearly bit his own tongue in half.

"Wha-?" Her face was so close, his voice left him.

"Stick your tongue out!" Nita's voice was sharp, her eyes wide. Her free hand pulled the curtain of her hair back so it all fell on one side, letting the faint sunrise glow in.

It already was, but he pushed it out further. He let her turn his head this way and that, those deep brown eyes of hers studying his mouth. It also meant she wasn't wriggling over his groin anymore, but over his stomach. Still dangerous, but not as bad. Surely, he could control himself better than that.

"Where did you get this mark?"

"What mark?" It was difficult to talk around a thrust out tongue, but he tried it anyway.

"The mark on your tongue." Nita said, her eyes narrowing as she looked from one of his to the other, then back down to his tongue.

Jasper gave up and pulled his tongue back in so he could speak normally, "There's a mark on my tongue?"

Nita sighed, rolling her eyes up.

His eyes, as if on their own accord, looked down her shirt. Why did she have to wear something with a loose neck while she was like this on him? She had definitely filled out nicely.

He said after swallowing down extra moisture in his mouth, his eyes still down her shirt. He couldn't not look. And he hated himself for it. "What kind of mark?"

"Don't you brush your tongue when you brush your teeth?" She squeezed her fingers into his cheek, as if she were making a dog open it's mouth for a pill instead of holding his face.

Jasper didn't dare let go of her hips, but he wanted her hand off his face, too. He jerked his chin; it didn't help. "Yeah…but…there's no mark!"

She sat up, and he heaved a sigh and he relaxed a little more. Except now she claimed he had a mark on his tongue. "Is it…like a bite because I just bit the hell out of it when you grabbed me?"

"No. It's a mark." Her eyes darted around.

She did that when it was witch things she wanted to talk about. "Nita, come on." He sat up, and she pulled away in his hold, but he held her fast. Something in him wanted her on top of him, and close enough to kiss. Another part of him wanted to push her away, so he wouldn't act on anything that his body wanted.

"It looks like a silencing mark." Her voice was low, and her body trembled over his.

"Silencing? As in, I should be mute? I'm talking. It didn't work." Jasper slid one hand to the small of her back, trying to comfort her because suddenly it wasn't fun anymore. She acted and looked like this was something terrible or scary.

"Not like that. Well, it could be. It's more like a certain thing is being kept from you or from you telling someone." Nita leaned toward him, her hands over his cheeks, "Stick your tongue out again."

He did as he was told, trying to think of anything other than her being so close. His body stirred, throbbing for her more than it had last night. If only Camden were here to rein him in.

Or make it worse.

"I'm not familiar with it. It feels…off." She said as her hands slid down to his chest. She didn't pull back or move to get up. "Maybe it's nothing serious. Maybe… maybe it's… I need to study the marks. I haven't seen them twisted together like that. The runes."

With a hard swallow, he asked, "Do you…ah…want to go with me to work? Just to see if it… does something?" Stupid. Idiot.

She laughed, "No."

That sound washed over him and made him warm inside and out. "I guess I better go…" he didn't want to, but duty called. The men on the mountain needed their clothes back, and he had to make some money.

"Right." She said, still not moving.

Jasper breathed in through his mouth, so he wouldn't take her sweet scent of eucalyptus and mint. "Bellbean, I'm about to do something stupid."

"Like ask me to go to work with you again?" Her voice was softer, made for the dawn cresting around them.

"No…worse, probably." He could feel the stirring of trouble within him. Nita on him, looking at him expectantly, and not a soul around to break them up.

"Like?"

He cupped the back of her head and bruised her lips with his. The memory of her damp from her shower and naked had him crushing her body to his. Her arms wrapped around his neck and he lost himself.

His fingers found the soft, warm flesh just over her worn jeans. He traveled his hand on until his thumb brushed the band of her bra. She whimpered. That sound had him wanting to tear her clothes off and make her his. He held back, barely. Willing himself to calm down, and hating that he had to, but knowing he should.

"How is this stupid? Still think of me as Camden's annoying little awkward sister?"

Her voice was like a candlelit bedroom.

"Hell no." He sounded ridiculous. Strained, and like an old man's. "Camden's gonna kill me, though."

"Why?"

Nita's fingertips threading through the short hairs at the base of his head distracted him. He imagined all he could do to her. All he wanted to do to her. "He thinks we'll be no good."

"He doesn't know everything."

Jasper wanted to taste her again, could feel the warmth of her lips on his they were so close. "No, no, he doesn't, but you are his little sister. His only family. Mine. I don't wanna hurt you."

She pulled back, and he swore the distance she put between them, the inches, were like a mile of ice. "Then don't."

"I don't wanna." His brain brought a thought screeching to the surface, "Wait…is this mark transferable? Catching?"

Nita shook her head, her arms crossing over her chest. Another sheet of ice added between them. This was the stupid thing he said he'd do. Whenever he opened his mouth, it was bound to happen.

"No. It's bound to you. Only for you."

He felt the grimace scrunch up his face as he explained, "Sorry, I don't know much about all this stuff."

"Stuff." She spat the word.

Another mile between them when she untangled herself from him and stood. "Nita, I don't mean it like… like others do. I have a hard time learning it all. Hell, I'm still trying to identify trees without cutting them down and seeing the color of the boards they'd make."

"I know." She wrapped her arms around her middle.

He stood, nearly tripped again over the long shoots of grass and a vine wrapped around one of his ankles. He stared down at it for a moment, settling his thoughts about her ability to do little things like that. As a kid, he thought it both fascinating and scary. Now he wanted to learn more.

Jasper sighed, trying to get himself to relax. To see reason. To not be such a fool. "See…this is exactly what I meant by doing something stupid. Maybe this mark should've completely muted me. I'd be better off."

"I'll do some research on it. I got a friend I can call who will know more about it."

"Need to borrow my phone?"

Her eyes narrowed, and he held his hands up, palms toward her, "Just sayin' is all." He pointed down to his ankle, "Can I or do you wanna let me loose?"

He thought she might not let him go. She took a long time, her cheeks reddening a little, before the greenery slithered away from him. "Can I…come back? Tonight?"

"Yeah, yeah, I should figure out the mark by then. Maybe."

"That'll be good." Now what? Should he hug her? Kiss her again? Just go? Should there be a Southern goodbye going on here or what?

"You're gonna be late."

"Yeah, I am." He stared into those dark eyes for a moment longer, then got into his truck. After pulling down to the end of her drive, he stopped and breathed. He could still taste her on his lips, on his tongue. He wanted nothing more than to turn around, bang his truck up on every ditch and pothole in the Bell drive and have her all day.

He couldn't.

"Damn Cam, maybe I should act on it. Maybe that'd bring you around the corner, breaking us up again. Always had a knack for showing up right when I was about to make a move on her," he muttered with a chuckle. Camden made him the khaki colored paracord bracelet with a large green jasper in the center when they were in middle school, he stared at it, hanging from his rearview mirror. He didn't like wearing it while he worked, and had forgotten to put it back on when driving to see Nita.

He drove to the gay men's house. They met him on the porch. Keeping his mouth shut, he leaned against the banister he built for them.

"Well?!" Gus finally broke the silence with a wide stance and threw his hands into the air.

"Spent the night with her." Jasper kept his voice neutral, not wanting to rile the tornado that was Gus' curiosity.

"Damn, kid, you got better moves than I thought you would."

The barb of Wade's words struck deep, "We fought. Mostly."

Gus dramatically heaved a breath, a hand going to his cheek, "My poor boy. Come on, tell old Gus all about it." He wrapped an arm around Jasper, guiding him into the house and sitting him at the kitchen table.

In true southern fashion, they placed more food in front of him than he could eat all day long. But he tried as he talked; leaving out the parts of witchcraft.

Gus bounced on his toes, hands rubbing together as he said, "I'm liking this girl more and more! You should bring her here to meet us. We can do a dinner!"

Jasper snorted, "Let's try taking you to her first, then we'll see."

"Ah, yes, that might be best with her introversion." Gus said with a nod.

"She'll come around." Wade murmured after a sip of his second cup of coffee. "I don't get Camden. I mean, how can he just up and leave? Stay there and not come back home? That's weird."

Jasper nodded, "It is. He's always been adventurous, but he's never stayed away long. He's always come back, kept in touch. Hell, he'd stop a hike to climb back down the mountain to find a pay phone before nightfall to make sure their grandmother and Nita were alright." He ran his hands through his hair. "He wanted to stay. I got it. It's beautiful out there. Even while we were gone, he called until Nita picked up each day. But when I left… nothing."

"So odd. Such a mystery!" Gus gushed with a small smile, "We'll help you figure it out, kid."

Jasper grunted when he stood, his belly full of too much food. "I'll get to work."

Chapter Five

Nita puffed out a breath and checked the little bars on her phone. "Finally." She took a few steadying breaths and found a nice rock to sit on. The mountain on the east side of her property blocked the tower on the ridge behind it. Halfway up and around the backside of the mountain, she got a full signal. She couldn't afford to drop this call halfway through.

The house had decided it was time to kill the landline for the day, so she had to make the trek up the mountain.

That mark on Jasper's tongue could explain a lot of things. It could also crush her. Either way, Jasper didn't know what it was, and they had to remove or deactivate it.

First, she listened to the voicemails that appeared on her phone, causing it to buzz and notify her for over five minutes. She contacted the park ranger, who had been reaching out to her the most through voicemails, and left one for him. Of course, this would be the longest case of phone tag ever.

She didn't find the message she desperately wanted. Camden, if well and able, would have called her. He never missed a day. Somehow, the mountains and signals sussed how important he was to her and his calls always came through. Even if they dropped somewhere in the middle, they always reached her.

With a deep breath, she dialed a number she only contacted every couple of months to catch up. The familiar voice wasn't as cheery as it usually was when she answered, "Hey, Megs, you alright?"

"No, no, I'm not, but you're in the same way."

"What's wrong?" Nita's heart dropped at the sorrow and anger in her friend's voice.

"Randy's gone. They found his car at Payne's garage, where they towed it from the bar. No one's seen him since that night, Friday night." Meg hiccuped, then sniffled loudly.

"I'm sorry. Any leads at all?" Nita asked, feeling her blood run cold. Why were there so many people missing? What was going on? Who was next?

"No. He just walked off. Disappeared into thin air." Meg's voice broke on the other line. "What about you? Any leads on Camden? Christy told me, hope you don't mind."

"No, I don't mind. No, no leads yet. Jasper came back though."

Meg made a half snort, half scoffing sound before asking, "Yeah, I heard. Want me to set him on fire?"

"I don't think he needs any more fire to him." Nita muttered, again her mouth running off before her brain could keep it in check.

"Huh?"

"Er…nothing." Her face heated, and she knew she was blushing for the mountain and trees to see. She rolled her eyes at herself. "Listen, there might be a lead, but I don't want to bother you-"

"Stop. I need a distraction. What do you got?"

Nita told Meg about the mark on Jasper's tongue and sent a picture to her she drew. While stuffing the drawing into her back pocket, she waited for Meg to check it.

"How did you notice it on Jasper's tongue, hm?" Her friend had a smile in her voice.

Her face would forever remain at an abnormal temperature. "I made him eat dirt, and he was spitting it out when I saw it."

"Riiiight."

Nita debated on whether to defend her honor when Megs broke the silence.

"Finally got it. Damn, do you not have a better camera on that brick? Wait, that looks like a silent mark."

"That's what I thought, but it looks weird." Nita felt a little spark of relief at knowing what it was, sort of.

"It's customized. The mark is preventing him from speaking of something specific." Meg explained, her voice closer and Nita assumed she'd stopped looking at the symbols.

"Like Camden's disappearance?" Nita asked, forcing the words out because the feeling of hope was a slippery thing.

"Yeah, or the fact he's back to rock your world."

"Thanks. Thanks a lot."

Meg giggled, "Oh, that's the first time I've wanted to laugh. I can't help it though. Jasper's cute. A good guy, too. You could do so much worse."

Nita made a face, "Yeah, I know."

"I think your thought is right, though. He knows something, and some witch doesn't want him to tell anyone. Camden piss anyone off recently?"

"Other than me? No. Not that I know of." Nita rubbed her temple where it started throbbing. "What about Randy? He make anyone mad?"

"No, I don't think so." Meg's voice broke as she said, "He's so young, Nita. Just turned sixteen. What if… what if it's those traffickers… you ken?"

"We'll find him. I'll help." Nita bit her bottom lip and chewed for a moment. Trying to form her thoughts together, "Hey, Megs, do you… do you think someone around you has a mark on them?"

"I… dunno. I guess I'm gonna start checking, though. You think they might be tied?"

"Well, they're both male and our brothers… who knows?" Nita hated the thoughts forming in her head. Because she knew they wouldn't get her much of anywhere unless she had something to go on. That something had to be what that mark on Jasper was hiding.

"Yeah, listen, I got an appointment to look through the stuff they found in Randy's car. I'm sending you a page from Momma's grim about how to break it. I'll call you later?" Meg said over rustling.

"Yeah, keep me posted." Nita's heart broke for Megs.

"Same."

"Be careful, Megs."

"You too, Nita."

She hiked further up the mountain. She had to wait for the file from Megs, anyway. Leaning against an old oak tree at the top, she observed her house and land below. Nita took a deep breath in, letting her little world soothe her as best as it could. She looked beyond, following the stream that made the northern border of her property, until something flashed in the sunlight.

She swallowed, calculating how close that metal roof was to her bathing hole. Again, her flesh warmed, and she groaned. "Times are changing."

A faint echo of a hammer reached her.

Her feet drew her to the holler and followed the creek at the bottom. Then up a deer trail until she was under the newly built porch. Sweat gleamed off his back. The tool belt made his fitted jeans ride low on his hips to where they bunched up over his boots.

"Go on, let out a whistle. Lord knows I have a few times. He'll appreciate it more from you."

As Nita looked up, she noticed Jasper doing the same in her peripheral vision. A kind smile met her gaze under soft blue eyes. He was leaning over the railing of the porch above her head. He gave her a wink as Jasper started grumbling.

"What're you goin' on about now, old man?" He bent, plucking his shirt from a hole in the lattice he was putting up and swiping it over his face.

His ass looked too good in those jeans. Nita swallowed and bent to grab his water bottle from his tool box at her feet. She popped the top open and squirted his back with it.

Jasper jerked, jumping with a slight spin to whirl on her. Then he froze, dark eyes wide with raised eyebrows. "Nita?"

"The basement has an open door and a cot. Just come on upstairs when ya'll are done." Gus grinned, then disappeared. Nita heard a sliding door close above them.

"Just wanted to tell you I got something that might help with the mark. Have to do it at midnight." It was the best time, honestly, not an excuse to have him stay with her all night. She had to keep telling herself that.

"You uh… midnight. Right. I was gonna come over, anyway. Bring my tools to help with the loose leg on your table." Jasper cleared his throat, glanced down at his shirt, still in his hand, and then back at her. "I uh… give me a sec."

He found the end and opened his shirt up.

Nita let her gaze trail over his chest. He reminded her of those pictures of models Christy showed her. But Jasper didn't have the deep cut of muscles like they did. He was softer around the edges, still defined. His chest had a fuzz on it and a trail of hair led from his belly button, disappearing into his jeans.

A dark mark on his arm drew her gaze up to his firm biceps. A large cat holding a bell with a swirl in the middle. Changing her position, she saw the match on his other upper arm. "Bells?"

His shirt caught on his head. With a soft curse, he pulled on it. He worked the shirt over his damp skin, and it kept sticking to him. Jasper glanced about.

Nita stepped in front of where his flannel lay half-hazard on his toolbox.

"Yeah." Jasper's eyes narrowed on her. He smoothed his hair back. The strands on his neck and around his temples were darker with sweat.

His family wasn't a bell. It was the mountain lion. An animal of leadership, power, cunning, and confidence.

"I should put my shirt on." He said in a low voice, motioning behind her as his eyes darted toward it.

"Why?" It was something she could ask to keep him talking, and hopefully not acting on his wants.

Jasper's Adam's apple bobbed as he swallowed before speaking, "Because you're here. Ain't proper."

Nita tilted her head back, noting how he watched her movements. "Being half naked around a gay man is? Isn't it just as improper to be naked around them as it is me?" What was she saying? Had that kiss made her go all nuts in the head?

"I- they…" he let out a long breath, "Dammit, Nita, you know what I mean."

"You have a shirt on."

He rolled his eyes. "Fine." He paused, "What are you doing here? I said I'd be back tonight. You didn't have to… did you walk?"

"Yeah." She had, and she didn't know why. Even kept asking herself why while she was walking, and still didn't have the answer. Other than that, she wanted to see him.

"Nita, that's a good mile. Drink." He motioned to his water still in her hands.

She did, and then wiped her mouth off on the back of her hand, "I was on the mountain making a call to Megs."

"Haven't seen her in years. How's she doin'?" Jasper asked, his voice switching from slight embarrassment to concern.

"Randy's been missin' since Friday." Nita answered, trying to keep the worry from her own voice and her mind from turning it over and over.

"Little Randy? He's what? fifteen?"

"Sixteen."

"Oh." Jasper picked up his hammer from where he had hung it in the lattice and put it in its holster on his belt. "I hope he turns up soon. She's probably worried sick."

Nita didn't know what to really say to that, so she just said, "Yeah."

"Wait, you came here from the mountain?"

"Yeah." She felt like a robot.

Jasper didn't seem to mind. "What she think happened?"

"Dunno. It's like he just up and walked off." And that was the thing. Randy was a good kid. He didn't go anywhere or do anything that was dangerous. He was shy, and too smart for his age. Too knowledgeable of the dangers of the world.

Jasper shook his head, "Like Camden."

"Yeah, that's what I was thinking." She waited for him to say something else, or ask another question. Not able to handle the silence any longer, she asked him, "Are you allergic to anything?"

Growing up, she hardly noticed her grandmother's cooking when he was around. It seemed that every other time he visited, she would make him spaghetti and an excessive amount of garlic bread. Nita didn't think he was, but people's body chemistry changed.

"No. Why?"

Nita pressed her fingertips against her palms as they itched to run through his hair. "If you're coming over, I need to cook, plus the concoction for tonight will not be tasty, at all."

"Oh. I can bring something from town."

"Or I could cook for you." Gus had snuck back out onto the porch, if he had left at all. Nita suspected he had just opened and closed the sliding glass door to pretend to be gone.

"I wouldn't want to impose." Nita tilted her head up, looking at Gus' grinning face as he leaned over the balcony.

"Oh, darlin' no imposition at all. Any hot little love interest of Jasper's is more than welcome in our home."

"Gus." Jasper's tone was close to a growl, "Don't make me drive a nail up into your foot."

"Finish your work, hired help!" Gus said with a chuckle, "I'll fix us something tasty."

Nita waited until she was sure he was gone before asking, "Got an extra hammer."

"Only the one in his pocket for you, darlin'!"

Gus wasn't gone, again. Nita thought Jasper's face was as red as hers was hot. "I think I'll go back home."

"Don't. They'll chase you down and just make the teasing worse." Jasper handed her a hammer. "You know how to make it stay still 'til you make it solid?"

Nita hefted the hammer. "Yeah, helped your uncle on the old Miller house remodel, remember?"

He nodded and smiled at her. "Yeah, I remember."

As they installed the porch lattice, the kitchen smells wafted down to them. Jasper had pre-cut each piece before he started putting them up. He didn't work with gloves on, and Nita didn't ask for any. She had thick enough callouses.

As she worked, she mentally listed what she had to do for that night. The spell required simple herbs, and she had ample time to brew the tea before midnight. Nita wanted to add a bit more, just to make sure he would tell her the truth once the mark was off. But she didn't want to ruin the spell to remove the mark. One herb could counteract if not planned perfectly.

She'd have to make another tea, a chamomile one, in the ruse of helping him sleep. Mentally she shook her head at herself. Did she really need that? It was Jasper.

His voice broke into her thoughts, "Done?"

She straightened and nodded, hoping the shame of her idea wasn't written on her face. "Yeah."

"Good. It's ready."

She stared openly as he pulled his flannel on. Jasper was always with a button up flannel shirt. And jeans. If he wore something else, something was wrong.

Noticing the pots next to the corner of the house, she asked, "Will these be planted to climb the lattice?"

"Yeah."

Nita smiled at the little potted clematis plants. She kneeled near them, putting her fingers into the damp, soft soil of each pot as she began humming her tone. Gus was likable enough, but all plants needed to be healthy and hardy.

She touched each pot, crooning.

"Nita…" Jasper's voice was low, "Careful."

"I am." She sang along with her humming tune, not changing the note that harmonized with the clematis starts. After touching the last bit of soil on the last plant, she stood, getting in Jasper's face. She stuck her tongue out, "See? No one came with pitchforks and torches."

Jasper's lips curled as he said, "Stick it out again and see what happens."

She did.

Then one hand slid into her hair and his lips fit to hers. His scruff tickled the tender flesh around her lips and chin. She felt herself lean toward him when he pulled back. She didn't know when she had closed her eyes, but when she opened them, his were looking deep into her soul.

Sam Wicker

His hand slid from the back of her neck, and the pad of his thumb brushed over her bottom lip. "Shoulda kissed you a long time ago."

"When?" Because she desperately wanted him to keep kissing her now.

"High school."

Thinking back, she remembered her teen jealousy. "You kissed everyone in high school."

His brows quirked, "No, that was Camden."

"Pretty sure you kissed plenty, too." Otherwise, she wouldn't have held back. Right? Right.

He shook his head, "What else did you assume I was up to in school?"

Nita couldn't keep the bite out of her voice, "Flirting with anything that had boobs and wore skirts."

Jasper laughed, "Were you jealous?"

She put his hammer into his toolbox, "The food smells good." Nita ignored his question, and his prodding after that.

After washing up, Nita sat with Gus, Wade, and Jasper at their smaller dining table near the kitchen. The wooden topped table held a large platter of grilled chicken in the middle, and bowls full of candied sweet potatoes, steamed vegetable mix, and dirty rice.

"Dig in. No need for ceremony here." Wade smiled, leaning back in his chair to take a deep sip of his red wine.

Nita felt something familiar about the older gentleman, like a distant memory hiding from her mind's eye. "Thank you for the meal, and allowing me in your home."

"You are always welcome." Gus gave her a wink. "It's nice to see the nymph up close."

Nita's body heat swarmed up to her face and neck, "I didn't think…I've always-"

"Oh darling, you may continue. Please do. We don't watch, per se, you've just become a muse." Gus waved a hand before placing it over his heart.

Jasper grumbled, "I'll fix your plumbing, or find someone who can, so you don't have to be stared at by two old pervy gay men."

Gus clicked his tongue before saying breathily, "Oh Jasper, my love, please don't be jealous. We look at you plenty."

Nita giggled as Jasper's face turned as red as hers felt. She dug into her chicken and rice. The vegetables were good, but the meat and sweet potatoes were quickly becoming her favorite. Other than the little meals she would purchase from the Greene's, it had been a while since she had someone else's cooking. And, other than Jasper's that morning.

"Gonna spend the night with her again? Why don't you just move in together? You're right there whenever I come up with a new project." Gus asked, his grin wider than the mouth of his wine glass.

Jasper's wine must have gone up his nose. He coughed a few times, his head shaking.

"He basically lived with us a few years back." Nita asked, "Once Camden comes back, you will again, right?"

"I dunno." He said, his voice a rasp before he cleared his throat again, "Maybe."

"Miz Bell, may I ask you something?" Wade's deep voice broke into the moment.

She looked at him, that feeling of familiarity bugging her again. "Nita, just call me Nita, and yeah, sure."

"Are the rumors true? Are you a witch?" His deep voice was even, neutral, and his eyes held no malice, just curiosity.

She stared at him for a moment, the quick quip she always spat out stilled on her lips. They were so near her home. She didn't need to make enemies here. Negativity could damage her boundaries. "Maybe." She said with a trembling of her lips as she tried smiling.

Wade smiled back, "Your Dad was an amazing witch. Or wizard. He always called himself a witch, though."

Nita's breath caught in her throat, "You remember my Daddy?"

"Yes, I do. We weren't the best of friends, but I considered him a friend. His goodness and comforting demeanor always helped turn my bad days into something more bearable." He said, staring into his glass, then his gaze flicked back up to her. "Being who I am, what I am, that is rare in these parts."

The memory clicked into place. "Wade? Wade Gregory?"

"That's me, darlin'."

"Oh. Oh, I remember you, a little." Nita sat on the edge of her seat. Remembering the soft deep voice, a larger-than-life hand ruffling her hair as she stared up at him from the floor where she was playing.

Wade chuckled, "As I remember you, a little."

Gus grinned, "Aww, this is so sweet."

Wade rolled his eyes with a sigh, and then another sip of wine, "I had friends, love."

"There's hardly any proof of that!" Gus held up a finger.

Nita waited for a breath or two, trying to remember more. When she couldn't, she asked, "What was he like? If you don't mind…"

Wade chuckled, "He was quiet. One guy that never picked on me for being different. Even though he was different himself, no one picked on him either, not really." He sat silent for a moment, before he began again, "When he met your mother, he came into himself. That odd boy became a kind and generous man. He had a voice with her. Got a few black eyes sticking up for people who wouldn't stick up for themselves." He shook his head, "Sorry, I can't tell you more. There're stories, but I barely remember the details."

Nita looked down at her plate, eyes burning. Her father was remembered as a kind and generous man, as Wade put it. That was enough to make this night worth every moment of embarrassment. "It's alright. It would be nice to hear someone else's take on him, rather than the ones I've already heard."

Wade added, "I'd probably remember more, going to the old grounds. The highschool. But we don't get out much."

"Safer that way," Jasper said before he tore a bite from a buttered roll.

"Our knight in shining sawdust." Gus patted his chest over his heart.

Wade chuckled, "Little does he know we can handle ourselves, but whatever makes him feel better."

Chapter Six

Jasper's face reminded her of a toddler's at the moment. "Did you really have to make it this foul?"

Nita bit her cheek to keep from yelling as he sniffed the mug. "Jasper, drink it. Now."

A muscle in his jaw clenched, but he did as he was told. She rang the bell after his last swallow, letting it hang above his head. She matched the tone with her voice as best as she could. Drawing on the magic of her land and mixing it with her own. She circled him, then kneeled in front of him.

As she explained each step to him before they started the ritual, he placed his hands between them on her knees, palms up. She smeared another concoction of her making over them. The pungent scents of ginger, onion, garlic, eucalyptus and rosemary permeated the air. She took the same mix and spread it over the mark on his tongue with her fingers.

She spoke the words of the spell, filling them with her power and that of her land. Nita closed her eyes, working through the intricate weavings and tones of the seal upon Jasper with the aid of the herbs, and the tone of the purifying bell. Someone powerful put it on him, and Nita's energy drained during the hour of work.

In that hour, she broke it. The mark disappeared as she opened her eyes and focused on it. "Drink this. All of it." She handed him another mug.

Jasper did as he was told, licking his lips afterward. "Peppermint?"

She hummed to herself and gave him a nod. "Tell me again what you remember of your trip with Camden." She steeled herself, not willing to hope, but it bloomed in her heart anyway.

He relayed to her the same information he had shared with her before, but this time, when he got to where he separated from Camden in Yellowstone, the story changed.

"We left and were comin' into town. It was late, and we were both a bit hungry. Kinda drove without stopin' the last leg just so we could get home. We stopped at the Waffle King. Still the only place open after midnight."

She nodded, and he continued.

"Weren't anyone in there, 'cept for the one cook. Can't ever remember her name, but she's been there for years? After we got our food, this couple in hoodies came in. Got a bad feelin'. You know, the nerves jumpin' up, hairs standin' kina thing. Camden looked the same. Kept lookin' at 'em." Jasper's words spilled quickly from his lips, his hands fists on his knees, trembling.

"We finished up pert quick, and got up to leave. One of the hooded people stood with us. And the next thing I know, I'm wakin' up in my bed in the apartment." Jasper shook his head, "Where... how did they do that to me?"

His face was pale, a little green as his eyes searched hers. "How did they have his camping stuff still in Yellowstone when we packed up?"

"I dunno, Jasper." Nita's skin crawled. She slid over, getting off her knees to sit on the ground. The grass was cooling, the air calm around them until a light breeze rustled through the leaves overhead. The old ironwood creaked and rumbled soothing tones through its roots beneath her.

Without thinking, she tugged on her braid, running her hands down the thick rope of it and twisting the end in her fingers. No one witch could do that. Two were at the Waffle King. Surely she could find some trace of them.

"We have to tell the cops." Jasper said, as if to himself.

She shook her head, "They'll only arrest you for changing your story." She looked at him after staring at the empty mug beside his leg. "You sure you don't remember anythin' from Waffle King to the next morning?"

Jasper rubbed his hands over his face, his eyes tightly closed. "No, no, I'm tryin'. It's like… I'm trying to recall a dream from years ago?"

She nodded, standing and moving behind him. She ran her fingers through his hair, tilting it this way and that so she could see to his scalp in the lamplight.

"You're getting that stuff all in my hair." He said and then groaned, reaching up to try to grab her hands.

"Suck it up." Nita growled, pulling his collar down to study the back of his neck.

"Your hands are cold. Let's go inside." Jasper shifted, then grunted as he stopped when she tilted his head back to scan the front of his neck.

When he was shirtless, she didn't notice a mark, but she was very, very distracted.

"Nita." His voice warmed her.

She was trying not to become distracted now. "Hm?"

"There's better light inside and you're cold."

"Right." She stopped, grabbing her tools while Jasper held the old lamp up. The path was so familiar, she didn't need the light to guide her, but Jasper did.

Nita listened to the plants and earth whisper sleepily to themselves and her. Camden was near. Closer than she expected. He'd almost made it home. She wondered if Camden and Randy were together.

She put the mugs and bowls in the kitchen sink, hearing Jasper blow the flame of the lamp out and place it on the counter to cool before putting it up. Nita turned to him, pulling out a chair and motioning for him to sit. She checked through his hair again, smirking a little to herself as the herbs coated his soft strands. Making the perfect hair imperfect.

"Take your shirt off." Nita demanded, waiting for him to do as he was told while keeping her hands to herself. She crossed her arms, locking her hands in place.

Jasper turned to look at her over his shoulder, his brows low. "Wha-why?"

"Just do it." Before I lose my resolve, she thought to herself.

He shook his head, refusing to do the simple task. "I was shirtless earlier today."

"Yeah… and… I need to see again." She dreaded having to do it for him. That might be too much for her moral compass. She'd break. Nita knew she would.

The red tinging his cheeks ruined his smirk, "What else ya wanna see?"

She smacked his arm, "Off or I burn it off."

His brows knitted together, "You can't make a fireball." He said as he tugged his flannel over his head, then his undershirt.

"I got a lighter, genius." She pulled it out of her pocket, hitting the flint and making the little flame pop to life.

He rolled his eyes, "Gonna let me shower after your inspection?"

"Told you to suck it up." Nita answered as she slid the lighter back into her pocket, trying to stay focused as she looked over his back. He worked shirtless enough that he still had a bit of a tan, apparently. His arms were darker, especially his forearms.

No marks appeared before her on his back, or on the backs of his arms. She moved to his side so she could check his armpit and ribs. After a full inspection, she shook her head. "Tilt your head back and open your mouth."

"I feel like I'm at a doctor's office." Jasper's voice was deeper with annoyance.

"You don't go to the doctor. Ever." She shot back, wondering why it was so easy for him to go from grown man to toddler in under three seconds flat.

"This is why." He said with a wide-eyed look.

"Just open your mouth."

Nita even checked under his tongue and in the dips of his ears. She didn't think a witch would put a mark in someone's nose, so she left that out of her inspection. "Alright, let's see your feet and legs."

Jasper grumbled, "What are you lookin' for?"

"Another mark, what do ya think?" Nita asked, and thought that her inspection was obvious.

"Just checkin'. Didn't know if this was some side effect of you doing magic on a smuggle or not."

Her brows drew together, "Smuggle?"

Jasper lifted a shoulder with a half nod as he said, "Yeah, you know. The regular people in that kid witchy movie?"

Nita raised her brows with a smirk, "Muggle."

"That's what I meant." Jasper grinned.

She observed him tug his boots off after unlacing them, and then his socks. "Well, that's not pleasant."

Jasper wadded up his socks and tucked them into his left boot. "Yours aren't made outta roses either, Bell."

Belsauros took that moment to stick his head in Jasper's boot. He popped back out, wiggling his nose, but stuck it in the other one, too. He then started playing with the laces, chattering to himself.

"Look! your little bandit don't mind the smell." Jasper chuckled and pointed at the raccoon.

"His nose is broken. Or he's overwhelmed by the stench that it burned his scenter out." Nita eyed the fur ball, fearing for his sense of smell as she checked both of his aromatic feet.

She dreaded the next step. She let go of his foot, "Pants off."

"Nita…"

"Jasper…"

He sighed, then cleared his throat as he stood. "I'll go look in a mirror."

Nita pointed out, "You didn't spot the last mark."

"I'll see this one." Jasper snapped back.

"No, you won't." Nita reached for his belt and he shifted away.

Covering his belt buckle with one hand, he held up a finger, "Just give me a damn minute, would ya?"

"What's the big deal?" It was pants, not like she was going to stick something up his ass.

"I ain't got… I didn't… dammit. Let me borrow some shorts from Camden. I'll be right back."

Nita grew annoyed with watching him retreat. Suddenly, she realized the problem and her blood ran to her face and ears. Her steady mantra of imagining dead puppies while looking over his flesh disappeared and was replaced with him. All of him. Bare to her.

She willed her thoughts back to safe ones. Squished bugs. Animal placentas. Clear cutting. Jasper naked on her bed.

Nope.

Camden missing. Burning trees and shrubs. Desserts. Jasper kissing her. "Dammit, focus."

"On what?"

She turned back to him. He stood in the hall, hands cupped over his groin, with a pair of Camden's boxers on. He picked the blue ones with shrimp on them.

After running her eyes over every inch of him, she found no mark. Only a few scars and his birthmark. The hairs on his legs weren't as thick as she thought they might be, considering his beard. They sure were pale, though.

"Nothing?"

"Nothing." Nita said, biting her cheek again and fighting with herself on the next issue.

"Whelp, guess that's done for then."

"I need to see…everything." She felt more than her face heat this time, and her heart began to beat even faster.

"Nope." Jasper took a step, then another, away from her.

"Yeah."

"Look, this has been fun and I'm sure you got somethin' recordin' this mess, but there's gotta be a line. This is the line. Here. Right here. A line. See?" Jasper pointed to an invisible line on the floor between them as he spoke. His neck and cheeks as red as hers felt hot.

"Gotta make sure you've not got another mark. That last one was pretty powerful. If they put another one on you to forget the time between Waffle King and your bed, then we need to find it and break it, too." Nita fought her nerves, and swallowed to try to get some saliva to make the butterflies drown in her stomach.

Jasper laughed in an odd pitch before asking, "What? They put a mark on my dick then?"

"I dunno… maybe?" Nita feared her face would scorch and her heart burst from her chest. She couldn't decide what was more embarrassing. "I just want to make sure."

"Can we get Gus to look tomorrow, or… someone?" He was on the verge of whining now.

"Gus doesn't use magic, neither does Wade. It's me or another witch."

Jasper muttered under his breath, "Coulda asked me out first. You know, chilled on the couch for a bit. Something."

Nita clasped her hands together to keep them from shaking. The lingering stickiness of the herbs made her palms damp. "If it makes you feel any better, I want what I see?"

The sound he made was somewhere between a growl and a groan. It made her peer into his face. His eyes were closed, and as she watched, he raked a hand over his face. "That's presenting me with the same, but bigger type of problem. One I had control over. Some."

She felt her throat grow tight at his admission. She admonished herself for the hope making her heart flutter. "It's fine. I mean, it's not like you haven't been naked with a woman before."

His eyes flew open and pinned her.

She swallowed, "What?"

"Nothing. Just… nothing." He shook his head. "Alright. Fine. Let's get this over with." Jasper shimmied out of his borrowed underwear and stood still.

Nita skimmed over the top part of his thighs, and just under his waist and into the dark curls around his penis and balls. She then looked over the muscular globes of his ass, running her fingertips over them because she had the urge, and he made a sound. Not a single mark.

What she did find was goosebumps rising over his flesh.

"Done?"

The word ground out of him as if his voice were metal gears in need of greasing.

"Yeah."

He pulled his pants on, "I gotta say somethin' here."

She turned her back to him, wondering why she was so disappointed. She knew nothing would happen between them. He only enjoyed seeing her reactions when they kissed. "Okay."

"This is… just what… dammit, Jasper, put the words together." He looked up at the ceiling. "Was this some sort of payback for me seeing you swimming the other day?"

"No." Nita turned, confusion curling over her, "I think they did something to you to keep you from remembering. I wanted to make sure you were unmarked. That means that they used something else to knock you out I'm guessing. You didn't bump your head, did you?"

Jasper looked as if someone had slapped him in the face for a moment, "No, no, I didn't."

"No headache?" Nita kept pressing, trying to think of the tasks at hand rather than what she wanted from him.

"No."

Nita pointed out, "That's why I looked for a mark."

"Right." He sighed, pulling his undershirt back over his head, "Good to know this is still entirely one sided."

"What's that mean?" A bit of anger threaded through the butterflies still storming through her.

Jasper chuckled, "Bellbean, you just had a guy in your kitchen, naked. You've kissed him and been kissed, so… yeah. One sided."

"How is that one-sided? yeah, we've kissed. I had to think of terrible things the entire time to avoid embarrassing myself chasing after a guy who's just teasing me." Nita hated the bitterness in her voice, so she looked away, fingering the now cooled lamp on the counter. Then she had to look at him, because it was killing her not to.

He dropped his flannel back onto the chair. Something in his eyes changed, "Teasing?"

"Yeah. I'm always expecting you to throw me into a mud hole again, or joke about how you kissed me and I liked it to your buddies in town." Her mouth was suddenly dry after being waterworks while prodding at his bare flesh.

He sat and then leaned forward, resting his elbows on his knees. His head hung low, and he shook it after sitting for a while. "Nita?"

"Yeah?"

He stood, stepping close to her and cupping her cheek in his hand, "I'm going to say this. You don't have to accept it. Rest assured, it is the truth and will remain so for a long time."

His fingers were warm, gentle as they slid up into her hair. The callous on the side of his thumb brushed over her cheekbone, and she leaned into his hand. Fixing her eyes on his; shade was lighter than her darker brown, a tawny color. She glanced behind him at the clock on the stove.

The truth potion wasn't in effect any longer.

"Why?" She cursed herself mentally. "I mean, what?"

Jasper's other hand cupped the top of her hip, over the waistline of her jeans, as his words began. "When we were younger, I grew fascinated with the way you made me feel. You anchored me down. Other times, when I was at my worst, lost, I saw you and those awful feelings just went away. Now, you're home." His arm curled around her waist, and he stepped into her, holding their bodies close. "You're the one I want to tell everything to. You're what comforts me and riles me at the same time. I want to see you every moment of every day, but I also want to see you after hours of being away from you because it makes my heart pound and my tiredness melt. You make me ache. You piss me off. You make me weak. You make me strong. I can't breathe without you, but you take my breath away, too."

"Look at you, all poetic and shit." Nita said to cover up the way his words made her feel. He was lying. Wasn't he? She couldn't tell. She hoped he wasn't. Was she dreaming?

Jasper chuckled, "And shit."

"Camden..."

"I know. We'll find him." Jasper said, his voice softening as he rested his forehead against hers.

"He told me to stay away from you. That you'd just break my heart." How many times had it been cracked because of him? Because she thought he only thought of her as a sister?

"Yeah, well, he's always been a bastard that way," Jasper said, closing his eyes, but he stayed put. "He always told me you'd never fall for me. That being a witch and the business were more important than anything and those were what you'd marry."

Nita sighed to relieve some of the pressure building in her chest. It didn't help. "Yeah, he's right, in a way. I always thought you'd just have sex with me and then move on to the next one."

"I'm not Mason."

She snorted, "No, definitely not."

After standing together in her brightly lit kitchen for a moment, she couldn't help but ask, "What do we do now?"

"Guess we do whatever it is you wanna do. We work to find Camden. We work our businesses. We kiss, hopefully a lot." He looked into her eyes and grinned on that last one, "And maybe have dinners and breakfasts… all of them?"

"Maybe." That was his test. If he could take multiple mornings of her being growly with him.

Nita yawned, wide enough that her jaw cracked and she grimaced.

The cook at the Waffle King topped off her coffee, "Don't ever see you out and about this late anymore. Now, I've seen you 'round five in the morning in that loud as hell truck of yours."

"Yeah, got a couple of questions for ya, Gladys." She curled her hands around the mug, her fingers warming against the cream stoneware.

"Shoot." Gladys cocked her hip, holding the coffee pot in one hand while the other rested on her hip.

"You remember Camden and Jasper coming in here late one night, close to a week ago?" Nita asked, wanting the coffee to wet her dry mouth, but knowing she'd burn her tongue if she tried it.

Gladys set the pot down, "I remember. I was glad they're back. I needed Jasper to fix my cabinets, you know, the ones my uncle made. During the move, a couple of them got loose and I shouldn't even try to figure out how to fix 'em." She laughed softly with a shake of her head. "They ate and left. Pretty starved from that drive, I imagine."

"No one else was in here?"

Gladys took a moment to think about that night, then shook her head as she said, "Nope, pretty quiet on Monday mornin's here."

"I see." Nita felt her heart drop to her belly.

"Why, darlin'?" Gladys asked, leaning toward her on the counter between them, her gray eyes searching hers.

"Camden's missing. Just thought you might've seen something."

"Oh! Oh, I thought I heard that, but I wasn't sure. I'm so sorry, Little Bell." Her hand pressed to her generous heart. "I hope he turns up soon. Maybe with a new girlfriend or something. Just got a wild bit about him and he lost track of time. Right?"

Nita tried a smile, "Yeah, maybe."

"Darlin' if there's anything? You eatin' alright? Can I bring a casserole over in the morning?" Gladys asked, her pale forehead creased in worry.

Sam Wicker

"No, I'm fine. Been eating well. Thank you though. Please inform me if you hear or see anything." Nita tried the coffee, and drank it down in one go. It helped keep the tears at bay.

"Of course! Now you scoot on to bed. You always rise so early. Sleep in now, you hear?" Gladys shooed her with one hand.

"Yes, ma'am."

Nita left the Waffle King and wandered around outside for a little. She found amusement in Gladys talking to a large group of high schoolers, probably coming back from some sports event or party. Jocks, with their fancy clothes and camaraderie.

Skinny shoots of grass struggled through tiny cracks in the parking lot concrete along with some hardy wildflowers, dandelions mostly. Nita reached out to their power as she let Belsauros out of the truck. He sniffed around, doing his thing.

Bel found a discarded half-eaten biscuit and paused to eat it.

She rolled her eyes at her familiar, "I should put you on a diet. You're already heavy to carry." A grin started at his little strangled noise. He turned, hiding the rest of the biscuit from her and finishing it quickly.

Not a single trace of the magic from that night. The grasses' memories were useless. Descriptions of boots filled her mind, and the scent of a man's piss that night. She walked through the parking lot several times. Using a flashlight from her truck, she picked up buttons and coins, just in case the witches or her brother carried them.

A young maple stretching toward the half moonlight drew her attention. It slept, but she could tap into the power running through it, listen to the tones of its memories. It witnessed more, and the description matched Jasper's recollection. A hooded couple, hardly any markings to make them stand out, except that one had a slight limp after dealing with Camden.

They'd also left in a car. A gold four-door thing that reminded her of a Camry by the shape and reverberations of it. Those were a dime a dozen.

It took her years to understand the perspective of plants and the earth. They perceived things, rather than saw them. She imagined it was similar to how a bat knew its surroundings with echoes, but she couldn't be sure of that either. Nita still had trouble translating the feelings of her friends into what she should look for, but it was getting easier. Her grandmother had been an expert and taught her well. Without her grandmother, she would still mistake car noises for thunder.

Nita picked up Belsauros and listened to his findings as she climbed into her truck and fired it up. In the mix of more crumbs, he'd picked up on something. A single footprint toward the edge of the parking pad before it bled into the little alley. A size twelve boot print beside Camden's cheap sandal print.

"What size does Jasper wear?"

Belsauros chattered at her, and she nodded. Size twelve. It could have been Jasper's boot. She would have to have Belsauros check the imprint.

Next was the bar.

Nita wasn't acquainted with Randy well. She saw him in passing. Like any typical teenager in Murphy, he spent his nights at the few spaces available for teens to hang out. Cherokee Bar and Grill allowed teens to play on the pool tables and arcade games until 9 PM each night. It was where Randy was last seen.

Bel was hesitant about exiting the truck this time. The scent of beer always made the raccoon recoil. At least there was a bit more greenery at the CBG.

Terrible memories flooded through her mind unbidden as she studied the bar. Nights where she hauled her brother away, bloody and reeling. Other nights where she stank of beer because some ass thought her mixed blood wasn't good enough to breathe the same air. A night where she found Christy curled in a corner stall, clothes torn, and blacked out.

The guys that did that hadn't lived in the county much longer after Camden, Mason, and Jasper found them. Christy barely remembered that terror, and Nita was glad of that. She still had bits of their hair and fingernails in jars deep in a cabinet in her greenhouse. Just in case the bastards crossed back into her magical reach.

Last she heard, they were still rotting in Florida somewhere.

She drew her memories back to the good ones. Few as they were. Winning a game of pool against Mason. She'd left that night fifty dollars richer and something she could shove in his face when she wanted. Her twenty-first birthday party, where she had gotten a bit too tipsy and Jasper carried her home and tucked her into bed. The night Christy threw a Coyote Ugly theme night, and they had sung and danced until dawn broke through the grimy windows.

Thinking of dawn, she glanced to the eastern horizon and frowned. It had been a while since she pulled an all-nighter. Nita began her search, unhindered as the bar was closed. Patrons didn't stay too late during a weeknight. A blessing a small town held. The majority worked day shifts, while only a few dozen were assigned to nights.

Many stories resided within the plants here. Their rumblings and songs livelier as they learned to stay alert through the night, unlike their counterparts. Nita struggled to describe Randy to the plants magically. Belsauros wasn't having much luck in helping her, either. She sifted through what they sensed the night Megs said he went missing. Trying to find the right tones and rumblings that might match Randy.

The town now has more teenagers than when she was one.

Frustrated, she tugged on the end of her braid.

"What are you doing here?"

Belsauros hissed, doubling in size as his fur stood on end.

She turned, slowly, to glower at a man head and shoulders taller than she. His aura made him like a tower compared to herself, and she kept herself from shrinking into his shadow. The fact he snuck up on her and Belsauros sent her hairs standing on end too.

"Could ask you the same thing." Nita drawled, pretending to not notice the threatening aura about the male.

"Witch?" The way his head cocked to the side slightly could have been endearing, if she knew him.

Nita squared her shoulders, stilling her fingers on the end of her braid. "Now, am I to take that as you being nice or you meaning something else?"

His smile made dimples appear on either side of his lips. His towering countenance seemed to relax into a homey brick house stock. "Green hair, raccoon familiar…I think you're a Bell Witch, right?"

"Depends on who's asking." She didn't think she knew him. He had some familiar traits, but she couldn't quite put her finger on the family she thought he came from.

"A Martin witch."

Martin. A name that was synonymous with the county as her own. Like her bloodline, Martins resided in the area prior to the emergence of surnames. One of her ancestors had married into the Martin family, too. "A Martin witch should've known better than to sneak up on a Bell."

His chuckle threatened her, yet made her relax. The conundrum yanked her in two different directions. Bel crouched between them, fur on end still, but no longer hissing. She sensed her raccoon's indecision about the man before them, too.

The Martin witch kept his smile, dimples and all. "Forgive me. It's been a while since I've been here. I forget how touchy Bells can be. One little tap and the sound carries for miles."

As she questioned whether it was a threat, he persisted.

"I'm Victor Martin. The head of District Two in the Southern Roots Coven."

The coven her great-grandparents had been part of and the one her grandmother had shunned. For what reason, she never stated, but Nita always thought it had to have been terrible for her grandmother to break with a fifty-year tradition. When Nita reached womanhood, the coven had sent her an invitation. Before she could even read the contents fully, her grandmother had snatched it away and threw it into the fire pit.

"Kinda young to be a head, aren't you?" Nita tried to give herself time to wrap her head around a coven leader being here. The coven's home was in Atlanta, two hours away on a good day.

"Thanks. I worked hard for it. How come you didn't join? We would've joined at the same time, you and I." His smile grew slimy with that revelation.

Something warm tickled low in her heart. She clamped down on her emotions, as her grandmother had taught her. "Not very sociable. I'm more likely to kill a group as to join them."

His smile faltered, and the tickle doubled.

"You're a little too grabby for my tastes. What are you doing here?" Nita narrowed her eyes on him, trying to figure out what was going on. What was so off about him?

The tickle stopped, and a shock of magic pulled away from her. He took a deep breath, his nostrils flaring with it. His aura grew again, going from homey to somewhere between a tower and the hulking mass of metal and concrete.

"Investigating. There have been a handful of missing persons cases in the area, in my district. I've come to see what I can find." His head tilted back, his eyes narrowing on her, "Seems you are here for the same thing. Or hiding your tracks."

She snorted, a little unnerved at how the shadows kept her from seeing much about him except for his smile and shape. He was making her perceive what he wanted her to. "Yes, I am so lonely that I need to replace my brother with a practical stranger who is an annoying teen."

"If that were true, then I would say you have company in the coven, and me." His countenance grew softer, what she could see of it with his back to the sunrise, and some magic hiding him from her.

Yet again, Nita puzzled over his words. She was torn between viewing them as a threat or dismissing them as mere smoke. "Have you found anything? Any leads as to where Camden might be?" She kept her arms loose at her side, even though she really wanted to create a barrier by crossing them over her chest.

"Probably no more than you have."

"Are you being vague on purpose, or are you tryin' to piss me off?" Nita grabbed for anger, it was always the safest bet.

That smile with the dimples appeared again, "That's the Bell fire I remember." He paused, stepping toward her while idly running a hand over her truck's fender. "We've met before. Do you remember?"

Nita felt her face twitch. "I'll meet you again, I'm sure. In hell, if you don't stop trying to make circles with words."

His chuckle was low, "I was eight years old when I visited my great-grandmother for the last time. Mother and Father took us all out for ice cream at this little deli or cafe. It was an odd name. You were there. With your brother and parents. We played together a little, after finishing our ice cream while our parents talked."

"No Name Deli." She spouted, and remembered a black-haired, dark-skinned, all elbows and knees boy with a dimpled smile and ice-blue eyes. Three months later, her family had a car accident and her world turned upside down.

"You remember." His voice warmed as his smile returned.

The tickle was back. This time, Nita broke it by crossing her arms and clamping down again. "Spirit witchery is forbidden without express permission. No matter if you're the coven head, a district head, or a nobody."

"I was wondering if you recognized it. Or if you're as dead to socializing as you claim." Another smile, and he leaned against her truck, crossing his own arms. Sunlight hit his face, and she could make out his features. The Martin roundness, but with sharp cheekbones and brows and a narrow nose with a flat end. The eyes remained icy, lifeless, and cold.

"Camden."

"Ah yes." He made a half sigh, half groan, as if she were annoying him with questions, "Camden Bell. He went missing from the Waffle King. I picked up on two witches, a Spirit witch, like myself, and an Energy witch. The same here, where Randy Haskins went missing."

When he said nothing else, Nita wanted to shake him by his neck. "Is the Spirit user a Martin?"

His smile twisted to one side, "Now, now, Miss Bell, don't go pointing fingers already."

Her eyebrow twitched, and she wanted to rub it away.

"Please, fret no more than you have to. My team and I are on these cases and we shall solve them. Quicker, if we do not have to worry about you going missing too, Miss Bell." His voice drawled, warm and low like someone pouring honey over a biscuit.

He was right on top of her, and she wondered when he had gotten in her face. Peppermint filled her nose as he spoke, and she stared into those ice eyes. "I'll do as I please. Camden is my brother and Randy is my friend. If I can help, I will."

His eyes scanned her face, down her neck, then back up, "You can help if you join the coven. But as you are just a lone witch, you will only impede our investigation."

"Don't you go getting in my way. Have a pleasant night." The way he looked at her felt all types of wrong, but warm too. She was tired. Too exhausted to put up with this man.

She picked up Bel, stepping back from Martin to do so, which irritated her pride. Nita slammed her truck door, smirking as it wailed on its rusting hinges and made him hunch as if to cover his ears with his shoulders. She drove off, her tires spitting gravel at the bar and the Martin witch.

She jerked as the phone buzzed in the seat beside her. Both she and Bel scrambled to find it amid her excess clothes and tools. "Hello?"

His voice held a yawn behind it, "Where the hell are you?"

She glanced at the eastern skyline and inwardly cursed as the first hues of daylight peeked through the buildings. "In town."

Jasper's tone livened up. "What? Why? Did they find Camden?"

"No. I was hunting for him." She hated to break his bubble.

"You coulda told me."

"You were asleep." Nita focused as her truck barrelled down the two-lane road toward a line of cars. The first dregs of the morning shifts going to work.

"Not when we were having dinner." Jasper bit out.

She rolled her eyes, "Look, if you're about to become one of those clingy guys or one of the control bastards, you best get that out of your system before I send you down to Florida."

Jasper barked a laugh, "Baby, you can try to get rid of me with all your might, but I'm here to make sure you eat, sleep, and are happy and healthy for the rest of my life."

Nita thought on those words, turning them over in her mind. The slick feeling in her stomach dissipated for the warmth he always brought there. "You're so weird."

"How am I weird?"

"The rest of your life, really?" She tried to keep the smile at bay, but failed.

Jasper half laughed before saying, "Yeah. Balls deep. Er…well, I um…"

"Fascinating."

"What?"

"I can hear your blush."

Jasper groaned. "Shut up. I'll see you when you get home. Which better be soon. The eggs are burning."

After the tone, she looked over at Bel, "How can someone burn eggs?"

When the raccoon just chattered with his arms out wide, she shrugged, "Yeah, I dunno, either."

Chapter Seven

"Hey!" Christy plopped down in the booth seat across from her with a wide grin. "Oh… have you had coffee?"

Nita's brow twitched, "Yes, why?"

"Cause you still look growly." Christy admitted, circling her finger to encompass Nita's face.

"I was up all night," she admitted, wishing for an intravenous drip of caffeine.

"Ooooh?"

Christy had many types of grins. The one she sported now was the pirate grin. The one where she always got herself into trouble with, because whatever was going through her head was not a good thing. Sometimes, that grin also led to some plan that got Nita in trouble, too.

"No."

"Huh?" Confusion replaced the pirate's grin for a moment, "What do you mean no?"

It was Nita's turn to motion at Christy's face with a single digit, "Whatever you're thinking, it's no."

Christy grinned again, "Oh, but I think it's all kinds of yeses. Maybe some moans too."

"Huh?" She needed more coffee. The pot she had downed that morning with Jasper's burned eggs was not allowing her to follow her bestie's thought processes at all.

Christy basically bounced in her seat. "Oh, come on! You got to tell me all the details! You and Jasper!"

Nita glared at Christy, trying to piece together what she could mean about the details of her and Jasper. She had just enough coffee left in her that her brain finally clicked into the same wavelength as Christy's. "Oh. It's not like that!"

"Didn't know that someone with a tan like you could still blush so heavily."

Nita swatted Christy's hand away when she poked her cheek. "I was up all night trying to figure out what happened to Camden and Randy."

Christy sighed, her lips puffing out.

Nita blamed her best friend's model training on how well the woman could pout at the drop of a hat. As soon as the server dropped off their coffees, Nita took down half of hers.

The model bestie waited until Nita was done swallowing before asking, "Mason said Jasper's been living with ya. Or with the gays. Which one?"

Nita took down the rest of her coffee so she wouldn't have to answer.

"Please, please, please don't tell me he went with the gays because you are too blind to give him a chance!" If she waved her hands around anymore, she'd have to get up on the table between them to keep from smacking things.

Nita had a hard time swallowing the last few gulps. She coughed a few times, until it settled into the right pipe, "He's living with the gays. He likes it. They're really sweet."

Christy leaned forward, the smile back, "Sooooo?"

"So what?"

"Does that farmer's tan go all over and we gotta call it a real tan now or what?"

She looked around, trying to figure out what could save her. Seeing nothing but the server and the barista, which would be no help as they were practically strangers. She explained weakly, "It doesn't go all over. But! It's not like that. I had to break a… thing… that was put on him."

She slumped, that model pout back again. "Sooo have you at least kissed?"

"Yeah."

"At last!" Christy flailed, "Thank Gawd!"

Nita rolled her eyes, "Maybe you should be an actor."

Christy snapped back without any hesitation. "Maybe you should let him live in your bed."

"Yeah, okay."

"Ditto for the acting thing."

They sat in a comfortable silence, enjoying each other's company, then Christy broke it.

"Did you find anything?"

"A little more than I had. There were two people who took Camden from the Waffle King." Nita explained, not sure if she had made any headway or not.

"Here?" Christy asked, her eyes wide.

"Yep."

Her brows drew down, and Christy said bewilderedly, "But he was left in Yellowstone."

Nita snapped her fingers, the sound weak, "That's what the thing made Jasper believe I had to take off him."

"Oh. Like..." Christy leaned forward and whispered, "A curse?"

She answered, "Yeah, exactly."

Christy turned a little green, "Is Jasper alright?"

"Upset with himself. And with me." Nita muttered the last bit, wishing she could magic more coffee into her cup so she wouldn't have to talk so much.

"Why with you?"

Nita looked down at her hands closed over the cup, "Cause I went out to search all night last night without telling him."

"You went alone?"

"I had Bel."

"Nita! That's dangerous! What if you were attacked or kidnapped, too?"

Nita glanced over at the two employees and watched as they tried to appear busy. "I'm fine," she said to her best friend as she motioned for another coffee to be brought to her. "I met someone."

"Oh?" Christy's brows drew together, "Like…like you're replacing Jasper met, or like you met someone new?"

She shook her head, "Chris, look, there's no Jasper and me. Not yet. I dunno if there will be. But it's… it might?" She still wasn't sure if Jasper was really in love with her or not. She hoped, but he had burned her before. "I met someone last night. A Martin. Head of the District."

Christy looked even more confused, "What district? Like school district?"

She'd never explained to Christy about the coven, so it was no wonder her friend didn't understand. "No, coven."

"Oh."

"Yeah, it's a bit much." Nita admitted, wrinkling her nose. Anything to do with the coven sent her into confusion mode as well.

"I'll come over…er… maybe tomorrow night?"

Nita nodded with a smile, "I'll make sure he stays the night with his boyfriends."

Christy laughed right as the bell over the cafe door tinged. Her laugh died down, "We might need to take that other coffee to go."

Before Nita could move, Mason slid in beside her, trapping her between him, the table and the wall.

"Hey." He said with a grin, draping his burly arm over the back of the booth.

Nita could feel the heat off of his arm on the back of her neck. His aftershave curdled her stomach as it filled her nose. "Just leaving. Move."

"Aw, come on little witch, spend some time with me." He turned toward her, instead of sitting in the booth properly. As the server set her coffee down, Mason moved it closer to her, "See, enjoy some coffee with me."

When he turned to place his order, Nita gripped her coffee cup. It was too good to waste on pouring it over him. Plus, that might put her in more danger. Never anger a bear unless you got some room between it and you. She had no room.

Christy piped up, eyes darting between her best friend, and her crush as she twirled her blond hair on a finger. "Hey Mason, guess what?"

"Hm?"

"You don't have to take me down to Atlanta anymore. Got my car fixed." Christy's smile was bright, somehow, it didn't reach her eyes at all.

Mason lifted a shoulder as he answered, "That's good, but I don't mind."

"I know."

"Sides, that little car isn't any good. Might as well keep ridin' with me once or twice a week. Hate for ya to break down in the middle of the freeway." Mason said, actually being a nice guy for once.

The only reason she ever tolerated Mason was because of Christy. The man would do anything for her best friend. And Christy liked him for it. Nita hoped it was a crush that would go away soon.

"And this witch's truck ain't no better." He said with a tug on her bun.

She'd fit all her hair on top of her head, for once, and it was a miracle it stayed with the tug. "Yeah, well, I don't enjoy going down to Hotlanta, anyway."

"You don't like goin' anywhere." Mason said with a snort. He picked up his coffee and took a sip when the server brought it over. "What are you two up to today? Brewing love potions?"

Nita rolled her eyes when Christy tightened her lips and shook her head at her slightly. Mason had a knack for irritating her solely through his presence. "Gonna come up with a way to make you mute."

"Don't like the sound of my voice? Not Jasper enough for ya?" He leaned in close to her, lowering his voice, "Does he still make you want him?"

She shoved at him, both of her hands flat on his broad chest. He barely budged, and she mentally cursed him, "Let me out."

Something crossed Mason's features before he said, "Talk to me for a bit. Hardly ever see you anymore."

"When do you want to see me?" Nita asked, hating her voice rose a few notes.

"Oh, I always wanna see you. Ever since you grew from the skinny little twig to the curvy thing you are now, you've been pleasing to the eye. Even with green hair."

She glanced under the table, wondering if she could slip under and out on Christy's side. Too much work. "So nice mother nature made me look good to you, I can die happy now." She muttered, trying not to snarl.

Mason's grin was feral and lopsided. "Not yet, been a while since we've spent some time alone. I'd like to do that again, a couple of times maybe, before you die or disappear again."

"Mason!" Christy's face was red.

"What? She ain't got anybody. Camden will snip Jasper's balls if he tries anything. Might as well give her a little fun." Mason spread a large hand wide on the table between them.

"Yeah, thanks. Perfect. Just what I want." Nita sneered, "Mason, a poor replacement for Jasper."

Mason turned back to her, leaning over her again, his lips twisted, "I'm better than that little bastard any day of the week, darlin'. Lemme show ya." He reached for her.

She swatted his hold away, kicking his knee at the same time. A tap. That's all she managed. The table didn't give her enough room to do much of anything. She couldn't breathe with his hot breath pouring over her.

"Mason, stop. That's enough. You always go too far." Christy was up, tugging at Mason's shirt to get him out of the booth.

Nita experienced the magic intensify within her and she pressed her eyes closed, striving to utilize the darkness to concentrate on suppressing the desire to use it. Suddenly, she sensed the weight of Mason being lifted off the booth seat. She looked, up and witnessed Jasper square up to Mason.

"Long time, Mase. How ya been?"

"Just fine, Jasper. Having a little chat with two of the prettiest in Murphy. You see?" Mason's head tilted toward the two in the booth.

"Yeah, yeah, I know," Jasper said, directing his gaze towards Nita. He paused, staring at her, "You alright?"

Nita swallowed down the bile, a burning threat that she was about to lose all her coffee. "I'm fine."

He turned back to Mason, "Mind if I join?"

"Nah, go ahead." Before Mason could make a move, Jasper slid in beside Nita.

He placed Mason's coffee cup to the inside on Christy's side of the table. "Now we can all catch up."

"Takin' a day off? Not like you," Mason grumbled as he slid into the booth after a glare from Christy.

"Runnin' a few errands for my current contractors. They wanted some good coffee, and I told them I knew just the place."

Mason groused, looking around the diner. "Ah. Where you workin' now?"

"You wouldn't be familiar with them. Far off the beaten path, not a townie like you."

Mason sneered, "You've become a townie now, too."

"That might change soon." Jasper smiled, glancing at Nita.

Nita shrank back into the booth, wanting it to swallow her even as Christy leaned forward with a strange gleam in her eyes.

"Yeah? Finally, making a move?"

Jasper whispered conspiratorially, "Maybe. Made plenty in the past few days."

"Yup. Time for me to go," Nita announced, sliding along the bench and into Jasper. She pushed at him, and he gave a little.

He wrapped an arm around her shoulders and kissed her temple.

Her face seemed to be burning.

"Want me to take you and Christy home?" Jasper asked.

"I drove."

"And?" His brow was up, hand tightening gently on her shoulder before rubbing a slow circle.

Nita reminded him, "You got work."

"My bosses aren't hard asses." Jasper said with a smile.

"Wait, aren't you working for the gays? I heard you were." Mason grinned, "Might not be hard asses, but they sure do like 'em. Bet they like yours."

"Yeah, they like lookin'." Jasper nodded, his arm tightening around Nita.

"Betcha it's more than a look. You've always been a softie for the different ones. Like that little witch under your arm. She looks like a freak. You like 'em like that, right Jasper?"

Before she knew what she was doing, Nita straddled Jasper. The table screeched toward the other side of the booth in her haste. His face was in her hands. Did he have some kind of magic control over her? Why had she sat on top of him? She understood the reason she was on top of him by observing the emotion in his eyes, the tightness of his jaw, and the twitching of the muscle beside his left eye. "Look at me."

His hands curled into fists on her hips, "I'm alright."

"He's not worth it."

Jasper smirked, "No? I remember you beating him a few times. Wasn't it worth it?"

"I- that's not the point."

"Sir, your order's ready."

Jasper nodded at the server. "Come on, walk me out." He said, patting her backside.

She wanted to stick her face in an ice bucket. Nita sensed her cheeks growing warmer as her best friend looked at her with mouth agape. She shrugged, grabbed her coffee, and walked beside Jasper.

Once outside, she took a deep breath of the already humid air.

"He touch you?"

"No."

"Tell me the truth." Jasper's tone darkened.

"He didn't. He pulled on my hair. That's all." Nita was thankful for town smells, for once. It was a lot better than whatever aftershave Mason used.

Jasper cursed, placing the tray of coffees into his truck through his open window.

The bell rang, and Mason was coming through the door. Christy behind him.

Jasper grabbed him by the shirt collar, hauling him over to the brick wall and slamming the bigger man into it. He stood in Mason's face, his fists in the polo shirt, "Touch her again and I'll kill you."

"Jasper? What the hell are you doing?" Nita felt her heart go up into her throat. It was always Camden that flew off the handle. Not Jasper. Jasper was always with her, playing referee and blocker to Camden's wild actions.

Mason laughed in Jasper's face, "You oughta be aware, if you touched her more, she wouldn't beg for me."

"What?" Jasper's hold loosened.

Nita rolled her eyes, "Oh please. Anyone who would want a Mason type is blind or…" her voice trailed off at Christy's wide-eyed stare.

"Or ain't gettin' what she needs from a Jasper type." Mason finished for her before turning his gaze back on Jasper, "What happened to your balls, hm? Scared to toy with the little witch? Scared she'll spell you into something slimy once you're done with her?"

"To hell with you." Jasper growled, slamming Mason into the brick again before letting go of him. "Never go near her again."

"Oh, I won't. She'll come to me soon enough, though. Once she sees your yeller belly."

"Jasper… don't." Nita tried stepping between the two men, but she was too late.

Jasper turned, slamming his left fist into Mason's jaw. The larger man smashed against the brick wall he had recently pushed off of and slid down a bit. He shook his head, rounding on Jasper. Nita jumped in between them, slamming her body into Jasper's, sending him stumbling back into the side of his truck. She experienced the brush of Mason's knuckles against the back of her head as he just managed to hold back his punch.

She turned, glaring at Mason, "Back off!"

He held up his hands, palms toward her as he took a step back, "Call off your little bitch." He pointed a thick finger at Nita, his dark eyes looking behind her.

"Remember who the witch is here? I'll do as I damn well please. You best pray to your pathetic god that I don't take a pound of your flesh." Nita hissed, showing her teeth and feeling more like Belsauros than herself.

Mason stepped into her, a sneer curling his lips and twisting his face as a bruise blossomed over his jaw, "I'll give you a pounding any day."

Nita grunted as Jasper tried to pull her out of the way. She hugged him to her back, nudging him back against his truck again with her body, "I doubt I'd call it that. Those steroids you took in high school has your dick lookin' more like a pinky from a baby."

Mason's sneer grew grotesque. She sensed the intense hatred radiating from him, as she felt her own towards him. Ice threaded in her veins, and her stomach grew solid as it sunk deeper into her.

"Once you have me, you'll never want another."

"I have had you. I've wanted others ever since. Wouldn't want you again if'n you became the last man standing on this earth."

"You've what?"

She detected Jasper loosen.

"Oho! She didn't tell you, hm?" Mason crowed with a laugh. "Oh, back in the day, we had a little fun."

Nita rolled her eyes, "Just wanted to see what it was like."

"To have a real man," Mason added.

The hatred and disdain she had for allowing herself that moment of weakness burst from her as a kick. She took all her weight and all the momentum she could to plant the top of her boot deep into Mason's crotch.

The big man doubled over, his breath leaving him in a half whoosh and half choking cough. He fell to his knees, then his shoulder hit the pavement. He lay in a fetal position. Every muscle and vein taught. His skin going from red to pale to red again.

She looked at her best friend, "I'm sorry, I didn't mean…"

"I know. You've never liked him and it's easy to insult a man by saying what wouldn't like him." Christy sighed, "Hell, I dunno why I even like him."

"I'll help you get him in his truck." Jasper murmured, leaning over to half haul, half be Mason's crutch while Christy took Mason's keys out of his pocket.

Mason's voice rasped, "I think she busted somethin', man."

"Probably."

"Hospital."

"Walk it off, dude." Jasper rolled his eyes, shoving the ass into his truck. "You gonna take him home?"

"Yeah, I guess," Christy said, slamming the door on a whimpering Mason. She turned to Nita, "Raincheck?"

"Yeah. Tomorrow night?"

Christy grinned, "Yeah, if you're not too busy." She waggled her brows at Jasper. Then laughed as Nita and Jasper both turned red.

Nita watched her best friend drive away in the large red truck. "You better get those coffees to Gus and Wade."

"Hold on." Jasper leaned against his truck, facing her, "You fucked Mason?"

"Yeah."

"When?"

"I-I dunno. Maybe two or three years ago?" Nita studied him, wondering why he was asking about it. "It was after Christy's birthday party... yeah, three years ago."

"Why?"

She lifted a shoulder, feeling a chill. She crossed her arms over her belly, not sure why this line of questioning was important to him, but his voice sounded angry. Perhaps wounded. "He was willing, and I was tired of being a virgin?"

Jasper rubbed the back of his neck after he pushed off his truck, "Hell, I was willing! Why not... why..." he threw his hands wide. "I gotta go." He jumped into his truck and sped off.

Nita stared after him, watching as he barely stopped at the sign that would take him the quickest way out of town. "Yeah, okay. So he was willing three years ago? With who?" Nita rubbed her jaws. The muscles were tight from biting her tongue to hinder her magic and to keep from saying words she would regret later. "I need sleep." She told herself, dragging her feet toward her truck.

"Shit. He has my coffee." She groaned along with her truck door. "Sleep it is."

Chapter Eight

Jasper didn't stay with her that night. It was for the best. She slept most of the day and well into the night, only waking at her normal time. As the sun rose, she sipped her coffee and dug her toes into the rich earth. The plants stirred awake, and she let them ease her into waking too.

She knew what she needed to do that day.

Upon glancing in her box, Nita realized that someone had taken the note for the couple with fertility problems, along with the herbs she had made for them. In its place was an envelope with the rest of her money. She tossed it into her house, not caring where it landed.

Finishing her coffee, she left the mug on the stoop and made her way into the forest. The dead leaves of years of shedding trees crunched under her feet while the dew coated her from her toes halfway up her knees. She was as bare as she dared to be. Short cutoff shorts and a thin tank top did little to keep the chill of the morning from goosepimpling her flesh.

She breathed in and out slowly as she took in her surroundings, becoming one with the earth, the little and tallest of the plants. She touched each tree and bush along her path. Nita hoped the little knowledge she held in this practice would be enough.

The old ironwood greeted her with a rumble. She hugged it, the rough bark biting into her flesh as she drew upon its strength. "Dear friend, do aid me in this." She smiled, pressing a kiss to the rough bark as the tree's power swelled with the magic of the land and ley lines running beneath it.

Drawing a portion of it into her body, she hummed with the tune of her land's magic. Centering it on her vocal cords. She turned, following the ley line deeper into the forest, until a small clearing opened before her. In the center was an old, ragged stump. The roots knotted and stretched to the edges of the clearing and Nita was careful not to step upon them lest it borrow her power too soon.

She leaned over the stump, feet planted and hummed into the hollow at the top, filled with the clearest of rain water.

The small pool rippled as she directed the magic from her cords to the pool.

A breeze whispered through the surrounding trees, telling her to ask her question.

She sang in the ancient tongue her grandmother taught her. The tongue of her family. Of the druids and natives. The pool shimmered and Nita placed her hands on the side of the natural made wood bowl. The edges smoothed by centuries of use and erosion. She asked for the missing.

Tones vibrated through the little pool, entering her hands and mind, trailing up her body and to her vocal cords until she spoke their names. "Essie and Ebony, Gail, Lilly and Evan, Faye, Randy, Camden, Leland, Vivian." The names washed through her.

Nita leaned on the stump, letting it eat away and gather her magic as she asked another question. She asked for the wellbeing of the missing.

Tears arced over her cheeks at some names, two, but the rest were fine. Gail and Leland were no more of this world. Pain shot through her in places at the others, they hurt three, and she would need to find them soon.

"Where?" she asked, slumping against the smoothed wood, her nose close to touching the rain water. She didn't see her own face in the reflection, but her brother's. Nita didn't dare touch the water. That way, souls got taken, pulled along the ley line until they were spit out. Lost. Becoming shades that tortured the living, feeding on magic and life to regain their own.

Another name bled from her vocal cords, tearing her tones with its own. Her throat was raw. A coppery taste on the back of her tongue. She didn't recognize the name. The magic didn't show her anything, still taunting her with her brother's face, pale in the water.

She asked in the ancient tones who was behind the kidnappings, pushing herself away from the water, her body heavy along the edge. The magic left her. Barren, she cried out as the emptiness tore through her. The ley line beneath her begged to be tapped into. She knew that if she did, she would no longer be her.

Something heavy gripped her shoulders and pulled her back.

Nita slipped from the water's edge, rolling along the knotted roots. Each bump and bark shred into her flesh, searching for more magic and finding nothing. It took her blood instead. The invisible, rough hands rolled her to the rim of the clearing, away from the roots.

The cool, soft touches of her land enveloped her body, now afire with the loss of magic. She cooled quickly, her blood leaking to her land from many cuts along her legs, sides, and arms. One thick gash across her temple she fingered, trying to staunch the flow of blood into her eyes.

Gray fur wove in front of her, shining black eyes in a black mask stared into her eyes. A pained sound reached her ears, and she couldn't determine if she was whimpering or if it was Belsauros. She hoped it was Belsauros.

Nita ran a hand over his head. Or wanted to. She ended up just plopping her hand on top of him. She also wanted to tell him she was alright, but no words came out.

Fear zigged through her like lightning in a bottle.

She couldn't speak. She couldn't hum. Nita pressed herself to the ground, the grass sawing, the dead leaves prickling, the roots of the trees and bushes around her. She experienced their magic as if it was a mile away.

She screamed a silent scream.

Christy paced the length of the old kitchen. The lights flickered above her head. She wondered if she annoyed the old house by being there without Nita around. She'd been on the property for an hour. Usually Nita would appear by now, called to her by the land. It always alerted her when someone was around. What was taking her so long this time?

She reached for the landline and dialed the number she read on her barless phone. After two rings, she smiled at the way he answered.

"What's wrong, Bellbean?"

"That's sweet."

"Er…Christy?"

"Yeah, have you seen her?" Christy tugged and twisted the coiled wire from the phone.

"No. She's not there?"

"No. Her truck's here. The kitchen light was on when I pulled in. I can't find her in the greenhouse. She's walking up to the house by fifteen minutes and some change after I arrive. You know…how she does that eerie thing with…yeah." Christy pressed her forehead to the wall, the hard but polished pine giving her the pressure she wanted to clear her thoughts.

After a pause, Jasper said, "Yeah, yeah I know. Look, I'll be there in ten minutes."

"Don't you dare crash."

"I won't."

Christy hung the receiver back on the wall. She strode out of the house, looking all around for the third time. She even dug under the greenhouse benches, just in case she had fallen asleep under them. Christy hated the cellar, but she even ventured down into it. She double and triple checked each room and the gardens and orchard. She was about to trek out to the ironwood, if she could remember the way, when Jasper pulled up.

His dogs barked twice each before he let them out of the cab.

They were so well trained, they stayed right by his side as he walked over to her, "Anything?"

"No, I was about to…" Christy motioned to the darkening woods.

Jasper nodded, "Let me grab one of her shirts. That fat rat ain't here either?"

Christy snapped, the irritation breaking her as she followed him back into the house, "It's a raccoon, dumbass, and no, he's not."

"Hey. Let's not start worrying until it gets dark."

"Right. Right. Not like her brother went missing or anything." Christy flicked her hand with a roll of her eyes at herself as she said, "Sorry. I'm sorry. I just… this isn't like her at all."

Jasper grabbed Nita's favorite sweater and let his dogs smell it. "Got a light?"

"No." Christy answered, holding her hands out. Her jeans and top were so tight that there was no way she'd have a flashlight hidden anywhere.

He dug around in a couple of kitchen drawers until he found the right one and pulled out two flashlights. He made sure they worked before handing one to Christy. "It's gonna be dark soon."

Christy drew a breath between her teeth, reminding herself that breathing was good. "She had a long day. She just fell asleep by that old tree."

"Yeah. Yeah, that's it." Jasper nodded, following his dogs into the woods. The path looked well worn, and he saw bare footprints in the softer portions of the path. Nita was always walking barefoot into the woods. In her garden. In her house. Everywhere. "Come on, Glory. Find her, girl."

He trailed behind his blue tic as she kept her nose to the ground and followed Nita's scent. His shepherd-labrador mix, Bones, kept lifting his head, sniffing around at other things, but always coming back to the fresh trail. Bones followed the old and new scents, but always circled back to the fresh. Glory always stuck to the fresh.

He circled the old tree when they came to it, then followed Glory as she took a turn down another path. "Where is this going?"

"I don't know." Christy whispered. She always felt like she was an intruder in these woods. Especially after the stories Nita's grandmother and Camden used to tell of their ancestors. She had no magic herself, but she could sense it in these ancient trees.

Glory gave a long deep bay and Jasper sprinted forward.

He almost stepped into the clearing, when something furred caught his foot. Jasper overcompensated, sprawling back on his ass and holding out a hand to stop Christy from getting any closer. He brought the flashlight up, about to bring the heavy thing down on the fur ball on his leg, when he recognized the dark eyes in the black mask.

"Dammit, Bel. Where's-"

Sam Wicker

"Nita!" Christy cried, scrambling through a laurel to get to a body lying on the edge of the clearing to their right.

Jasper was right beside her, gathering Nita to him. Her flesh was cold to the touch, her breathing shallow. Cuts flared all over her legs and arms, one on her face poured into her eyes and down her cheeks. "She's alive." He stood, cradling her to him. "Put that over her, will ya?" He jerked his head to the sweater he'd left on the ground in his fall.

"Good girl, Glory! Good boy, Bones! Good job, guys!" He said through the knot in his throat, praising his dogs as they should be. Something to keep the panic from taking over his mind.

It seemed Christy was trying to do the same by saying, "I'll get them some chicken when we get back. Or if she has any beef."

"Thanks." Jasper watched as Christy draped the sweater over Nita. "Damn, she's half naked. Why?"

Christy shrugged, "Some kind of spell? She sometimes wears shorts so she can have more of her skin touching the ground and grass on some spells."

Jasper hissed when he touched her, "She's so cold."

"She's lost a lot of blood. Maybe we should take her to the hospital."

"You think so? What… what if they ask questions?"

Christy led the way, turning on her flashlight and letting the beam swing toward him so he could see. "I… I dunno. We've never been over if something were to happen to her what she would want me to do. Cause… well… Camden would know."

Jasper gritted his teeth, "Yeah."

They made it back to the house quickly.

Once inside, they looked at each other over Nita.

"Bath?" Christy asked.

"Yeah, probably best. Not scalding hot. Just warm so we won't shock her." He tried to remember what little emergency medical training he had while on his contract jobs and in school. He'd once thought he would make a paramedic, but the first time he saw someone he knew in a car wreck, he knew it wasn't for him.

Christy padded up the stairs to the largest of the bathrooms and started the bath as he followed.

"The first aid kit is under the sink. We'll need it after we get most of this cleaned off her." He wasn't about to leave her in there for long. Fear gripped his heart in icy fingers as he realized she hadn't woken up yet.

Nita was such a light sleeper. She woke if Belsauros walked across the room in the kitchen while she was in bed. "If she doesn't wake up in an hour, we'll take her to the hospital."

Christy cried in frustration as Belsauros started chattering and jumping around her. "I think he wants something?"

"Yeah." He grunted, positioning Nita on the lip of the tub. "Can you strip her with me and then see what he wants?"

Christy wrung her hands together, looking from Jasper to Nita and back again. "I might need to do this alone?"

Jasper raised a brow at her, "Can you move her without causing more damage?"

"Probably not." Christy nodded, and then shook her hands out.

"Then just let her beat me when she wakes up for me manhandling her, kay?"

"Sounds like a plan." Christy muttered as she helped Jasper pull Nita out of the two pieces of clothes she was wearing. She followed the raccoon downstairs then.

Jasper lowered Nita into the tub, half full of water. He shucked off his long sleeve shirt and began washing the dirt and bits of leaves and grass off her so he could see what the damage was. He cursed himself for not checking for broken bones.

After a quick check, he continued studying the tone of her skin all over, and each cut to make sure they were clear. Satisfied, he pulled her out of the tub and tried not to think too much about the color as it drained. "Jesus!" He cried as her head snapped back and stayed there with the weight of her hair. "Way to go Jasper, break her neck while you're at it," he muttered to himself, leaning her against him so he could wring the thick strands out.

Grabbing a towel from a nearby stand, he dried her off the best he could and debated on how to work on her wounds. He nodded to himself, boosting his own confidence before lifting her and the first aid kit into his arms. Jasper carried her across the hall and into her room. He pulled the cover off, knowing better than to stain the quilt on it, and lay Nita on the top sheet.

He flipped open the kit and shook his head. "Gonna have to learn to restock, babe." Jasper retreated into the bathroom to pull out the box of gauze and rubbing alcohol. He rummaged around, looking for anything else he might use. Not finding anything, he went back to Nita and began working on her cuts.

The one on her temple was already coloring her green hair. He cleaned it again, dried and covered it with a thick pad of gauze. He grabbed one of her headbands and used it to help hold a little pressure to stop the bleeding. "That might need stitches." He talked to her, willing her to speak to him, "Might need to take you to the hospital after all. What were you doing out there?"

He heard the ruckus downstairs. The sound of a kettle blowing and Christy saying things to the raccoon as they seemed to run out to the greenhouse. He sighed, "Of all the times for Camden to not be here… this is probably the worst."

He worked carefully and tried to be quick about it. After a half hour, he rolled her onto her back again, satisfied he'd bandaged her cuts and put an antibiotic ointment on all of them. Jasper was about to set her up in her chair and strip the bed so she would have clean sheets when Christy entered.

Christy held a steaming stoneware bowl in both hands, a kitchen towel draped over her shoulder. "This… I have no idea what this is, but he made me make it."

Jasper made a face as the stench hit him from the steaming mug. "Okay…" He said while eying the animal. "Is she supposed to drink that?"

The raccoon opened its mouth and smacked it with a nod.

Jasper took that as a yes. "Perfect."

Christy's voice finally gave way to her worry as she asked, "She didn't wake up yet?"

"No, but I can try something."

"Do it."

Jasper groaned, "Just… make sure there's something nice on my tombstone, will ya?"

"Sure."

Jasper sat on the edge of the bed and pinched her fingertip. When that didn't work, he tapped her cheek with his fingers, harder, and paused. Nothing. He reached down, tickling her feet, then pinching in the fleshy arch. Again, she didn't move. "Alright." He took a deep breath and dug his knuckles in her sternum.

Her sharp intake of breath made her arch, and she nearly sat up. Jasper held her down, "Easy. Easy. Hey, can you hear me?"

She nodded.

Jasper felt tears sting his eyes, "Good, baby. I have something for you to drink, can you?"

She nodded again, and he shifted to sit behind her, holding her up. He nodded at Christy, who sat beside her best friend. "Geez, Jasper, couldn't you dress her by yourself?"

"I was about to I just-"

"Yeah, right," Christy rolled her eyes as she settled the bowl against Nita's lips and tilted it to allow her to sip.

Jasper pulled the edge of the sheet around and draped it over Nita, "Better?"

"Some." Christy snorted with a shake of her head.

Each sip of the magic drawing concoction was hell. It burned her lips, tongue, and all the way down her stripped throat. No pain, no gain, as her grandmother always said. She drank it down.

As soon as the last drop hit her stomach, Belsauros jumped on the bed and pressed his paws to her throat. He licked her chin, his paws lightly patting her neck, before he chattered and moved to play with her hair. She made an effort to pet him, but the sheet held her hand captive.

"How do you feel? What happened?" Jasper's lips moved against her temple.

Nita tried to speak, only a hoarse whisper came from her lips. She shook her head.

"Shit." Christy leaned close, "Nita… how can you lose your voice! You've always been so careful!"

She tilted her head again, wanting to push them both away, but her muscles were as raw as her throat. Nita found out the reason her grandmother told her to never use the stump. Ever. She probably ruined it all by using it.

Nita would lose everything if she couldn't make the tones.

"There should be a notebook on her desk," Jasper said, shifting Nita to lie on her back. She caught the movement more than saw Christy get up. Then Jasper walked out of the room. Christy sat back down just as Jasper came in with more pillows. The two stacked them behind her, asking several times if that was better and finally, they found a sweet spot where she could recline in bed.

She took the pad and pen from Christy and lifted her brows. Something along her temple pulled, and even the muscles there were tight. What had the stump and roots done to her?

"What happened?" Jasper asked again, sitting on the other side of her.

She wrote on the pad, *Bad spell, gone wrong. Took everything.*

Christy rested a hand over the sheet on Nita's thigh. "That doesn't sound good. Even your voice?"

Nita nodded.

"What was the spell for?" Jasper asked.

Finding Camden and details about what's going on with that.

Jasper leaned forward, "Did you find him? Do you know where he is?"

No. There are others missing. When I asked who was behind it, this happened to me.

"What others?" Christy squeezed her hand on Nita's leg, "What else can we do to help? More tea?"

Nita shook her head and started drawing on the pad. She drew the bookshelf downstairs in crooked, slanted lines. In her mind, she counted the books on the third shelf, drawing them in as best as she could, until she reached the one she would need. She put the mark on the spine on the drawing and pointed to it.

Christy nodded before getting up and running down the stairs.

Jasper cupped her face in his hands and made her look at him, "Don't ever do anything like this again. What if Christy hadn't come around? How long have you been out there?"

She tried to shrug him off, but he held firm.

"It's dangerous. Christy and I don't understand what to do when we find you like this. Camden did, we don't." Jasper's lips were tight after he stopped speaking, his eyes narrowed under drawn brows.

She rested her hands on his wrists. The pulse under her fingertips was strong. Hers was like a butterfly fluttering in her chest.

"This it? Oh… should I…" Christy half turned back out the door.

Nita held out her hand for the thick book. Jasper dropped his, one slid over her thigh, and stayed, resting close to her knee. Christy dropped the book in her lap and she flipped through the pages until she found the recipe she was looking for.

Her great-great grandmother was a master at making teas and ointments for everything that could ail her family. Including a tea and poultice for those that dared use the scrying stump in their woods. There wasn't a guarantee that it would work quickly, Nita found as she read the scrawl along the edge of the recipes. The time it took for these two to work depended on how much magic and energy the stump stole.

It could take up to two weeks. She hoped it would take a day. Nita translated the scrawl onto a clean sheet of the notepad and handed it to Christy. She then grabbed her friend's wrist and held up three fingers on the other hand.

"Enough for three batches?"

Nita nodded.

"On it." Christy gave a curt nod before turning.

She gripped Christy's wrist, glancing at Jasper before motioning to her dresser with a meaningful look at Christy.

Her bestie grinned, "Alright." She looked at Jasper, "Out. She feels shy now."

"What the- I've seen everything and I'm not gonna paw at her. Besides, it's easier to change the bandages this way." Jasper said even as his ears reddened.

Nita glanced at her arms and saw some gauze held on to them with medical tape. She observed the others on various parts of her body and tried to whimper. The stump took a lot out of her. She glared at Jasper, jerking her chin toward the door.

"Fine." Jasper stood, walking out and taking the note with him. "I'll get started on this then."

Nita whimpered, relieved that a small sound came from her, but still worried Jasper would somehow burn water.

"Don't worry, I'll be there in a minute to make sure he doesn't screw it up." Christy said as she moved over to the dresser. She dug in the bottom drawer and Nita frowned. The bottom drawer was full of things Christy gave her she never wore. Ever. But didn't have the heart to throw away or burn. They were gifts, after all.

"Oh, this might do it." Christy held up a little thing that was all see-through, a mesh type fabric that Nita had only seen used in fancy underwear. Useless.

Nita shook her head, motioning to a cut on her wrist and trying to raise her brows as Christy showed her the thing while shaking it out.

"It's fine. He has control. We just wanna put the thought at the front of his mind for when you get better. Besides, the magic juice will have you right in no time.

Right?" Christy's grin was toward the pirate side of her dangerous zones.

Nita snorted with a roll of her eyes. She didn't know how many times she had told Christy that magic wasn't instantaneous in a lot of things, especially healing.

"Fine. Something a little more solid, but still with easy access."

Nita wanted to strangle her.

"For changing your bandages. Honest!"

Whenever Christy said the word 'honest', she wasn't.

"Here we go." Christy pulled out a thin thing of forest green.

Nita loved the color, just not it. The fabric, while not sheer, clung and was still very thin. It also had the thinnest straps on it that led to practically nothing. It barely covered her breasts, had strappy things over the back, and it only reached to her knees. She shook her head.

Christy's smile faded a little. "Work with me here."

Nita shook her head again.

Her bestie sighed, "Fine. This then." She dropped the little forest green babydoll back into the drawer before pulling out another one.

Christy was already pulling the sheet away before Nita could react. It was far better than the others the model had held up. Nita counted it as a half win. Lifting her arms into the short sleeves was about all she could do. She had to lean on Christy when she sat up so her friend could pull the soft jersey cloth down.

Frowning at the deep V of the neck, Nita plucked at it, trying to pull it up so it didn't show off anything, but Christy swatted her hands away. Pain shot through her as Christy leveraged her hips up to pull the gown down over her hips and thighs.

Her back must have experienced severe bruising.

Christy grimaced right with her, "I'm sorry. Are you okay? Do you need an ice pack?"

Nita nodded, feeling like a heavy log against the pillows. When Christy left, she eyed the book lying closed at her side with the notepad on top of it. Most of it was recipes, but there were a few warnings and procedures in it too. She pulled it back into her lap and found the recipe page again, and flipped to the next page.

Ways to regain magic after being drained, in black inked curly letters atop the page, made her smile. Until she started reading the list. She wanted to throw the book.

This was why there were so many terrible movies about witches.

Lay in the moonlight of a hunter's moon surrounded by hardwoods and grasses, naked, over a ley line if you can. If you have a mate, have them bring you to orgasm as many times as possible for as long as the moonlight shines on you.

Bathe thrice in a pond under the light of a full moon, once at the moon's apex, the other two halfway up the sky and halfway down. Each time sip a tea of ginseng, peppermint, and cordyceps mushroom for fifteen minutes before each bath.

Partake of six-ounce infusions of above tea every hour for three days for eight hours a day. Drink two gallons of pure water each day.

Nita groaned silently, closing her eyes and just resting for a moment. Her body was heavy, her head heavier. She debated on whether a modified version of all three would work. She didn't have time to rest in bed. Camden needed to be found, and so did the others.

Whatever had taken them was dark. Foreboding. She had inferred that from the spell, and it wasn't just the magic eating stump.

The half chuckle woke her, not the book being lifted from her lap. She rolled her head on the pillow to the right, looking at Jasper reading the book. Her book.

His eyes met hers. "I suppose the first one is the most powerful?"

She didn't have the strength to glare at him.

Jasper used the page she had written on as a bookmark. Closing the tome, he placed it gently on her dresser. "How are you feeling now that you've been awake for a little bit?"

If she were to be honest with herself. She wasn't sure. Fear kept creeping up on her, making her want to curl up and cry. If she didn't regain her voice, she might as well die. Camden wouldn't be found if she didn't have a way to find him. The thought of living without him, or her magic, made her lungs seize in her chest.

"Easy." Jasper sat beside her. The pads of his fingertips swiping away the dampness on her cheeks. "I'm here. Christy's here. We're going to do everything we can to help. Don't you worry. You just gotta rest and tell us what you need."

She closed her eyes, letting the comfort of his words wash over her. Nita tried shutting out the fear, but it curled around her heart and sank deep into her stomach. She experienced her hair being gathered, pulled toward him. She heard, then felt the brush scrape against her scalp and down the length of her hair until it reached a tangle. His fingers worked the tangle out.

"I remember your grandmother used to brush your hair when you were feeling bad. You've always had such long hair. She hummed too. I don't have the voice for it. She was probably using magic, though, right? Tones, as you call them, to help you feel better?" Jasper's voice held a warmth to it that washed over the ragged edges of her panic.

Nita studied the movement of his fingers, her eyes burning with more tears as she nodded.

"You're gonna have to teach me. If they can be taught." He said with a small smile and another gentle swoop of the brush from scalp to tangle and then to the end of her hair.

He cleared his throat, "The uh… there's gonna be a good moon tomorrow night. Supposed to be clear. Was gonna take the dogs for a hunt, but I can help you…"

His voice trailed and softened the more red entered his face.

Was he for real? Part of her wanted to laugh it off. As she usually did. The other part of her rose to the challenge and it won. Panic subsided at the thought of gaining her magic back. She nodded.

Jasper gaped.

Something inside her, dark and twisted, made her smirk.

Chapter Nine

That morning had been hell. She drank all the concoctions she could handle and gave herself two stitches in her temple while Jasper held the mirror for her, and three stitches in a nasty cut on her left calf. Nita bathed and walked with the help of Christy. Her physical strength was returning faster than her magic.

Her voice was the slowest of all.

She could whisper. Trying anything more felt like claws running down her throat instead of words. She kept the earthy scented poultice on her neck, renewing it as soon as it started drying.

At nightfall, she watched Christy's rear lights bounce along the drive toward the road. The rich soil of her garden was cooling from the sunlight it baked in. Throughout the day, Belsauros chattered incessantly, occasionally touching her with his dirt-covered paws. Each time he did, she recognized a little more of her magic power build within her. He curled in on himself in her lap, his chattering turning to the deep breaths of an exhausted familiar.

She hugged him to her, worried that she would drain him of all magic if he kept trying to take care of her.

"You're gonna get cold just wearing that flimsy thing." Jasper said, leaning against a fence post behind and to the left of her. The scent of soap and Jasper's musk filled her nose as a light breeze blew from him toward her.

She hadn't changed out of another one of Christy's gifted nightgowns. It was thin enough for her to feel the earth and power around her. Feeling it was almost as comforting as it was infuriating. Nita observed the mug in his grasp, and wished for something other than the medicinal potions.

If she moved, she would slosh with the tea and water she had drank. She held out her hand, and he put the mug gently in it. Nita drank it down as quickly as she could. The taste wasn't the best, the smell was like a skunk took a piss in it, but it wasn't as bad as the tea her grandmother had made her drink for her first ritual.

She couldn't even remember that ritual, but she could the tea.

Nita handed the mug back to Jasper and sighed. She'd been sighing a lot that day, too. The fear of not regaining her brother, her voice and her magic twirled in an angry dance with the nervousness of tonight in her stomach. She told herself Jasper would back out. She had nothing to worry about.

Another ritual performed alone.

What was it that sex did to have her gain magic, anyway?

Right. Her mind dredged up the most uncomfortable conversation she'd ever had with her grandmother. She heard that raspy voice tell her again, "An orgasm makes you open to the universe. You are so sated and relaxed that the world's power and will effortlessly flow in you, as your earthly thoughts fade away."

Perfect.

She wondered how many thought of their grandmother's words while thinking of sex, too.

"Earth to Nita."

She turned to look at Jasper.

He was grinning, "Just what were you thinkin' about, hm?"

Nita brushed her fingertips around her lips to make sure she hadn't been drooling. Nothing. She raised a brow at him.

Jasper's humor faded when she didn't talk. "I asked you if you were ready to go in and change or wash off. Or whatever it is you need to do before we head out."

Oh. Wait, he said we. She needed the earth to swallow her. Even with her voice, that had never happened before.

Before she drowned in her nerves, Nita nodded.

His arms were bands of steel under her knees, and across her back as he lifted her. She lay her head on his shoulder, suddenly feeling as tired as she had the night before. His heartbeat was strong, and a little fast under her hand. Eucalyptus melded with his scent and she smiled. He'd used the natural body wash this time, instead of his store-bought stuff.

His long legs made quick work of the path from the garden to the house. He bent, letting her feet hit the ground before he steadied her into a standing position beside the tub. Nita used him as a balancer as she turned the knob.

The house groaned. The pipes shuddered. Mud spat into the tub once, splattering over the white porcelain.

Nita glared, slapping the wall.

The house did nothing but flick the lights.

"Well, that's a bust. Did I use all the water?" Jasper asked as he turned the faucet off.

Nita shook her head and flipped the room off. She whispered, leaning close to his cheek, "Creek."

"Right." He grabbed the little shower basket she used to carry her things to the creek in before swooping her back up into his arms. "Do you, uh…need anything else?"

She shook her head, then paused and nodded, pointing to her bedroom. Once he took her into it, she pointed to her dresser and he stabilized her in front of it. Without thinking, Nita bent down to search the next-to-last drawer. His hands shot to her hips, the roughness of his jeans pressed against her through her nightshirt. She froze.

He stepped back, still holding her hips. "Sorry," he muttered with a half cough.

Her face flushed as the room spun around her. She cleared her mind, then slowly straightened herself, using her hands to crawl up against her dresser. Nita dug in the second drawer and pulled out a set of underwear and bra. She fumbled with them, and he handed her the basket.

Nita stuffed what she had grabbed into the basket, only then noticing the forest green color and the odd feel in her hands.

As Jasper lifted her, all thoughts vanished except for anticipation. Down in the kitchen he looked at his dogs, "Stay. Good dogs. Be nice." He said the last sternly as Belsauros swatted at their wagging tails.

Nita smiled at the animals, even when Belsauros huffed at Jasper for telling him how to behave. Jasper turned, shifting her world as he stooped to retrieve an item from the floor. She raised a brow at him.

His face was red as he said one word, "Supplies."

Jasper swiftly reached the creek, not using his usual leisurely stroll tonight. "Alright. How do you… can you float?"

She nodded.

"Good cause… yeah. Not gonna finish that thought out loud." He cleared his throat again and set her on her feet at the water's edge. He took her clothes from her basket and stuffed them in the bag.

The water was chilly as she stepped into it. It brought out the gooseflesh all over her, but she pressed on, using Jasper's outstretched arm to steady herself. The scent of wet earth and the smell of fresh clean mountain water filled her nose. When the water reached her waist, she let the basket float. Planting her feet in the soft mud of the bottom of the creek, she unbuttoned the nightgown until she could pull it down off her shoulders. She lay back, letting the water help her pull the garment off as she floated.

Wadding it up, she half pushed, and half threw it back toward the bank. She watched Jasper fish it out with a stick he found nearby. The water made her flesh feel as tight as her insides felt. Taking up the soap she made herself, she washed as quickly as her tired and sore muscles would allow.

Nita didn't bother with her hair. The weight of it alone wore her out, much less trying to wash it.

She swam lazily back to the bank, pushing the basket ahead of her.

Jasper reached out for her, and she handed him the basket first. She grabbed his hand and relied on his strength to pull herself out of the water. The mud was gone off her legs, her thighs especially, from where she had sat in the garden all day.

He wrapped a towel around her. "Got a place in mind?"

She nodded.

Jasper's voice held a slightly worried tone as he said, "Please don't tell me it's near the ironwood. That old tree watches me."

Nita laughed, with little sound, and shook her head. She pointed to a little deer trail to the east of the bathing spot.

Jasper nodded and picked up the basket and bag, slinging the latter over his shoulder this time. He licked his lips as he studied her, "The clothes you grabbed, they for now or… after?"

"After." She pushed through her lips and hoped he could hear her over the babbling water.

He nodded and lifted her, cradling her to his chest again.

She felt the towel shift in unpleasant ways and whimpered, trying to cover herself.

"Stop wigglin' or I'll drop you."

She did, going stiff in his arms.

He chuckled. "I kinda like you being all silent and needy. I get to manhandle you, touch you all the time, see you naked, and you don't say a damn thing! Even make all kinds of little sighs."

Nita was glad the sun was setting. Maybe he wouldn't notice her surefire worst-ever blush. If she smacked him, would he drop her? Now under his power, she had to carefully consider the aftermath of her actions.

Pointing her finger further into the woods, off the path, he turned and picked his way carefully over roots, rocks, laurels and vines. He breathed a sigh of relief once he stood in the clearing. "Thought I was going to drop you two or three times."

He gently placed her on her feet.

Looking up into his face, she patted his cheek.

He leaned into it, turning his head to kiss her palm. After he scanned the clearing he said, "Looks like that might be our best spot, in the middle and to the left. Moonlight's already started there."

She nodded and leaned on him as he walked her a few steps into the moonlight. He handed her the thermos and she reluctantly drank its skunky contents. After she finished, he closed the thermos tightly and put it back in the bag.

Nita stepped into the moonlight, letting it spill over her face. Soft pincushion and haircap moss tickled her feet, and she wriggled her toes into it. A hunter's moon shone down on them and she drank it in like the gallons of water and herbs she'd been drinking all day. Power whirled all around her, whispering in the gentle breeze that tapped and clapped the leaves and branches of the trees around the clearing.

A gasp parted her lips as fingertips touched the tender skin behind her ears and the fine hairs of her neck. They trailed down her bare flesh under her hair, lifting it and creating a fist in it. His other hand cupped her bare shoulder, the pad of his thumb raking a tight little circle before his hand slid down her arm.

He nuzzled into her neck and her toes curled deeper into the soft moss. A light tug on her hair had her tilting her head, giving him free roam. His lips touched behind her earlobe, then his tongue flicked her ear before he sucked her lobe into his mouth gently.

The towel loosened in her grip with the heavy breath she took in.

When his teeth scraped, she placed her hands in his hair. Her towel fell free, forgotten. His hot breath bloomed over the back of her neck before he nipped the space just below the shorthairs on her neck. With his one hand still in her hair, his other slid up her ribs, fingertips teasing the flesh just under her breasts, and she arched, trying to force him to touch her more boldly.

"Why have we waited so long?" He said with a moan against her shoulder.

He cupped her breast, her nipple pinched between two fingers, and she arched into his hold again. Every muscle screamed. He pulled his hand through her hair, down her back, and across her hip. He pulled her flush against him and she leaned back heavily. Her legs beginning to feel like noodles.

His fingers trailed into the curls between her legs. He parted those lips and the callous of his index finger brushed over the peak.

Her breath caught, and body convulsed. She turned to whisper against his lips, "I want you."

"I want you too. Not yet." He kissed her, deeply, his tongue rubbing hers in the same rhythm as his finger did her clit.

She whimpered, her knees knocking.

"Hold on to me," he murmured. His hand slid over to her other breast and he pressed her back against his chest with it. Holding her to him with his arm as he still fondled her.

She dropped a hand from his hair and slid her fingers through his belt loop on his hip. Nita couldn't release her hold in his hair with her other hand. She needed another kiss. She pulled him back to her mouth so she could taste him again.

An orgasm sent her sliding down him, but he held her tight.

He chuckled, "Easy does it. That's my girl."

He let her come down from the orgasm before he spoke again. "Let's lie down. Hm?"

She nodded, her body still wrecked from the orgasm. Her mind twisted with pain and the glory of finishing. She felt torn, yet whole. Empty, but she was filling.

She let him guide her down to the damp moss. It was so soft against her tender flesh. She lay back, the moss now her bed. She stretched in it, letting the earth and moonlight hold her.

His hand rested on her stomach, and she wanted more of him on her. His mouth found hers, and he drank from her, deep before he kissed and nuzzled down her neck to her chest.

When his lips wrapped around her nipple, she pressed into it, willing him to take, to suck. He did. Long, languid strokes of his tongue over her breasts before suckling hard, and more kisses and tastes. He then moved to the other breast, and she moaned. Only, little sound came out.

Her body ached to have his pressed against hers again. But he kept himself scarce. Hands and mouth on her only. That mouth kept trailing further and further down.

She whimpered. A wave of embarrassment as she tugged at his hair, trying to stop him from doing what she feared he would.

He kept on. When his tongue flicked her clit, Nita arched off the moss. After the initial licks, kisses and nips, Nita lost track of orgasms.

Thoughts circled back to her once she lay fully in the moonlight. Jasper beside her, a grin on his face that she'd never seen the likes of before. She wanted to wipe it off his face, but adored it, too.

Tonight was a night of halves and tearing of emotions and thoughts.

She waited for him. Throbbed for him in her core and heart. A thought occurred to her. She didn't have the strength to strip him.

"Clothes. Off." Her voice was mildly stronger than it had been. It didn't sound at all like her, but some raw, unforgiving thing.

Jasper shook his head.

Nita glared at him, "Now. Strip, for me."

He stared at her for a moment, then took her hand and kissed it. He sat up, pulling his boots off and tossing them toward the bag they had abandoned just outside the circle of moonlight. "You want something to drink?"

She shook her head.

He raised a brow and then strode barefoot to the bag.

Nita noticed the way his butt made his jeans tight. They were dark, wet all over from the moss and damp ground. Closer to the stream, it was always wetter. She watched him pull a bottle of water out of the bag and palm something else.

Jasper pulled her up to a half sitting position, leaning her back against his thigh and knee. After taking a sip, he held it out for her to drink. Once she took a few swallows, he capped it, tossing it to the side as he nuzzled into her neck.

"You are so beautiful. I didn't think you could get more pretty, then I witnessed you cum, and it took my breath away."

Nita snorted, turning her head away.

Jasper sighed, "I see what I see."

She fumbled over the buttons of his shirt, pleased to find he didn't have an undershirt on.

He helped her, slowly undoing the buttons as she trailed her fingers down his chest. He wasn't hairless, but not hairy either. It was like fuzz, a little thicker than what everyone in the south called peach fuzz, until his stomach. His hair turned darker and thicker in the trail that led to his groin.

She saw him peel his shirt off. The marvelous show of the muscles from a working man, defined by his work, with them being thicker in the shoulders and biceps, wiry in the forearms, and his chest muscles kept him firm. She knew he worked to keep his stomach flat, but there was little definition to it, unless he was curled back.

She slid her hands over the tattoos on his biceps, feeling the muscles and imagining them tight around her as he slid inside. His chuckle made her pause, and she looked into his eyes.

"That's why I put them in that spot. Your bells, marking me, Bellbean."

She gasped. The age of the tattoos was clear in the slight fade. At least a few years. He'd marked himself, permanently, with something of hers.

She remembered his words in the kitchen.

Then she heard them again.

"I love you, Nita."

She wanted to weep. She wanted to cry out in joy. Her emotions tore and split in her, to bounce back into each other again. Nita always told herself it would not be possible. Here it was. Now that she knew it, she didn't know how she believed.

Scared. Thrilled. Hopeful.

No longer doubting.

She couldn't say words with such meaning in a whisper. They were powerful. Meant to be sung. Screamed.

So she kissed him.

He kissed her back, long, hard, and then stood.

She lay on the moss. Watching as he studied her. Her gaze flowed to his hands. His jeans spread once he had the button and zipper undone. The bulge freed.

He peeled out of his wet jeans with some difficulty, and Nita bit back a giggle. Men's pride suffered when their private parts were exposed with a giggle accompaniment. Not that there was anything funny about it.

It was just as she expected. Not huge, not big, nothing abnormal. An average cock, for a guy that thought of himself as an average guy.

She wanted it inside her.

Nita reached for him when he drew near and he shook his head, taking her hands and kissing them. "I gotta last a while, love. You touching me with that look on your face is gonna have me act a fool."

"I need you." She mouthed, not a single sound forcing its way out of her throat.

"Oh, I've only ever seen that look you have when you've seen one of those cheesecakes you hoard and eat the whole thing in one sitting."

She rolled her eyes, glaring at him.

Jasper chuckled, "I just wanna know… am I strawberry or caramel to ya?" He waggled his eyebrows at her.

Nita slipped her hands free and wrapped one around his cock.

He moaned a curse, stopping her in mid pump on the second pull.

She gasped as he pulled her up, only to sit her back down on top of him. He positioned her in the moonlight. His cock pressed into her folds and she ground herself onto it with a whimper. Then his hands were between them, working something over his penis, and she realized with whatever low percentage of her brain was still active that he was putting a condom on.

And it was back. His hands were on her hips, holding her upright as he lay down. Then he slid into her. His hips met hers in a rocky, unbalanced rhythm at first, then they found their way. Nita felt like she couldn't keep the pleasure inside her. She tossed her head back, bathing in the moonlight as she reveled in the feel of him inside her. His cock stroking her closer to another orgasm, the grind of him between her legs driving her wild. With each stroke, the moon and earth pulsed with him. Filling her again with the lost magic.

As she climaxed, the magic spilled into her, filling her soul and throat. Her energy bolstered, she grinned as she watched him under her. His muscles taught, bunching and releasing with each thrust. She rode him harder. Pushing him faster as her body slapped into his until a look crossed his face as his body lurched and trembled under her.

Nita hummed, taking in his pleasure and adding it to her own as she let him ride his feelings out. "On your knees." Her voice was still hoarse, but the magic strengthened it, more her. Nita slid off him, stretching out on her back in the soft mosses.

Jasper swallowed, visibly, as he stared at her, his eyes trailing over her body. "It's like you're glowin'."

She smirked, trailing her hands over her breasts as she watched him slide the condom off. Once he reached for her, she rolled to her hands and knees. Digging her fingers into the earth, she arched her back and looked at him over her shoulder, "See if you can make me orgasm again, Jasper."

The sound from his throat was half whimper, half growl as he pumped more life back into his cock with his hand. When he was hard enough, he slid another condom on. "Yes, ma'am." He grabbed her hip, pressing the head of his cock until it parted her slit and slid inside her, then his other hand joined on her other hip.

Nita stretched out, pressing into the earth while rolling her hips back to take Jasper deeper inside.

With each pounding thrust, magic and Jasper filled her as one until she could take no more of either, but didn't want to stop. She begged and cried for more, even while moaning for him to stop. The first hints of dawn peeked through the trees at the tops of the surrounding mountains. The valley shaded them from the light of the sun as they lay spent on cool earth.

Chapter Ten

Jasper stayed with her the next day, sleeping sporadically after a sleepless night. Nita stayed awake, pulling out notepads and cards to write what she could remember from the stump. And her dreams.

Often, when magic returned to one's body, it brought news with it. Nita's magic was no exception. She couldn't make much sense of it all. What she saw in the stump's water bled into her dreams and her magic news.

She drank a sip of her tea. A concoction to soothe her throat and restore her voice's strength. Licorice root was not her favorite flavor, but the hefty dose of slippery elm, peppermint and lavender helped. She kept the warm mug in one hand while she moved the cards around with her other.

Trying to piece together names and where they might be was giving her a headache. Another reason she added the peppermint this time. "Doesn't matter the age?" She glanced at the names, trying to recall the approximate ages of those she knew or had heard of.

The Little's lived on the other side of the county, but she'd seen them often enough. If she figured it out right, the twins were missing. Twin sisters who were about twelve, maybe thirteen. She remembered them getting a terrible case of poison oak and the Littles had called her for help. Oatmeal and calamine weren't the only things she had in her arsenal that could help those poor girls out, and she'd helped the best she could.

Bel stirred beside her, pawing at a card.

She looked, shook her head, and said, "I don't know where it is."

Her raccoon sniffled, rubbing his nose, then pawed at the card again.

"It smells?" She studied the card and wrote the word 'smell' with a question mark. She and Bel shared a special connection. Sometimes he was in her dreams, guiding her, and he had been in them early this morning. She wondered if he saw the stump images and what news her magic brought back to her, too.

There were many things her grandmother didn't finish. Plenty of teachings not taught. At least Nita had all the books and resources at her fingertips, though.

She looked up as Jasper leaned against her doorframe.

His lips tilted up at her as he asked, "How you feelin'?"

"Okay. A little sore. Weak. But okay."

"That's good. You sound a lot better," he entered as he spoke, leaned down and kissed her forehead. "Another tea?"

Nita answered, "Yeah, different one this time."

"Yeah, I smell peppermint."

She smiled at him, "What's peppermint for?"

"Uh…pain?" Jasper raised a brow, not sure of himself.

Nita nodded, slightly proud of him for knowing little things about her life when he had so much going on himself. "Among other things, yeah."

Jasper motioned to the cards as he spoke, "Still not makin' heads or tails?"

"I think I've made a little progress. Bel says the place they're at smells."

"Lots of places stink, but it's a start." Jasper sat on the bed beside her, careful not to disturb any of the papers. "Smells like what?"

She glanced at Bel and the raccoon puffed up, looking all around. He jumped toward her, pulling at her bracelet, a single bead in particular.

"Beads?"

Her raccoon stared at her for a moment, completely still, before one paw lifted and smacked his forehead.

"I've never been good at charades, Bel."Nita glared at Jasper as he shook the bed with snorts of laughter. "Well, what do you think he means, genius?"

Jasper snorted from holding back his last laugh, "I dunno…maybe the color or plastic?"

"It's metal. Copper."

Bel jumped, patting his paws against the back of her hand.

"Copper?"

Bel chattered happily.

Nita clarified, more for herself than the animal and man in the room. She was ecstatic to have her voice back. "So the place they're being held, or at, or something smells like copper."

Jasper said in exasperation, "That's a whole two towns, plus anybody that strips copper for salvage and all the salvage yards."

Nita shook her head, "It kinda reminded me of a factory building. Windows were high up and square, the crank kind. Concrete and brick feeling."

Jasper pointed to the card, "So why's that not on the card?"

"It's coming to me," Nita growled, writing it down.

"Yeah, well, if you want help, you gotta share all the details. Not some here and there, genius." Jasper sneered at the last word, mocking her strained vocals.

"Is that what you think I sound like?" She raised her brows at him.

"You sound much better."

Nita nodded, gazing at the cards, urging her mind to remember more.

"Faye Stalcup?" Jasper asked, pointing to one of the cards.

"Yeah, you know her?"

"You do too." He tapped the corner of it, and raised his gaze to her with a slight tilt to his head.

She shook her head and Jasper began explaining, "Remember the girl that was between us in school that transferred out when I was in fifth grade, then came back when I was a senior?"

She feared her mind would break. "I…no, not really."

Jasper's brows drew together, "She's kinda sandy blonde, a little shorter than you. Oh! She drove a Jeep!"

Nita groaned, "There were a hundred people in our high school that drove Jeeps, Jasper."

His hands were in front of him, molding something in the air between them as if it would help her remember the girl. "It was blue. Like baby blue."

He was trying so hard to help her remember she wished she actually cared for some of her schoolmates back then. In her mind, she excluded dark-haired Jeep owners from the list. "Wait. Faye. Stalker Faye?"

Jasper's brows drew down over his eyes, "Stalker Faye?"

"Yeah, she used to just show up wherever you and Camden were. Well, except here, obviously."

She observed him as he sat in silence for a moment.

Jasper shrugged, "Huh, now that you mention it, yeah."

"She had pink hair her senior year. You couldn't bring that up?" Nita muttered, writing herself a note on the card with Faye's name in case she forgot again.

"Oh yeah! I remember that. Camden called her Bubblegum or something stupid every time we saw her. Which… was a lot. Guess she liked Camden."

Nita rolled her eyes and muttered under her breath, "More like you, Mr. Oblivious."

Jasper shook his head as he said, "Nah, it was bro."

She wrote the details she could remember about Faye, the important ones, on her card. "I didn't realize her family was magical."

"They are?" Jasper asked, the confusion she felt in his voice, too.

"Well, the Little twins are part of a magical lineage. So's the Martin here, Camden of course, and the Everwood. I'm assuming they're all from magical families. That's got to be the connection. If not for this, why would the coven be investigating here?" Nita half explained and half thought out loud.

"The coven is investigating? Wait, there's a coven?"

Nita realized her mistake. She hadn't told Jasper that, just Christy. "Yeah, there's a coven. A few, actually."

Jasper's brows drew together. "When do ya'll meet?"

"I'm not in a coven."

"Why not?"

"Grandmother left it, so did my parents. No need to join something Grandmother didn't want to." Nita lifted a shoulder, feeling justified in her grandmother's decision still.

"So they're bad?"

Nita thought about that for a while, "I dunno. Maybe she had an argument with them over something. She never said why she left and cut ties."

Jasper sat silent for a while, as if soaking up the information. Then he asked, "What about Megs, is she part of the coven?"

"Yeah, she is." Nita answered, wondering where he was going with this.

"Would she know why they're investigating, too?"

"I'm hoping because she told them about Randy missing." Nita lifted a shoulder, "I didn't find out, until the other night."

The night you stayed out all night?"

"Yup."

Jasper pinched the bridge of his nose to keep from lecturing her. "Alright, we'll talk about your safety and all that again later, I'm sure. What else you got?"

She let him read the cards that she had, adding details when she remembered them, and realized she hadn't written them down. Nita had always been terrible at sharing.

After studying all the cards and prodding her for information, Jasper asked, "So there's ten missing, right?"

"Looks like."

"What powers do they have? Or their families?" Jasper pointed to one of the name cards again, "You don't have that down here."

Nita blinked, staring at the surnames. "Martins are Spirit." She wrote that down, "I didn't know Stalcup's have powers, so I'm not sure. Randy and Megs are Fire bloodlines. The Littles are Water. Everwoods are Energy magic." She pulled the older lady's card, Gail Stiles. The Stalcup card and the Wright card, too. "Some Stiles are Air witches." She wrote that on the card. "If these other two are from magic lines and they are the elements I think they are…then there are family members missing from each elemental bloodline."

"What… what can that mean?"

Nita shook her head, icy, spider-like legs crawling down her spine and making her shiver. "It's not good. Powerful spells require a witch from each bloodline. It's rare for us to work with each other. It's dangerous. All that power can… it can rip the world apart and make it anew."

Jasper let that sink in for a moment. "But Camden couldn't use magic. How is he needed in all this?"

"Randy and the twins couldn't use magic either." She shook her head, "If all these can't use magic, but are of the bloodline… it doesn't make sense."

"Unless it's some kind of trap."

She looked at Jasper, something needle sharp trailing down her spine after the ice, "Trap?"

"Yeah, think about it. All of you powerful witches have someone missing that you love. You all hear that they're… somewhere. You go there. Boom. Trap." He said, snapping his fingers with the word 'trap'.

Nita groaned, pressing the cooling mug to her temple to relieve some of the pressure steadily building. "It's smart."

"Damn right it is. That means that whoever is doing this knows their targets well, too. I mean, at least you. They knew Camden would be the only person in this world that you'd do anything for, to protect."

"Not the only person."

Jasper grinned, "Aww, thanks babe."

"Christy. I meant Christy." She couldn't help the grin.

He rolled his eyes, "Thanks, thanks a lot."

Nita peeled her fingers from the 'oh shit' handle and bolted out of his truck. Not that Jasper was a terrible driver. It was that he was driving. In his brand new, weak vehicle. Not her tank of a truck.

She sucked in a lung full of air and let it out slowly. They hadn't died. Jasper was actually an excellent driver.

"You alright?"

She nodded, feeling the warmth of his hand on her back, rubbing a soothing circle before running down her spine. "I'm good."

Jasper's hand rested just below her bra clasps. "Alright. Take another minute or two if you need one."

"No, I'm good." She straightened and marched toward the little white house. A tin roof glinted in the sunlight. Box bushes, carefully trimmed in neat little squares, stood around the front of the house. Long stemmed, bright red poppies waved at them from the side and in a few of the flower beds dotting the lush green yard. The Littles always had well-groomed yards with pretty flower beds in every season.

She knocked on the door.

Looking through the screen into the mudroom, she saw several pairs of boots, sandals, and other types of shoes neatly paired on mats lining the wall by the door. Straw hats and caps hung on pegs between the square windows. A grill squatted in a corner, covered still from the lack of use in winter.

Shuffling feet drew her attention to the front door as someone entered the mudroom. She smiled, only for it to falter at the haggard face that was once bright, smiling, and always welcoming. "Mrs. Little! It's me, Nita Bell. I'm sorry to bother you."

"It's alright, dear. Come on in."

Nita's heart cracked at the weariness in the voice. She opened the screen and entered, "Jasper's with me. Remember him?"

"Of course, Nita dear." The woman shuffled back through the door and Nita followed her with Jasper right on her heels.

Mrs. Little asked weakly, her hands rubbing her cream colored apron, "Just finished making some juice. Do you want any?"

"What flavor?" Nita scented nothing in particular when entering the kitchen. It always smelled like an old house. Subtle hints of baking and frying, with the dash of age that only old ones held the special scent of.

"Apple cherry." Mrs. Little said with a sigh.

Nita nodded, "Sit down. I'll pour us all some. That alright?"

After she got permission, she pulled three glasses from the dish drain. She took the juice out of the fridge and poured each glass half full. She sat down with Jasper and Mrs. Little at the kitchen table, placing their glasses in front of them. Nita took a sip and smiled. Perfect.

"What troubles you, honey?" Mrs. Little asked, her light hazel eyes meeting her gaze through thin bifocal glasses.

She smiled at the elder, "I'm here to listen to your troubles."

Mrs. Little's eyes watered, and Nita noticed they were rimmed in red. "Bah, there's no need for that. We all have troubles."

Nita placed her hand over the lady's and gave it a light squeeze, "I know. I want to help. Maybe they're with Camden."

Mrs. Little nodded, "Maybe. I heard he was a missin' too. I'm sorry dear."

She refused to draw away. "Do you remember where the girls were before they disappeared?"

"The Murphy 'n Andrews game."

A Friday night. Hundreds of people around. Unlike Camden and Randy's disappearance, the girls being taken from there were a bold move.

"Can either of them do magic?"

Mrs. Little's eyes automatically shot to Jasper, then back to Nita. At Nita's nod, she shook her head, "Not a bit. Can't even water-witch."

Nita nodded again. Many believed the age-old talent of finding water underground to be witchcraft, but it wasn't. A chemical imbalance, a genetic trait, separates those who can and cannot do it. "Anyone else missing or hurt in the family?"

Mrs. Little shook her head in a slow methodical way, "No. But there's plenty missing. Last I heard, there were nine or ten missing from the area."

"You remember who?"

Mrs. Little rattled off the names that Nita already knew. Her goal was to compare notes and verify the truth behind the magic and rumors. Seemed like both were true.

"Lord, bless those missing. Watch over 'em." Mrs. Little murmured, her hands rubbing together in her lap. Her eyes grew sharp on Nita, "What are you thinkin'?"

Nita smiled, "I don't know yet. Do the Stalcups, Wrights and Stiles have magic?"

Mrs. Little chuckled, "Your grandmamma sure didn't tell you a thing about anybody else, did she? Always teaching you her ways and how to be safe. I don't blame her. Not at all." She nodded, then went back to answering the question. "They do. Stalcups are Light witches, while the Stiles' are Airs. Now the Wrights are Dark workers."

"The missing ones from the other families, can they work their magic?"

Her brows furrowed, "Not that I know of. I think they're all like my grandbabies." Her hands rubbed together more slowly, "None of them can even protect themselves."

"If Camden's with them, he'll protect them." Jasper stated quietly.

Mrs. Little smiled, her eyes lining with tears again, "He would do that, wouldn't he?"

"Yes, ma'am," Nita's reassurance felt weak, even to herself.

"The coven has been lookin'. Studyin' this mess. Nita, you should talk to the coven. We'd like to have a Bell back in our midst." The wrinkled hand turned, clasping Nita's.

"I'll think about it." Nita finished her juice. "Thank you, Mrs. Little. I'll get outta your hair."

"Oh, don't mind that." She said with a wave of her hand after getting up. "I like visitors. Come by again, when you have more time. You seem like you're on a bit of a mission today, so I won't ask you to stay." She paused, holding Nita's hand in both of hers, "You be careful. Do talk to the coven."

"Okay. You take care, Mrs. Little." Nita followed Jasper out as he held the door open for them both.

Jasper drove them away from the Little home, going a mile or two before stopping to look at one of the many dams nearby. The lake water sparkled under the sunlight. Not that many boats out on it, as it was a weekday, so it was quiet, save for the occurrence of a passing car or two.

He sprawled in the driver's seat. His arm snaked over the back of the bench seat and she could feel the heat from his hand on the back of her neck. He didn't touch her, though, not yet.

Nita tore her gaze away from the beauty and calm of the lake to look at him. "If they aren't magic users, maybe your trap idea is more correct than I thought."

"I hate to say it, but I think it is." Jasper sighed, "With so many missing, you'd think someone would have seen somethin'. Like one of them almost running away and getting caught again, you know?"

"We aren't in a movie, Jasper."

Jasper kept it going, "Just sayin', though. Someone somewhere shoulda seen somethin'."

Nita bit back her smile as, through his frustration, his country accent was stronger. Most of the time, Jasper tamed it. Not that he was ashamed, it was the way they were taught. Keep the slang and twang strong at home, but out and about, better be respectful and proper.

Unless you're in a fight, then give 'em hell.

"Spells. Remember how you remembered nothing because of a spell? That's probably what they're doing to witnesses." Nita pointed out, trying to think like a kidnapper. A witch kidnapper.

"Can't catch all eyes." Jasper muttered, "As nosey as most of these old bitties are… really?"

Nita said, "You know as well as I do there are plenty of places to hide 'round here if ya don't wanna be found. Some are in plain sight, while others only vermin can get to."

Jasper cursed under his breath.

They sat in silence for a while. Looking out over the lake. She listened to the sounds of the lapping water through the open windows. Copper smell.

Something clicked in her mind. "You remember a black house?"

He snorted, "You mean like a burnt one?"

"No. It's black. Like old black." She struggled, "Pine and tar old."

He frowned, "Yeah, there's plenty. Why?"

"Around some place that looks like a factory or school that smells like copper?"

He groaned, leaning up and hugging his steering wheel. He ran a hand over his face as he thought. "Can't say as I do, Bellbean. Wanna drive to a few?"

She glanced at his gas gauge. "Might need to get Christy to drive around and take pictures in her little car. Otherwise, you're gonna spend your whole paycheck drivin' us all over the country."

He raised his brows before starting the truck, "If it finds Camden and the others, it's well worth it."

Chapter Eleven

Nita's stomach flipped and gurgled strangely. Sliding from the truck, she stumbled into the woods through the grass, away from the narrow road. A few lengths in, she leaned against a tree and toed her boots off to dig her feet under the dead leaves to the dirt underneath. Taking a few deep breaths, she let the earth and plants around her soothe her frayed nerves.

"Here, drink some water." Jasper's gentle voice was at her side.

She took the bottle and drank from it.

As Jasper screwed the cap back on after she was finished, he said, "I know you don't usually wanna talk about it, but I think you're doing good. Considering."

She shook her head, more to keep away the awful memory of watching her parent's car burn than to disagree with him. The old truck that had run them off the road sat untouched, save for a dented bumper and grill. That's why she had an older truck and kept the thing running as best as she could. The new cars had nothing to them. They shattered. Crumbled down until there was nothing left inside them but ashes.

"I think they'd be proud of you. I am." He cupped her cheek.

She wanted to say something similar to him, for him, about his parents. Yet, those two were not the finest individuals. Hence why Jasper practically lived in the Bell household most of his life.

She only witnessed her father's anger once, when he discovered bruises on Jasper after they all went swimming. That night, she heard the car start and watched as he drove away. He came back as the gleam of the sun started along the horizon.

He had bags of Jasper's things and a bruise blooming over one cheekbone. Bruises and cuts covered his swollen knuckles, mostly on his left, and the stench of magic overuse emanated from him. When she went into town with Grandmother later that day, she overheard the cops talking in hushed tones in Greene's diner about how the Prices were unrecognizable, as was their house.

Their time in the ruined house was short-lived. Later, cops found a hidden building stocked with meth and its production supplies. All thanks to an anonymous tip, they stated in the paper.

"Whatcha thinkin' about, Bellbean?"

"Nothin' much." She leaned into his hand, still on her cheek. "Camden didn't see it. He wasn't around."

Jasper acknowledged her torture with a furrow of his brows. "No. I'm glad. I hate you saw it."

Nita shook her head, "I am too, but not."

What she hated was that instead of saving herself or her husband, Nita's mother had saved Nita. The cops and investigators said it was a miracle that she survived. The miracle had been her mother's air magic blasting her out of the back window of the car to safety.

Nita had only suffered a broken arm and a concussion.

And a lifetime of nightmares of screeching tires, her mother screaming, metal cracking and bending while glass shattered, and the zap of electrical wires as they set flame to the drought dry grass.

The drunk came up on them. Going one hundred miles per hour. If not more. He didn't hit the brakes. Just swerved and hit their back left, crushing the bumper and trunk into the tire and sending them flipping and rolling off the embankment.

"If I hadn't seen them… die, I don't think I could have accepted it and kept on living." Nita admitted, feeling the tears in her throat and behind her eyes.

Jasper shook his head. "You would have."

Nita knew where the argument over 'what-ifs' and 'should haves' would lead. It was never pretty. She shrugged it off and focused on what was important that day. Camden and the others.

Each place they found didn't strike her as the one from the image the magics gave her.

She needed a win today. Besides, the other vanished individuals did not possess magic. She wanted another thing to point her further along the path she needed to take. They were going to drown in the not knowing, or they were about to become as lost as the missing.

Staring at the latest factory with copper scents, she hugged her arms around herself. Nothing. Between her and Jasper, they should know every inch of the country for a hundred miles. But they didn't, apparently, because none of the dilapidated buildings matched the one the ley lines gave her. "The Everwoods are near here, right?"

"Yeah, about five miles off Friendship." Jasper said after finishing a long stretch.

Nita nodded, "Let's go there."

"Hey, Vivian." Nita greeted the woman when she pulled the old red oak door open.

"Nita? What're you doin' here?"

She tilted her head with a slight smile, "Wanted to check in on ya. Brought you a pie." Bags shadowed her friend's blue eyes, and her perfectly smooth skin sported signs of stress in its paleness.

She was glad for the store beside their former high school. About the only thing she remembered of Vivian during their school days was the love the girl had for sneaking off campus to go to the store. She'd bring back all kinds of things for them.

She handed Vivian the paper bag full of fresh apple pies.

"Oh, oh, these smell so good. Come on in. I can't possibly eat all these. How are you doing? Jasper?" Vivian talked as she stuck her nose in the bag and breathed in the apple and cinnamon scents.

Jasper answered as he shut the door behind them and followed the two ladies through the foyer to the pristine country kitchen on the right. "We're good, Viv. Nice to see you again."

"You too. Are you two finally together? It's about time. Always figured you'd either live your lives alone pining for each other or you'd have five little tree huggers by now."

Nita nearly choked on her own spit.

"Well, we're not either. Five's not a bad number." Jasper grinned.

She would kill him and drive his truck home. Nita was pretty sure Vivian would have a shovel she could use to hide her crime. Vivian placing plates and smoky glasses out on a lace covered round table drew her from her thoughts.

After Vivian finished, she asked, "Milk or somethin' else for ya?"

"Milk'll be good." Nita nodded. "Now those are for you."

"Hush, sit and catch up." Vivian waved her off before pouring out the milk. When she finally sat down with them, she gave them two pies each. "Now then, these bring back memories."

Nita smiled. She remembered the teachers lecturing Vivian plenty until they gave up. It was difficult sneaking in pies and the like with them smelling the whole

school up like some bakery heaven. "How you holdin'
up?"

Vivian shook her head, tearing a corner off one of
her pies and popping it into her mouth. "I tell ya, I dunno
how momma ran this household and worked, too. That's
what I focus on. Keep tellin' myself she's went on
vacation. Just for a little bit."

Nita could hear the tears in her voice. She and
Vivian hadn't been close, but they weren't complete
strangers. They'd been friendly. Never a cross word, but
no secrets passed between them either. "I'm sorry, Vivian.
It's hard."

"Yeah. How are you holdin' up?" Vivian's swallow
was hard, and her long fingers fiddled with the rest of the
pie.

Nita lifted a shoulder, a small smile trying to
comfort them both, "Like he's gone on vacation for a little
while."

The woman nodded. "I can't place it. Momma never
hurt nobody."

"Could she use magic?"

"Naw. It skipped her. Her sister and one brother got
it. And she passed it onto three of us kids." Vivian shook
her head. "Ya know, Little Jake was with her? Right in his
car seat when they yanked her outta the car. Left him in
there."

"He alright?" Nita's heart was in her throat, worried
the toddler suffered needlessly.

"Yeah, his screaming brought someone outta the
hardware store. That's where she'd been. Getting a fittin'
for the old sink cause it started leakin' a week back."

"Did ya fix it? Need me to look at it?" Jasper tensed
like he was about to leap up out of the polished, intricately
carved wood chair he sat in with them at the table.

Vivian narrowed her eyes as she said, "Ya know,
women can fix a leak just as good as you men. I handled
it fine."

Jasper chuckled, holding up his hands.

"Anybody see anythin'?" Nita asked around a mouthful of juicy apple and pastry.

She sighed and shook her head. "They saw a gray mini-van, a white ford truck, and a little red four-door car pass the store. The cameras they had on the parkin' lot didn't capture a thing. Wires cut."

Jasper slumped, "Figures."

"That's the way I feel." Vivian ate a few bites before asking, "What about Camden? Anyone see anything with him?"

Nita shook her head, "Magic erased it."

Vivian stared at her for a moment. "You sure?"

"Yeah." She pointed to Jasper, "Took a mark off him that kept him from telling and knowing the truth of what happened. He thought he'd left Cam in Yellowstone, as Camden wanted. But someone took Cam from here, the Waffle King."

"Well, shit." She muttered, slumping back against the rung back. "Wait... you think it might be the same people?"

Nita spread her hands, "Small town like this and over ten people missing? It's gotta be, right?"

"Wait, ten?" Her friend's eyes nearly popped out of her face.

"Yeah, all from witch families."

Vivian frowned, pushing away her plate. It took a long time for her to get her last bite down. "I think... I think I need to show ya somethin'."

Nita shivered as a trill of ice ran down her spine, but still followed Vivian to the garage. Jasper was right behind them, finishing his last pie. She blinked as the lights flickered on and gasped.

Vivian's car was always a pretty little thing. A navy blue Toyota that her parents had helped her pay for after graduation. Now it had become a wrecked mess.

Black and red sprayed letters stained the once pristine paint. Nita read some words, then all of them. 'Filthy witch!' 'Go back to Salem!' 'Wait for the bonfire!' 'Thou shalt not suffer a witch' and many more insults all over it.

"You guess who done it?"

"No. But not two days after, I saw Mason had some black stains on his fingers. Jacob and Matt Dower too. I told the cops that day, but they aren't doin' anything about it." Vivian shook her head. "Been drivin' Dad's car. He retired this year."

"I heard. Glad he did." She folded her arms over her chest, staring at Vivian's car. "I hate to ask this, but… did you show anyone your magic?"

She snorted, "I tell all my clients that it's massage, reiki and crystals. My job is enough to set stuff like this off, you know that."

She knew all too well. "Yeah, sorry. I just… haven't seen nobody lash out like this in a while."

"Yeah. Me neither. Dad says the Martins got graffitied too."

"Really?" Jasper asked, resting a hand on the fender of the vehicle.

Vivian nodded, "Their house. Covered it in shit like this and pentagrams. TP'd the trees and egged it too."

"Assholes." Jasper muttered with a shake of his head. "Need to do the same to them. See how much they like shellin' out for the cleanup and new paint jobs."

"I'd like to skin 'em alive."

Nita raised a brow at Vivian, who shrugged. "Was this about the time your mom went missing?"

"Two days before."

Nita rubbed her temples as she asked, "You think this is related, too?"

"I dunno. I can't wrap my head around anything anymore. The only reason why it's so calm here now is the kids are at school and Dad took Little Jake to the baseball field with the dogs in the truck."

Vivian was the eldest of seven children. Each time Nita thought about that, she wondered how Vivian had any sanity left. Or hair. Or anything not broken. She still lived at home, too. Nita would have been out the minute she turned eighteen if she had been Vivian.

Then again, Vivian probably felt the way about her siblings as she did about Camden. Love. Family. Those were the most important things in the world. And Vivian had always had an amazing sense of responsibility and a giving heart, too.

"You need anything?"

Vivian followed them out and shut the lights off and the garage door behind her. "No, I'll be alright. We'll be alright. How about you? Need me to reset some of your energies? You been through hell and back?"

"She has." Jasper muttered.

Nita lifted a shoulder, "Did some magic I wasn't supposed to do is all. I recovered."

Vivian shook her head. "Get on my table. Back inside. I'll be better if I work on you a little bit." She waved them back up the steps and guided them with directions to her workshop. Upstairs, to the right and in a practical made over closet.

Vivian admitted with a slight chuckle, "If Mark hadn't moved out to live with his girlfriend, you woulda had to lie down on the couch."

"Didn't think you had anyone coming to your home to work on them."

"I don't. This is mostly used to train the little ones and myself. Grandpap comes here or we go there." Vivian clarified as she set up and lit the candles.

She looked at the table, then down at her clothes. "Shoes off or on?"

"Naked." Jasper said with a grin, leaning on the doorframe.

Vivian laughed, "Shoes off, please. Might want to loosen your hair too. Lying on the table with it in a tail is gonna hurt."

Nita nodded and pulled her tie out of her hair as she kicked off her shoes again. "Feet are dirtier than my shoes."

Vivian nodded with a small curl of her lips. "Of course they are, you are an Earther."

Nita grinned and lay on the table. "Do I need to hum with you?"

"No, well, not unless you really feel like you need to. But make sure you stay open. Don't shut down on me." She said as she rubbed her hands together, warming them.

"Right." Nita closed her eyes. Having someone as close to her as Vivian did not make her serene. She was already having to grow accustomed to how often Jasper touched her. She'd never been a touchy, feely, kinda person.

She sensed Vivian start before she heard her. The woman could begin energy work without tones, or maybe it was just the act of finding where to work. Whichever, Nita sensed something like strings and film move all around her and inside her.

Once she got over the initial shock, it was easy to relax with Vivian's singing in the warmth of the little room.

After an hour, Vivian stopped humming. "Damn, what in the hell did you do?"

Nita stared up at her and asked, "That bad?"

Vivian's face was strained, and she swiped a few strands of her honey brown hair back. "I haven't had to work that hard since Grandpap drained himself trying to keep the rescue squad energetic."

"She drained herself too." Jasper piped up, still leaning against the doorframe.

Vivian sat down on a small stool in the corner, picking up a church fan and waving it around her face. "Doing what? You can plant fields without magic these days, right? There're these things called plows and tractors…"

Nita rolled her eyes as she sat up. "I tried something to figure out where the missing were. That's all."

"Did you?"

"Not really."

Those light eyes of Vivian shot daggers through her as she said, "Then it wasn't worth it. You better be more careful. With how wrecked your energies were, it's a wonder you could walk in here."

She hadn't thought of that. She'd only been worried about regaining her voice. Paralyzation hadn't crossed her mind. "I won't do it again."

"Good." Jasper and Vivian both stated.

They said their goodbyes after Nita and Vivian haggled a payment. Nita was going to bring by sage and energy boosting teas and bath salts for Vivian to use even if Vivian didn't want any payment. Nita insisted. Besides, Vivian couldn't stop her from shipping the goods or dropping them off at any time.

She was much lighter, and ready to take on the world as they walked to the truck.

"Energy witch?"

"Yeah, that's what they're called. Although, I think some call it yin yang or chakra work. Depends on the coven, heritage, bloodlines, and area you grew up in." She shrugged, "Like some call Earth witches, Green witches or Natural or Herbal witches."

Jasper paused after he opened her door, a contemplative look on his face. "Right. So it sounds simple, but it's always much more complicated than that."

Nita chuckled, "Yeah, it's that way."

That night, she lay awake in Jasper's arms. Sated with her energy and magic aligned, she couldn't bring herself to sleep just yet. She listened to his deep breathing, the soft snores that could turn thunderous at any moment, and wondered if her life was real. If any of this was real.

Nita slipped from bed and pulled one of her oversized shirts on. She slipped downstairs and curled up in an old armchair by the window. The lace curtains let the moonlight through, bright and clear. She looked up at the moon, a waning face, and let its light wash over her.

Into the trees, hugging up close to her house, her gaze drifted and paused. A great horned owl perched on a branch just above her window, in the shade of the mighty oak. Instead of dreading the message it could bear, Nita was wrapped in warmth, like a hug, and the faint scent of eucalyptus and cinnamon tickled her nose.

"Hello, Grandma. What do ya wanna tell me tonight?" Nita asked the owl in a low whisper.

The feathers fluffed, making the raptor look round and twice its normal size.

Belsauros climbed up into her lap and curled up, staring out the window, too.

Nita divined the message into form with her familiar's help. Images and feelings poured to her. Distrust. Unease. Anger. She curled into a tighter ball around Belsauros. She was doing everything wrong.

The memory of the magic drain flashed through her, and the anger surged.

"I'm sorry." Nita whispered to the owl that carried the news from her grandmother.

The message changed. Adrenaline pinged through her along with a coppery smell. Nita blinked, "That smells like blood."

Was the place they were looking for something to do with blood instead of copper?

Belsauros chattered quietly, pressing the top of his head under her chin.

Her grandmother's old coven book flashed into her mind and another surge of anger. "Don't trust the coven. I know."

Then there was nothing but the warmth of a hug for a long time.

Chapter Twelve

Mr. Greene fed Belsauros two ears of corn. Nita discussed raccoons getting fat with the old man. Of course, Mr. Greene suddenly turned deaf not hearing a word she said as he walked back up the ramp. She sighed, shaking her head as she loaded the cart up with this week's goods. She also had supplies for the Greene family that day. Stickers for them to use with Bell's Herbs & Spices printed in pretty font, along with more spices for Mrs. Greene to use in her diner that she ordered last week.

It fell short of a grand delivery. Nita had neglected her plants for a few days and it tore at her insides. To heal, and to find Camden. It had to be done. They were hardy things, her greens, and didn't need her gentle touch and care every day.

She was the one that needed it every day from them.

She bit back a laugh as Belsauros attempted to eat two corn ears together instead of one by one, and shook her head. "Just eat that one, and then that one. Don't stuff them both in your mouth, you're gonna choke! Here, gimme that."

Nita made a grab for one ear only to have Belsauros roll away from her, clutching the ears of corn as if they were lifesavers and he was drowning in the deep waters of Notley Lake. She chased him around the truck twice, then stopped as a chuckle reached her ears. A slight rise of neck hairs made her turn.

No one was near.

Not able to shrug it off, she stood still, listening to all the surrounding sounds.

Cars on the highway offered no help in pinpointing abnormalities for her. Mrs. Greene kept bird feeders, about fifteen of them, full to the brim and the birds crowded around them and carried on with loud squawks and trills. She studied each bird, looking for any that could mimic a laugh.

The itch of being watched did not go away.

She looked in each window of the Greene buildings. Each door. Every crack. Nothing.

She stupidly wished Jasper hadn't gone back to work and was with her. She clamped down on that ridiculousness and straightened her spine. Nita Bell didn't need a man to protect her. Never had. Never would.

Feeling partly a fool, she turned and pushed the cart into the packing area, grabbed an empty one and returned to her truck to load the last of her shipment. Shooting a glare at Belsauros, who sat under her tailgate, eating the cobs with juicy smacks and soft whimpers of joy, she folded the tarp up and put it behind her seat in the cab.

Nita waited on Belsauros to waddle his way up the ramp before closing the roll-up door and locking it. She gave a nod to one of the Greene's grandsons, already sorting her product and wrapping them in little pound baskets. She couldn't remember if he was Todd or if that was Ben. Thankfully, he didn't speak to her, just kept right on working after giving her a smile.

Entering the diner, she grinned at Mrs. Greene.

The hairs on her neck were still standing. Someone had eyes on her still. She kept looking around, trying to catch whoever looked at her. Hardly any people in there today, and none of them were as interested in her as they were their food and drinks.

"You alright?"

"I am. How're you?" Nita focused on the older woman in front of her who was in all her prim cotton dress and white apron glory.

Mrs. Greene waved off the question, "You look a little pale. Did you eat today?"

Nita nodded as she said, "I had some breakfast."

Mrs. Greene put a hand on her hip, "Some?"

"Yup. Honest." She felt like she needed to put her hands up, so she shoved them into her jeans pockets.

"I'll fix you a sandwich. Sit down dear, I'll be right out. Oh! And thanks for the extra lemon pepper mix. I hadn't thought about it and didn't order any. How'd you guess I was low?" The lady asked with raised drawn brows over sharp eyes.

Nita smiled and tapped her nose, "Witch's secret."

Mrs. Greene laughed, "I swear if only that were true. I'd pay you for all your potions and brews!"

"If only she knew..." came the guttural whisper right behind Nita's ear.

She whirled. Lungs catching on her breath. Heart jumping into her throat. Nothing. Her body racked itself in a shudder as she studied each person in the diner. She turned back to the counter, resting her palms flat on it. It was cool to the touch, but not cold enough to settle her nerves.

A laugh and now a sentence. What was going on? She glanced down at Bel. *Was she finally hearing him?*

No. She hadn't had the power to understand the thoughts of her familiar, she wouldn't grow them now. Would she?

She toed him.

He swatted at her with a back paw, still not willing to loosen his hold on the nearly finished corn.

He chattered at her, but no remark came from him. It wasn't him. Even as an Earth witch, the plants didn't communicate with her in words. Not human words. These were definitely human phrases.

Plants didn't watch. They felt. Something was out there with eyes on her.

"Nita?"

She blinked, drawn from her panic by the soft voice of Nikki Greene. No, she was a Graham now. "Hi. Sorry."

Nikki's customer service smile didn't reach her dark eyes, the worry settled thick in her gaze on Nita. "It's ok. Momma said to grab you a tea. What would you like?"

"Oh, no need to go through the trouble." Nita cursed herself mentally as her voice shook on each word like a scared little girl.

Nikki motioned behind her to the little boxes and jars with neat typed labels on bright white paper. "You know how Momma gets. So best just choose one."

"Um…whichever will go best with the sandwich she's making. I trust you."

Nita waited as Nikki began to boil water in a clean kettle and grab one of her tins off the shelf above her head. A fine choice, Earl Grey Lavender. It would help calm her nerves and the flavor wouldn't overpower the meal coming her way.

Speaking of the meal, the mother of the diner exited the kitchen with a small plate in her hand. "Here you go dear." Mrs. Greene said with a smile as she slid a plate in front of Nita.

She stared at the flatbread filled to bursting with egg salad. She smiled and said, "Thanks," and again when Nikki brought her the white mug. Taking her time, the witch finished her tea while pondering the source of the voice. It had to be someone in the diner.

She paid her tab, picked up Belsauros, and took him to the bathroom to clean him off. "You are an absolute mess." Each piece of kernel she plucked out of his fur, he grabbed and ate. After a good rinse, she held him under the hand dryer.

He lay flat in her arms, letting the warm air blow the fur of his belly and arms dry with coos of contentment.

"You're such an odd beast." She murmured with a small smile at him. He wouldn't dry fully, and that was alright. She took him out, but in the hallway, a woman and a man appeared. She recognized them as natives to the county, but couldn't place them. She really wished she wasn't so bad at names.

"Get that rodent out of here. You're disgusting!"

"He's cleaner than ya'll are right now." Nita rolled her eyes, but the instigators spread, blocking off the whole hall. "Find it funny you're blocking the way out if'n you think we're so disgustin'." She drawled, leaning casually against the wall.

The man sneered, "Make a good pelt. They still make a bit of money."

Nita quipped, "Get more off your skin. Maybe. Got an awful bunch of blemishes and you're way too pale."

He snarled, putting a finger in her face, "That a threat, ya damn witch?"

Nita grinned, "Betcha you're more of a mutt than me, inbreed."

He pulled his hand back and Nita pushed off the wall, squaring with him, "Go ahead! Slap me! I will start and finish it, no matter what, I swear."

The man paused, his red face going slightly pale.

"Nita? You a'right?" Mrs. Greene's voice cooed from behind the two.

They turned, and Nita grew sheepish at the woman's presence. What had she been ready to do in the Greene's lovely business? "Just fine."

Mrs. Greene stood, hand on hip, gripping a large serrated bread knife. "That's good to hear. Hate to see someone being mistreated in my place. Cause if'n they were, we might have a fried green tomatoes moment or two."

"Mmm, you make some good barbeque, Mrs. Greene." Nita added to the threat. She doubted the couple knew what they were talking about.

"Now move along, you two, I'm sure you got someone else to spit at. Try to find one that actually deserves it." Mrs. Greene said with a sweet smile, but the bread knife flashed in the light as she motioned to the front door with it.

Watching them leave, Nita wondered about their involvement in the earlier whispers. "Sorry, Mrs. Green. He'll stay in the back from now on."

"Nonsense, that little rascal has been coming in here for longer than they have, and Belsauros actually pays his tab."

They laughed together.

Nita added, thankful for the kindness of some, "Alright. If he can't pay his tab next time, you can set him to washin' dishes."

Mrs. Greene chuckled, "I'll bet he'd be good gettin' every last crumb."

Nita nodded with a tight hug on her too fat familiar. "See ya next week."

"Take care, dear."

Nita took Bel to the truck, avoiding confrontation with the couple in the parking lot, and scratched his ears. She took one long, slow look around and listened. No more whispers came to her. Not a soul appeared suspicious hanging around, either. Besides a few morning doves and a couple of crows, there were no other lurking animals. She saw song birds flitting through the trees, but she couldn't make out what species they were.

Surely a witch couldn't latch onto flighty song birds.

"Stay here." She whispered to Bel and began her slow walk around the Greene's store.

Luckily, the troublesome individuals had departed. In her slow wander around, she pretended to look at several things. The hanging baskets of flowers, the paving stones with little art pieces on them, and the homemade signs another local made that the Greenes sold for him. Still no new whispers. Nothing in the plants and grasses around her trembled. No one posed a threat to them.

She bit back the aggravation at not being able to find the culprit. As she circled back to her truck, she gritted her teeth. Willing her nerves to calm, and the feeling to go with them. Part of her wanted to stand with arms wide and scream her challenge.

Camden would have. He would have stood in the middle of the parking lot, shouting for the threat to emerge. And continue until someone showed up.

Her cell phone rang, causing her to nearly jump out of her skin at the sudden loud noise. She fumbled it out of her back pocket and answered, "Hello?"

"Nita? This is Eve, you gave us some herbs to get pregnant?"

"Hi, Eve. Yes, I remember. It's only been about a week… is everything alright?" Nita felt the muscles in her face tighten with the stress of possibly doing something that would harm the couple. It was always a fear for her, no matter how much she knew.

"Oh! Yes! I just have another customer for you. They're visiting us tomorrow, will it be alright if we bring them by in the morning?" Eve's voice was toward the excited end of the spectrum.

Nita did a quick run-down of her schedule in her head. "Of course. Nine or ten sound good?"

"We'll see you at nine!"

"Great! Thank you and be safe."

Nita shook her head as she slipped her cell phone back into her pocket. The hairs on the back of her neck were no longer on end. She didn't feel like she was being watched anymore. Climbing into the driver's seat, she stared at Belsauros, who stared right back at her. "You're a lot of help."

Bel growled at her.

Nita growled back at him as she started up the old truck, let it roar to life, and began her way home.

Halfway home, pausing at one of the few red lights outside of town limits, Nita noticed the thing shudder right after something popped. She groaned, letting off the brake and moving around a little Honda car to roll into the parking lot of a gas station. The truck started hissing and smoking before she could pull it into a safe spot and cut the engine.

"Hush, it's alright." She muttered to Bel as he began chattering loudly, his dark eyes as wide as his reaching arms.

The door whined as she opened it, and groaned as she closed it. Popping the equally noisy hood, Nita stepped back as white smoke pooled out and spread with the creak and grind as she lifted it. "Well, got my sauna treatment this year." She coughed, waving the smoke away until it settled into a steady stream. She immediately spotted the culprit.

The top hose had a long crack in it, and she cursed. She'd forgotten to order a new one. She'd noticed the hoses getting worn and the little hairline surface cracks in a few spots. Propping the hood up, she strode to her bed and dug around in the toolbox. She hoped that Camden might have ordered one and stashed it before he went missing.

No luck.

She heard the scuff of footprints on the crumbling concrete pad around the outskirts of the gas station before the steps settled into the gravel of the parking area she was in. "Ye alright?"

She turned, smiling at the middle-aged man, "I am. Just got a cracked hose."

"Ah, they don't make them things like they used tuh." He took off his cap and scratched at his brown hair turning salty gray. "Think I might have an extra one in the ole box. Lemme see, might be shorter'n yourn though."

"Oh, that's kind of you, but you don't-" Nita stopped when the man waved her off as he walked back to his truck. She shrugged knowing the type. It would be useless to argue.

Country living meant that you were either stranded for hours, or you had help coming around the corner. Few left someone in need for long when it was a broken down old truck. Especially other farmers.

After a little while, he came back holding a roll of duct tape. "Ain't got one, but this outta do the trick."

"Thanks! I just have a pile of rags. Dunno what I did with my tape."

"Ah, done that before, too." He chuckled.

She took it from him and together they wrapped the cracked pipe as best as they could. "Thank you, mister."

"Anytime."

"How much do I owe ya?"

He shook his head, "Just if'n ya see someone else broke down, stop and give 'em a hand. Especially me."

She laughed, "Will do."

After fixing the truck and seeing the man off, she went inside the gas station to indulge herself. And to get room temperature water when her radiator cooled a bit more. It had been a weird day, and she wanted junk food. While grabbing chips and searching for donuts, she overheard a conversation.

The gas station had a little eatery attached to it. The eatery frequently changed ownership since Grizzle's, the original burger place, closed down. Now there was a little hot dog joint in it.

"Gotta be careful who you hang out with, boy. There're witches and wizards that'll carve you up before you can blink. We need to burn 'em all out."

Nita paused, moving slowly so as not to make too much noise. She peered through the rack that rested on top of the shelf that separated her from the dining area. Mason and his dad were sprawled out, sipping on Cokes with their hot dog wrappers and napkins all over the table.

Mason snorted, "I know Dad. None of 'em can do anything. Hell, Jasper was the one that kept me from taking that Bell witch."

"Jasper? Thought he was smarter than that." The older man shook his head gravely, as if Jasper had committed the worst sin.

"He's been after that little witch ass for years. Figured after he humps her enough, he'll come back to his senses." Mason muttered, then sipped on his drink.

"Probably has him under some kinda spell."

Mason grinned and shrugged. "Got some of 'em outta town now. Heard 'bout that, Pops?"

"No, what?"

"Some of 'em's been missin'. Camden, the Bell boy, he's one of 'em. Got that little witch all tore up."

Mason's dad grunted, "Good."

Nita growled under her breath, snatching her donuts and marching to the cashier. She glared at the men. Mason had enough sense to look like a sheepish dog, but his dad stared right back at her, a snarl curling his lips. She added a few ice creams from the cooler by the counter and paid for her purchases.

Using her back, she pushed the door open and sauntered to her truck while flipping off the men.

Sam Wicker

    "Bet they got some white robes with pointy hoods in their closets, too." Nita muttered, putting the bag behind the seat so Belsauros couldn't tear into her goodies.

Chapter Thirteen

"Welcome back, Eve." Nita smiled, rubbing her hands together to force the dirt from them before wiping them off on a towel. She tossed it back inside the greenhouse, onto a table.

Eve gave her a wave with her free hand, helping another woman out of her car. "This is my friend, Gretta."

"Hello, Gretta, it's nice to meet you." Nita waited patiently, not wanting to rush forward and unsettle the woman as they made their way toward her.

Gretta smiled, "Same."

Nita studied Gretta for a moment, already picking up on her pain. The lady hunched her body, muscles tightened, and her hands shook. Her smile was bright, and a warmth exuded from her like no other Nita had met.

"Come on, let's sit over here for a bit. Can I get you anything?" Nita asked softly, motioning to her usual table to see clients.

"Some of that water would be good." Eve mentioned.

Nita nodded with a smile, "Gretta, are you from the city like Eve and Derek?"

"I am," she said, her nodding not stopping once she began, "How did you tell already?"

Nita grinned, "Nah, I didn't, not really." She grabbed a fresh pitcher from the mini fridge and three glasses; she filled them up before sitting down with the two ladies. Nita noticed a grimace on Gretta's face. "Can I get you a cushion to sit on?"

"No, it's ok."

She got up and got the woman one, anyway. And a blanket to put on the back of the chair to help soften it in case she wanted to lean back. "Now, how may I help you?"

"I'm not sure you can, but Eve insisted." Gretta looked down at her hands. "I have MS."

"I see." Nita sat forward, "I have to be honest with you. I have had little experience helping people with MS, nor have I studied it. There's inflammation, but that's about all my knowledge. I'd like to have copies of whatever your doctors have given you so that I might build from it, along with the normal list I need that I'm sure Eve has told you about."

Gretta stared at Nita, her brown eyes wide in her round face, "You want to help?"

"I see you're in a lot of pain, and that breaks my heart. I will do everything I can for you, but I cannot make any promises. Just like I told Eve, sometimes herbs work just as well or better than the modern medicines, work well with them, or they just brush the surface of the ailments or not help at all. We'll figure out what helps, if anything. If you're willing. Do you think it's worth a try?"

"I do. I'm willing to try anything." Her voice trembled along with her lips.

Nita smiled, "Good. I might have to take some extra time on your case. Actually, I know I will. I'm going to study up on MS and your case. There might be things I don't have that I need to order, too. I can give you what I give my arthritic patients to help with pain."

"That sounds good." Gretta paused, then added, "I live on a fixed income. So please, don't go out of your way too much. I fear I cannot pay you for your time as Eve and some of your other patients can."

She tilted her head to the side. "Payment is not a problem. We will come up with something."

Eve chimed in, "She makes these lovely tissue box covers."

"Eve! They're… okay." Gretta's rounded freckled cheeks reddened.

"I'd like to see them. We can trade." Nita patted the table between then as she said, "Let me go get you the cream and tea. Hopefully, one will ease your daily pain." She stood and went into her greenhouse to gather the pre-made items she had. With an abundance of elderly and labor-intensive workers, she always had a supply of arthritis medicines on hand.

She found an accordion file folder on the table upon coming back. She stared at it for a moment, then smiled. "I see I have my work cut out for me."

Gretta's features drew in, concern clouding her happy demeanor. "Eve insisted, is it too much?"

Nita flipped through the folder and shook her head, "No, it's perfect. This should help me understand what you are going through, and therefore what you need."

She paused, studying Gretta briefly. "If anything is unhelpful or overwhelming for you, please tell me. Honesty is going to be key, and nothing you say will harm this relationship. But I also want to ask you to please talk to your doctor about everything I'm suggesting before agreeing to use it."

"Of course."

"I mean it. If it makes your poop a weird color or makes your mouth dry, I want to know." Nita raised a brow, handing the small brown bag to Eve that held Gretta's medicines.

Gretta's laugh was as warm as she was, "Alright, I'll try to share all the little details with you." She pointed to the cream and teas, "How much do I owe you for those?"

"Twenty and next time I send you anything or see you, I will have you an official receipt so you can see if your insurance will pay for it."

"Thank you." She smiled and pulled out a twenty from her small wallet with pretty flowers on it.

"Whatcha readin'?"

Nita felt his lips against her forehead and grunted. She finished the paragraph before answering, "About MS."

Jasper's brows drew down, but he didn't make a move to read over her shoulder. He knew better than to dig into patients' issues. "MS, like multiple... what is it?"

"Sclerosis. Right." She nodded, "One of my clients brought me another one."

"Isn't that somethin' that's still being studied?" The concern laced Jasper's voice. "It's gonna be a lot to take on with everything else..."

"Yeah, I know. Part distraction, I guess. And the challenge. I think that it's been around for a while, just misdiagnosed in the past. If I identify what certain previous clients of my grandmother took, it could assist my new client. I've read her file twice, and the printouts she brought me on MS that she had a few times already. Just to wrap my mind around it."

"Once you got your mind set, the magic can explore."

Nita smiled, hearing her grandmother say those words instead of Jasper. "Right."

Jasper tapped the corner of the papers and asked, "Wanna pause for a sec?"

"Yeah." She pushed the papers back into the accordion file folder and secured it with the stretchy string attached to the bottom.

Jasper crouched in front of her, "I found something." He grunted as his dogs ran up and rubbed under his arms, begging for attention since he was close to the ground, and them. He pet each one.

"What?"

"Found out where one of your other names lives." He said, resting his hands on top of his dog's heads and rubbing with his fingertips.

"Oh?" Nita asked as she leaned toward him, petting the dogs, too. They leaned heavily against Jasper and the chair in delight.

"Yeah, they lived alone. I dunno where they were taken, but it might help check out their house to figure out why they were targeted. Maybe there's something that's similar to somethin' of Camden's." Jasper explained, a certain look on his face she hadn't seen since the last time they'd snuck into a place. She chuckled as Bel climbed up the dogs and began petting them, too.

Nita lifted a shoulder, "They're all related to witches. But if there is something else, like some store they all frequented, then it might narrow down who done it." She smiled, "You're smart."

"Hold on, say that again." He pulled out his phone and tapped a few times on the screen.

Nita rolled her eyes, nudging the dogs away. "Dumbass."

"Dammit, that's not what you said five seconds ago!"

She laughed.

Jasper stood, "Lemme shower. Then we can grab somethin' to eat in town."

"Yeah, I lost track of time." Nita glanced at the old cuckoo clock on the wall that had quit making noise years ago, when her grandfather died.

"It's fine. You're workin' still. I'll be ready in a few." He leaned down and pecked her forehead again. He headed upstairs, his dogs following him with a fat raccoon trying to ride both of them at once.

Sam Wicker

Nita witnessed the mess between the dogs and the raccoon, grinning the whole time. Who knew that a coon dog wouldn't mind having one as a buddy? She shook her head at the irony and went back to studying up on her new client and making a few notes on some thoughts that might help off the top of her head.

Hearing the shower stop, she went upstairs to wash in a different bathroom. It was normal to have Jasper in her home. Just abnormal that he now slept mostly in her room. And kissed her. And touched her.

She realized as she got dressed in jeans, boots, and an old T-shirt, that their conversations were the same. About their days and wants. Now, they added in a few planning moments of figuring out when and how to spend time together other than their nights. That was odd. But not unsettling.

"Camden should be here making fun of us." She whispered to herself as she twisted her hair into a braid. She could almost hear him. But she didn't want the scenario to play through her mind. Not yet. It made it seem like she was giving up on seeing him again.

A week. No, ten days.

"Ready?"

She nodded, swallowing back the tears and some of the fear that rode them.

"We don't have to go…" Jasper started his eyes trailing over her face then back to hers.

Nita shook her head, "I'm fine. Just got lost in my thoughts there for a moment. Let's go."

The more they looked for clues, the closer they would get to finding Camden. Soon, he would poke fun at them. She wouldn't miss him for long.

With those thoughts running through her head like a mantra, Nita squared her shoulders and followed Jasper down the stairs. "Let's take the animals."

"K." Jasper nodded, picking up the harnesses and slipping them on Glory and Bones.

"See, that's how it's done." Nita pointed to the canines while talking to Belsauros. She stuck her tongue out at her raccoon as Bel chattered angrily at her and curled up into a ball.

Jasper chuckled, "You tried putting him in a harness?"

"Yeah, a few times."

"Is it still in one piece?"

"Nope."

He laughed as he opened the door for them, watching as Bel climbed up on Bones and shook his head. "Well, he's prolly gonna ruin my good huntin' dogs."

"Yeah, well, they turned out to be good at findin' me. Maybe we need to join the rescue squad or somethin'." Nita said with a lift of her shoulder as she watched the dogs trot toward the truck in front of them.

"Nah, they're doin' away with it. So I heard."

Nita snorted her disdain for poor decisions. "That sucks. Let's put more on the volunteer fire and the cops."

Jasper nodded, "That's what I said when I heard."

They piled into the truck, the dogs in the back of the cab and the humans in the front seat. The raccoon couldn't decide where to sit, so he kept hopping over the bucket seats.

"Where ya wanna eat?" Jasper asked as he moved the truck out of the driveway and onto the pavement.

"I dunno."

He made a face, "That don't help me out none."

"What do you feel like?"

"I dunno. You want burgers, chicken, fish, what?" Jasper asked as he looked both ways before pulling out onto the two-lane road.

"Um… burgers?" Why was it when someone asked what she wanted to eat she no longer had much of a desire for anything?

"'Kay, so cheap and greasy, or fat and greasy?"

Sam Wicker

Nita laughed, "Uh cheap and greasy?"
"Wendy's or McDonald's then?" Jasper smirked.
She rolled her eyes, "Wendy's. I want a Frosty."

After they and the animals ate their fill of cheap greasy food, Jasper took them all to the house of one of the missing. It was a Wright, a Darkness worker. His daughter, an only child, was a witch and lived with her mother somewhere down toward Atlanta. His mother had been a witch, as were some of his brothers and sisters.

Wright's house sat about two miles off the road; the drive was partly paved, but mostly gravel and mud. The trees with their thick summer undergrowth gave way to an overgrown field, heavy with tall grasses, briars, and what most called weeds. It was an old house, not half as old as the Bell home, but still old. It had the blocky look of a house built in the 20s with a bungalow roof of coated tin and a wide front porch. Box elders were a bit of a mess and bordered the porch.

Jasper left the truck lights on, the beams shooting into the darkened house. It sent an eerie thrill down Nita's spine. "How we gonna get in?"

"We'll check to see if there's a loose window. If not, we'll make one." He sounded so confident, yet he hadn't got out yet either.

"We should probably let the dogs out. Let them sniff about." Nita suggested after neither of them had the courage to get out.

Jasper nodded, "Yeah, that's what I figured."

He finally made a move and opened his door. He then opened the back cab and told the dogs to stay close.

Without anyone appearing with a gun, Nita slipped out of the truck. She grabbed Belsauros and made him sit on her shoulders. An extra set of eyes was always a boon, especially nocturnal eyes.

She followed Jasper around the house as he checked for a loose or damaged screen. Finding one in the back, he pried it loose and tried the inside storm window.

It didn't budge for the longest, then he finally wedged his knife under it and it screamed its way up the tracks as old wooden windows do.

They paused. They waited, keeping an ear out for anyone inside who might have finally been disturbed by the noise. Nita kept looking out across the land, especially toward a barn that looked newly built. Who was to say that they had moved out of the house and into the barn?

City folk were doing that. Taking the old barns of the country, renovating them, and living in them. Or building brand new ones. Why someone would want to live in something that housed equipment or several animals was beyond her ken.

Then again, most of them had about as much sense as a mad cow.

Jasper peered inside, and then turned to whisper loudly. "I think we're clear. Here, I'll give you a boost inside."

Nita shoved Bel into the house first, then hopped up, pulling herself into the window. Jasper's hands on her rear gave her pause, and she mule kicked. He dodged. Had the audacity to laugh, too. Regaining her balance, Nita grunted as she slid onto the floor, crawling awkwardly into the room.

A living room. The couch had a dark color, brown in the gray darkness, and a comfy suede look. She breathed in, smelling the hint of dust. Chairs matched the couch, pillows piled on one, tables with lamps and various clutter. A large flat screen dominated one wall.

At least it hadn't been robbed. She looked down at her hands, "We shoulda wore gloves."

"Damn. Why didn't we think of that sooner?" Jasper whispered after making a far more graceful entrance through the window.

Nita grew curious. "How many houses have you broken into?"

"None!"

"One, then."

"Yeah, this one." Jasper shrugged. "All well, here now."

Nita pulled the little flashlight she had taken from her kitchen out of her back pocket and began looking around. Bookshelves lined one wall, full. Completely, hopelessly full of tomes, papers, pamphlets, and notebooks.

Not a single grimoire.

Made sense. Nita looked over some spines. Classics, mostly. Well read if the wear on the spines and edges were anything to go by. Plenty of westerns crowded the shelves, some mysteries, and a handful of non-fiction books. Most of those were on how to deal with divorce and connecting with your kid after one. Her heart broke for him.

She found three small shelves full of children and teen books. Not as well read as the others, but they were getting close.

Jasper sifted through clutter on the tables, checking the mail. "Nothing out of the ordinary. I don't think."

Nita shook her head, "Nope." She moved on into the kitchen. It was clean. No food left out other than the basket of rotting fruit. She held her nose closed. Bel climbed back up on her shoulders and stuck his muzzle in her hair.

The ice maker turned on. Nita's heart went up in her throat and she figured if Bel hadn't weighed her down, she would hang from the ceiling. The electricity was still on, obviously. She rolled her eyes, then went from the kitchen to the dining room.

She poked through some more mail she found laying on the four seater wooden dining room table. Nothing threatening stood out to her. Normal junk mail and a couple of bills. Mr. Wright had missed a sale at Dick's Sporting Goods. He'd cut his coupon out and left it lying.

Jasper was in the nearby bathroom, so Nita went down the hall to the next one. She opened a door on a closet. Mostly cleaning supplies and house tools. She shut it and Belsauros tightened his hold on her.

She paused, listening. Jasper's dogs growled outside.

"Nita." She turned, looking at him. He motioned toward the window and she nodded.

They growled again, and Jasper sprinted to the window to look out toward his truck.

Right behind him, Nita observed two long shadows passing before his headlights. "Shit."

"Let's go." Jasper grabbed her elbow and half jogged half walked back to the window they'd opened.

She watched him as he took a dive out the window. Again, looking more like a swan than an idiot like he should have. Nita followed and Jasper pulled her and Belsauros out. He pulled the storm window down and replaced the screen, cussing under his breath as it didn't want to sit properly.

Nita punched a corner, and it stuck.

They went to the front of the house, pressing their backs to the wall. Jasper peered around the corner, looking toward his truck again. Nita watched his hand make a fist.

Sam Wicker

The shadows were still there.

Bones gave a sharp bark.

Nita jumped at the nearness of the dog. He was right in front of them, barely six feet away. He looked twice his size in the dark, and with his neck fur bristled. His teeth gleamed in the headlights as he snarled. She assumed Glory wasn't too far away.

"Come out, Ms. Bell."

The drawl made her hairs stand on end.

Jasper turned toward her and whispered, "Who is that?"

"Someone I don't wanna know." She muttered and stepped out. She rounded the corner and stood beside Bones. "What are you doing here, Martin?"

"I should ask you that, Bell. Shall we not go by first names now? It is our second meeting." She couldn't see any of him, except the solidness of his body against the bright lights behind him.

She narrowed her eyes, not willing to be on such relaxed terms with him.

"Mr. Martin, who is this?"

"Oh, forgive me. Allow me to make introductions. Mr. Kent Allen, this is Nita Bell. Nita, darling, this is Kent. He's an associate of mine. You could say my right-hand man for coven business, and a close friend for personal." One hand motioned between them, palm up.

"I'm not your darlin'." Nita nearly spat as oil slicked through her belly at the thought of him calling her something so tender as that.

She felt his smile more than she saw it. His face was always in shadow. As was this Mr. Allen's.

"Shouldn't you introduce us to your friend? Or shall I say friends?" He asked, his head tilting slightly to the side.

Nita observed his gestures towards Jasper hiding in the shadow, then Bones, and finally somewhere behind him. A good hunting dog, Glory, but she was also an amazing snoop and protector. If Nita was to believe she was there, she had flanked the two men, blocking them from getting back to their car behind Jasper's truck.

She turned her head, waiting until the last moment before looking at Jasper. "Come on out." She wasn't about to say it was going to be alright. She didn't know that.

Jasper pushed off the side of the house, his walk was more of a saunter as he slipped past her to pet the ruff of Bone's neck. "My name's Jasper Price."

"Ah, it is a pleasure. I've always liked someone with the last name Price. Met a few very powerful witches with that last name, though, I believe not of your particular bloodline." Martin's voice was smooth as silk still.

"Guess not."

Nita gazed briefly at Jasper before turning her attention to the shadowy Martin and Allen witches. "Just checking to see if Mr. Wright's home."

She noted his smile again. Her nerves clanged with the unsettling realization that she was in tune with him. He was angry. But he was smiling. How was she picking up on this?

"You know he wasn't. He hasn't been for weeks now."

Mr. Allen's voice wasn't as smooth as the Martin's. It was a higher pitch, and not as debonair. Mr. Allen wasn't as full of shit as Mr. Martin.

"Come now, Kent. Let's not point fingers." He said in his slick voice again. "Let's see what they were really here for and go from there."

"You had the house bugged?"

"You Bells are always quick to figure out the little things." The silken voice held a note of amusement and awe.

Something zinged through her, and Nita noticed herself drop with an abrupt jump of her stomach. The ground caught her, softening her blow with the excess of soft grasses, but it still knocked the wind out of her lungs. She clutched at her chest, half expecting a knife to be protruding from it, such was the pain.

"Nita?!"

Jasper's voice seemed miles away. But he was running toward her. He was well.

"Nita? What's wrong? What happened?"

She let him pull her into his arms as he kneeled on the grass beside her. Nita finally fought a breath into her lungs. "Spirit..." she couldn't manage more words. She needed more air. Something was taking her air.

"Stop it!" Jasper bellowed at the two shadows.

Her ears rang with his voice. When did he gain that tone? That power in his words?

The surrounding air stirred again, and she sucked some of it into her body. It clicked in her mind then, an Allen must be an Air. Air and Spirit witches worked best together. Their magics were basically untouchable and untraceable. Both could render other elementals useless. No air, no tone. No spirit, no magic or emotion for the tones to work off of.

Quite a pair.

Chapter Fourteen

Nita sat up in bed. Her lungs filled to the point of pain before she pushed the air out. Panic clawed through her chest and mind as she took in another painful lung full. Darkness surrounded her.

"Nita? Nita it's okay."

Jasper's voice?

"She's just fine."

That was the soothing, but shit-eating Martin voice.

"Where am I?"

"You're in my home. Welcome. Although I wish it was under better circumstances." The Martin drawled, sounding metallic.

Nita blinked, wide, making sure that she was actually opening her eyes. "Why can't I see anything?"

"Ah. I forgot."

The sound of clapping hands came from the same direction as the voice. She ended up blinking several times as the light hit her irises and set them aflame. She found herself in a room with twin suns. Her heart beat in her ears, quick and thundering like a drum. Her lungs refused to fill with air. Through tear-filled eyes, she discovered a whitewashed room. She sat on a small bed, resembling a cot, and faced the door.

Nita lifted her hand and could touch the other side of the room. She frowned. Where had the voices come from? She turned, spotting the mirror behind her.

If she could place a bet, she'd bet it wasn't really a mirror.

"Better?" The voice was behind the mirror.

"Sure. Now let me out." She looked down, finding that her clothes were still on, some of the panic ebbed a bit. Nita focused on her breathing as she waited for an answer. She could breathe. She was alive.

"In a little while. We need to have a chat first."

"Get her out! The room is too small!"

Why was Jasper in there with the Martin witch?

She turned, placing her boots on the white tiles. Nita breathed in. She let the breath out. She repeated the process, slowly. Willing her mind and adrenaline to slow its roll. She focused on her boots. Her boots on the white tile. Not the fact that she was in an unknown place.

"What kind of house has a room like this? You own a prison?" Nita asked flippantly.

A laugh. She pictured fecal matter sliding down a tube with that kind of laugh. He had a certain something that made her constantly think of feces. She'd never had a person do that for her before. Not even Mason and his little redneck cronies.

Victor Martin answered her, "I only have two rooms like this. I run a rehabilitation center, of sorts, for witches in need."

Nita's brow tightened, "I'm in need?"

"Intervention perhaps. You are determined to stick your nose into coven business. Therefore, I brought you here to talk you out of continuing your investigation or to join us."

Nita snorted, "Fat chance of either."

His voice dropped, holding a mild threatening tone. "Choose one or the other."

"I told you she would laugh in your face!"

She gritted her teeth, "Why is Jasper in there with you?"

A heavy pause. One that settled like a weight over her already pounding heart.

"He's in the other room."

Lie.

The lie worked under her skin like she read his anger and that smile in the dark. Why would he lie about that? Why was she sensing his intentions again?

She deepened her breathing, humming a little with her exhale out. The dirt beneath the house was far away.

As if another story or two were between this room and the ground. Like she was in the attic at home. Third floor.

Beyond that was a small plant, a succulent, nearly five hundred feet away. The next was further than that. A tree that was young but weak. City.

The coven was housed in Atlanta. She was in Atlanta. The panic roared to life, and she stood. She paced to the door, then back to the mirror. Her nerves making her muscles and powers twang like bells at a celebration.

"Let me out."

"Now, Nita…"

"Out!" she screamed, slamming her fists into the mirrored glass. Pain shot through the sides of her hands and wrists, into her arms and fingers. She pounded at the glass again. It reverberated, but held.

"She's panicking."

She could hear his footfalls behind the mirror. He was running. He was running to her. But should she let him? Why was he in the room with the Martin?

Where was the Allen that could render her unconscious?

"Nita, calm down." That itch started against her sternum. The same itch from the bar that night.

"Don't you dare."

"Let me calm you."

"Fuck you!" She spat.

"You're only hurting yourself, my dear."

She wished she was strong enough to crack the glass. Nita whirled when she heard the click of the lock on her door. It was locked. Had she even tried it? Part of her was glad she didn't. Her panic would be worse.

Sentience. She needed thought. More thought.

Jasper stood in the door, his eyes wild under a mass of mussed hair.

"What were you doing with him?" Her voice rang in her ears.

"He just let me be." Jasper rushed forward, arms out for her.

"Did you hit him? Kick him? Anything?!" Nita hugged herself, feeling the panic tear apart her emotions and thoughts as she tried to focus on breathing.

Jasper held up his hands, "Nita, I'm just a normal guy. What am I supposed to do when you pass out and he's… they're…"

"Witches."

The panic raged, but something also shattered inside her. Always different. Always alone. She'd never met another earth witch outside of her family. It was as if she was the only one.

"You are not the only one." That voice purred from behind her. Warm. "Let me help you."

Was that the shattering inside her mind? Had he finally broken into her?

Another person came up behind Jasper and moved him to the side with a shove. She growled at her. Her head had one side shaved, with a tight braid against her skull just above the shaved part. Above the braid, colors erupted and flowed down half of the woman's face to her stomach.

Viking came to mind.

The woman's stance was threatening or protective. Nita couldn't place it as her lungs refused to fill up with enough air. Her eyes. Those eyes were a bright sky in the fall.

Something clicked inside Nita again. She was calm. She had enough air. The room wasn't threatening to close in on her. The woman was just standing there. "Who?"

"Vash."

"Energy?" Nita wondered at the sudden calm.

"Yeah, you got plenty of it. Ready to talk now?" The woman's voice was deep, an oddly soothing sound.

"No."

"Too bad."

After a few tones, a rune on the woman's right hand tinged red as she reached for Nita. Once it landed, Nita's energy drained from her. She fell to her knees.

"Grab your girl and follow." The striking woman barked at Jasper, who did as he was told.

Were they manipulating him? Was he cursed again?

She slumped against his chest, finding small comfort in the familiar musk. Him carrying her was also becoming commonplace and comforting. Something that she never thought would occur. Strange how time changed things from absurd to reality. But how come he was with the Martin witch in the room behind the mirror? Watching her?

At the end of the plain hall, no decorations in sight, not even a picture or painting, was a room with a circle of couches. These were navy. Plain. Made more for durability than comfort. Jasper sat with her on the closest one, across from Victor Martin.

"Now let her have her own space, Mr. Price."

Jasper slid out from under her, making sure she was comfortable on the couch, and made himself at home beside her.

He had to be under a spell. He wasn't even saying anything.

She pointedly stared as the Energy witch sat down to her left.

Victor's smile slid onto his face like oil poured into water. "It will be just a moment. My colleagues were discussing you in another room."

Sam Wicker

That was not comforting. "What do you want with me?" Forming words were sluggish. She could barely hold her head up.

"Like I said before. We're going to discuss you joining the Coven."

She trembled, "Not happening."

"Never say never." Martin smiled.

"I didn't."

She watched as six people came down an opposite hall. Nita recognized some of them, vaguely. They arranged themselves on the couches. None joined her and Jasper.

"Now then, let's begin. Introduce yourselves."

The man sitting beside the Martin on the couch gave a smug smile, "We've met. Kent Allen, Air Witch, second in command of District Two of the Southern Roots Coven."

She recognized his voice. Had he not lurked in the shadows at the Wright house, she would have instantly punched him for that smarmy smile.

The Energy witch was next, "Vashiana Everwood, Energy Witch and third in command."

"Hugh Haskins, Fire Witch, Enforcer Commander." He oozed military training and hard-assedness.

"Ginger Black, Light Witch, Head of Healing for District Two and Three."

Under different circumstances, Nita was certain she would have liked this woman. She was grandmotherly, a kindness in her eyes that made her distinct.

She might have liked Vashiana too. The punk look and strength would have made Nita interested in knowing more. But she never would now.

"Ash Kelley, Water Witch, Resource Allocation and Recruitment Head." The girl turned to her and smiled. She wasn't much older than Nita. Her almond colored eyes were kind as well.

"Zee Levitas, Earth Witch, Treasurer and Secretary." Nita wondered if the irony was lost on Zee for being a treasurer.

"Raven Reid, Darkness Witch, Event Coordinator and District Liaison." The facial features of her people were strong in Raven.

"Great job. Everyone, this is Nita Bell, an Earth Witch."

"And everyone knows Jasper by now." The Martin continued.

What was that supposed to mean? She wondered as she looked at Jasper. The man was looking straight ahead. As if he hadn't a care in the world.

"Nita here is lost. We must regain her trust in order to bring her back into the fold and protection of the Coven." Victor Martin smiled brightly. "I'm sure with all of us here, we can come up with something to convince her to join us."

Ash was the first to speak, her smile even brighter than her leader's. "Of course! There are all kinds of benefits to joining the coven! We are like a family. Close-knit. We take care of one another. Need help with a problem, worry, or deciphering a spell in your great-grandparent's grimoire? We're here for you! Our network is boundless. We trade amongst each other, too. But more often than not, it's just friendly help when we can." She continued after a while, "There're classes, mentorships, and the like that members of the coven offer at great discounts if they charge at all. Free healthcare. Free business advertising if you have a business. Free school for children up to the age of eighteen in our privately run schools across the district."

"Protection." Hugh chimed in gruffly.

"Yes! Protection! If you are being harassed, we work with your local forces to squash it." Ash nodded with a smile to Hugh.

Sam Wicker

"What was the reason behind my grandmother leaving, then?"

Silence fell. The room seemed to grow darker, smaller. The coven members glanced at one another.

Victor Martin leaned forward, placing his elbows on his knees. "I think that is irrelevant to our time here."

"I don't think it is." She met his gaze, noticed his harden, then that smile tried to make her melt. "What was her reason?"

"If she didn't tell you, why should we?"

Nita looked toward the Energy witch, Vash. "Because she was probably still too angry, if this is how you all talked to her."

"I believe she left because of the new leaders." The voice was soft, but had iron underneath it.

Nita turned to the healer. "Meaning? Just because they were new to her? Or because they are corrupt?"

Ginger shook her head, white curls bouncing, "No, neither of those. I think she just wanted to retire. To be out of it."

Nita narrowed her eyes, "That's not my grandmother. She worked until her last breath. Someone here should tell me the reason she left, the honest one."

"Nita." Jasper's voice pooled toward her like a warm blanket.

"No." She bit out the word. She looked back at the coven members, staring them down one by one.

"She left because she believed we were losing our way." He paused, as if for dramatic effect instead of needing to have a moment. "At the time, we were recruiting a lot of new blood. Investing in private schools and tutors for the young." He should smile less.

"She wouldn't be against that."

"No. No, she shouldn't. But she was."

Nita shook her head, "What are these schools teaching then? How to take over the world?"

"No, nothing like that." Victor chuckled with a shake of his head, "They're teaching the fundamentals that every school does. But also witchcraft. Protecting themselves in a world that still views us as dangerous. Teaching them how to read and use spells, runes, and empowering their tones."

Things that schools for witches would do. Nita frowned, there was something else. A thing they weren't telling her. "That's not losing your way." She blinked, then narrowed her eyes on him. She discovered the lies again. "How, exactly, were you recruiting?"

Ash looked away at that.

Nita hit the mark as a spike of anger lanced through the connection she had with the Martin witch.

"At the time, we were enrolling all children of all known bloodlines."

"Without the consent of their guardians?" She asked when the dark witch didn't expound.

"Yes."

She snorted. It angered her grandmother. "And now?"

"We are far more lenient, of course." Ash piped up.

"Of course." Nita tensed up, "And these missing persons cases. Are they part of some forced recruitment too? Is that why you want me to stop looking into my brother?"

"No. No, they are missing. We are searching for them. Your involvement is hindering the investigation." Victor's words spilled out of his mouth.

"How so?"

"Well, for one, you could be damaging evidence." Hugh muttered. "For another, you are a civilian and understand little about these disappearances. We work closely with the police and the victim's families. We have more knowledge than you ever will, and your lack of understanding is dangerous.

Nita snorted again, "That just sounds like you're worried I'm going to find Camden before you will. Sorry, I don't need a knight in shining armor that comes as a coven of lackluster promises."

"No, you have one in flannel and sawdust." The Allen witch sneered.

When Jasper still didn't say anything, Nita staggered into a standing position. "Release him from whatever spell you have him under."

Victor stood, as if he was about to stretch instead of face down an angry woman. "We don't have him under a spell, Nita."

She pointed to him, "He's listless, pretty much."

Jasper smiled up at her, "I'm fine, babe."

She rolled her eyes, "Fine, keep him. I'm going home."

"You will join the coven." The Allen witch insisted.

"No. I won't."

"Nita, please. It is for your own good. We can help you find Camden. You will know all that we do and have all our resources." The grandmotherly one cooed.

Her energy drained again and she glared at Vashiana. "Is this how you recruit?" She sat back down on the couch, barely able to sit up. Nita thought she could sleep for a year. "Where's my brother?"

"We don't know." Their leader crouched in front of her, "I wish we did, my dear." His voice was a purr, and he reached for her.

She recoiled, "Let me go. This is against your bylaws!" She realized she couldn't feel Belsauros near her. The spike of panic returned as her magic stretched thin to find her familiar.

He smiled, "Not entirely. If a witch is deemed a danger, we can hold them."

"I am no threat!"

"No? You broke into someone's house. A victim. Someone who has been missing. How are we to know that you didn't do something with Mr. Wright? Or your brother?"

Nita gritted her teeth, willing her energy back. "I have nothing to do with the missing. What do you have on Camden's case?"

He smiled, "Join, and you'll have exactly what I do."

"Who is the threat here? You're telling me to join a group that I have no interest in joining and withholding information on my brother's missing person case. If I were to go to the cops with this, who do you think they would deem unsafe?"

His smile stayed, "You, darling."

She stared at him, "You kidnapped me!"

"For your safety. When I found you, you were breaking into a home. You began saying strange things about magic and familiars... what was I supposed to think? And seeing as how I am a spiritual leader... I couldn't help but be concerned. I've helped many like you."

She swallowed the bile that threatened to erupt in her mouth. How long had she been here? Where exactly in Atlanta was she? How many could she take down before she was back in that tiny container?

She flicked her gaze to Vash and met the woman's stare. Not a lot. One wrong move and she'd be in the room. Concrete hell. That's what she was in.

"Let us go." Nita demanded with hardly any weight behind her voice as she couldn't muster enough energy.

"Not yet."

When she frowned at him, he continued, "I promise I will let you go soon. You're weak. We'll feed you and talk to you some more. Then you can make your final choice."

He stood, holding a hand out to her. "Come. We have some things to show you that may change your view." He looked at Jasper, "Go back to your room. A tray will be brought to you soon."

Sam Wicker

Nita watched, her heart dropping to her stomach as Jasper just rose and walked down the hall. "Release him."

"When he will not tear this place down to protect you, yes, we shall." Vash's voice whipped out.

Outside, the sun was bright between gray clouds that threatened to bank into a rainstorm. The shadows did little to settle her fear as they led her from one building to another. The plaza between the concrete buildings reminded her of a college campus. Bricks placed in neat circles around some point of interest. This one was a fountain. A plain one.

She reached for the dirt beneath them. She touched the clay and clenched her teeth as an obstruction silenced her connection with the earth. Powerful. Those of the coven were formidable together.

Inside, the sounds of children screeching and laughing filled her ears. She pulled back, pressing against the glass door. Victor squeezed her hand, and she tore it away from him. How long had they been holding hands?

"Come, darling, this is what we wanted to show you." He motioned to a hallway that spoked off the foyer. He reached for her again.

She pressed against the door, stumbling as it opened.

Hugh's large hand closed around her forearm and pulled her into the circle of the coven officials. His eyes, dark but flecked with gold, held hers as he spoke, "Miss, this isn't harmful. This is kindness. You are twisting it in your mind."

"You're a Haskins?"

"Yes."

"Randy?"

His lips thinned. "I was adopted into the Haskin family by Randy's great-uncle and aunt. My parents abandoned me at one of the schools the coven built as soon as I started showing abilities. I was born a fire witch, and the Haskins were kind enough to take me in and teach me their ways. Randy is a beautiful and kind boy. I remember him playing with my son at family reunions. I remember his laugh." He smiled, for the first time since meeting him, "And I will hear it again. Unless some little earth witch messes up our chance of finding him."

As soon as it had appeared, the smile disappeared into a snarl. It caused Nita's heart to squeeze and her breath to catch. "I understand."

He let her go and turned.

Nita followed them. Victor opened a classroom door with a smile, "Hello Mrs. Graham and children! Sorry to interrupt, but we have a guest. This is Nita Bell."

He flung a hand toward her, beckoning her into the room with a flick of his fingers. She stepped inside and his arm immediately wrapped around her. The classroom didn't have many children in it. She guessed about a dozen. The teacher was smiling in the back, a book in her hands that she seemed to have been reading to them out of as she walked down the aisles of desks.

"Children, are you learning a lot?" The Martin witch asked in a light tone, obviously made for talking to kids.

Most nodded shyly, a few rolled their eyes, and the majority responded positively.

"That's good! Which one of you will share with Miss Bell what you've learned?"

A little girl raised her hand, slowly.

"Go ahead, my dear little Yvonne."

He knew her name?

The girl stood. "We're learning about the Egyptians this month. They wrote in pictures kind of like our runes, but more elaborate sometimes. They had many gods, but also had slaves. They built many cities. Had large trade agreements and were very smart for a people living during their age." She paused, looking sheepishly at her teacher before continuing, "Mrs. Graham showed us how some of our marks and tones came from all the way back to the Egyptians. They are some of the most simple spells, but powerful. She says some of us might be able to trace our lineage back them if we want."

"Beautiful, Yvonne." Victor smiled, "I'll make sure you receive an extra muffin in the morning."

The child beamed.

"Mr. Martin, sir?"

He nodded to a boy who raised his hand, "Go ahead, Wade."

"Is Miss Bell gonna be a new teacher?"

"She might." He grinned, "We're showing her around so she can decide on whether or not to join the coven. What do you think about our family, Wade?"

He grinned, "It's fun! When we gather, there's always lots of food, dancing and music. Some learning too." He added after a soft throat clearing from Mrs. Graham. "We help each other out. No one is alone anymore. No one teases us about being… different."

"No! We just tease him for having buck teeth." Another boy sucked on his teeth while making an odd face at Wade.

Wade glared at his bully, but then went on, "My momma is a teacher. She has blue hair."

"Yes, she does. She's a wonderful teacher." Mrs. Graham added with a smile. Then she pointed a finger at the boy who spoke out of turn, "Corner. You know how I feel about you teasing others."

The boy sulked as he wandered toward a corner and stuck his nose in it.

Nita shook her head, "Why are you showing me this?"

"Well, we shall not interrupt any longer. Keep learning children!" Victor led her out of the classroom.

Nita shrugged off his arm he'd slipped around her while they left, and faced him. "Well?"

"Just wanted to show you we aren't holding any kids hostage. They're healthy. Happy."

She would not get out of this with her freedom. Nita knew that now. They would have her.

Grandma, forgive me. "What do I have to do to become coven?"

Victor grinned, "Excellent choice." He loomed toward her, a hand heavy on her shoulder, "We have a custom, a tradition. The same one your grandmother did when she was of age. It will be nice to have a Bell in our midst."

"Her spot on the inner circle is still open."

Nita turned, looking at Kent.

He leaned against the wall, arms crossed, head back, and his eyes were half lidded as he looked at her. "The position of Balance. Work hard to gain it. The Bells of old were powerful, and well learned. No one has filled their shoes within our circle."

Her grandmother held the balance? The ring of truth in his words echoed through her. Grandmother was a strong wielder, and often could work her power to emphasize Nita's magic or rein her back into safety. Her grandmother could also work the stump without collapsing, too.

"The Bell tone resonates with all, calls us all, keeps us safe and grounded." Victor's voice was soft, as if in a chant, "Without the Bell, we are all lost. Halved of power."

That wasn't intimidating. Nita swallowed, the prickle of panic started again in her toes and fingertips. "When can the ritual be done?"

All of them looked at Raven.
"Tomorrow night." The dark wielder said with a smile.

Chapter Fifteen

Nita could not see Jasper. They allowed her to stay in one of the guest rooms of Victor's house instead of the small torture chamber she had woken up in. It was Ginger who kept her company.

Ginger helped her wash and pick out the robes she would wear during every coven gathering. Nita remembered the beautiful forest green of her grandmother's robes and chose similarly. She yearned for her land and sensed the old Ironwood summoning her.

"Soon," she whispered, closing her eyes and imagining her land. She pictured being home, comforted, with power coursing through her and around her. How anyone could survive in the concrete was beyond her. Yes, it was dirt, but it was like the pounding feet and cars made it dead.

In her mind, she rehearsed what to say during the ritual. Nita shook her head, knowing she was about to be bound to a group she did not trust. A group her grandmother left. A coven.

It would be nice to have contact with other witches. Wouldn't it? She was pretty sure that she would not be pleased with the amount of talking they would demand of her. Once a week. More than that, and she'd plot to kill them.

A knock sounded at her door and she turned toward it right before it swung open. "Ready?"

She nodded to Ginger. Gripping the black robe, she followed the old woman along the hallway and stairs. Her inner mantra kept telling her not to trip over the flowing cloth.

Through the back door, into the greenery. Nita breathed it in. How had she not noticed this spot?

Sam Wicker

With the touch of earth and grass on her bare feet, she found her answer. Fake grass. Barely any dirt. Only a small peace lily plant in the corner held life. She reached out, touching their tones with her own. Estranged. A muscle not used to using the power tightened. They were still holding her back.

Her fingernails dug deep into the palms of her hands through the thin cloth of the robe.

She paused outside a circle of white stones. Within stood a person in a purple robe, the large hood drawn low over their face. To the right, Zee, in a lime green robe, stood holding sand and a jar of white. To the left was one in red robes, Hugh, holding a candle and a folding fan.

A deep voice boomed from the one in purple robes, asking, "Who is to become one with the sacred coven of Southern Roots?"

"I bring you a Bell to enter into the sacred circle to join our sacred Coven." Ginger answered at her elbow.

"What name shall the Coven recognize you by, unsworn?"

"Nita."

"Enter and make your pledge with me." The hand reaching for her was familiar. She felt a sliver of ice run down her chest.

That was wrong. She paused before entering the circle. She stood before the one in purple. The gleam of a smile solidified her suspicion. The Martin witch would take her oath. As was fitting. But it did not sit well.

"Ready yourself for the purification of these elements. Become one with them, as you will become one with the Coven."

The three men took turns. Pouring water over her, then sand, letting the flame lick the flesh of her hands and edges of her robes, fanning air over her, allowing the tickle of a spirit magic tease her heart as the energy, light and darkness of all surrounded her. Pressing against her like a heavy weight.

"By joining the Coven of Southern Roots, you will become family. You will enter the circle of kinship, never ending even in death. United, we will confront the mysteries of life, both present and future. You will learn and grow within this Coven each day. You will seek knowledge and earn it as you work. Let us, the Coven, and the gods aid you in your journeys. Will you pledge to be part of this circle, offering your knowledge and backing, becoming family, Nita?"

"Yes, I swear."

"Then begin your life anew as part of us. Take up your mantle and name."

Ginger brought her the robe she chose, and she changed into it with her help. Three more men and a woman to see her naked. Perfect. Family indeed.

Nita was about to exit the circle when Victor cupped her face and placed his lips over hers.

Everything froze.

She couldn't breathe. Nita wondered if her heart still beat. She only had consciousness of him against her. Every fingertip, every breath curling across her cheek, and the warmth of his lips on hers. He pulled back, resting his forehead against hers, he whispered, "Welcome to the family, Nita. You have been missed."

"Don't kiss me again." She hissed.

He chuckled, "I cannot make such promises."

"Release Jasper." Nita pulled back, glaring into the depths of the hood to see the slithering smile of Victor gleaming like a Cheshire cat moon.

"He's free." He released her face.

Nita turned and stopped. Jasper stood just outside the back door. His fists shaking at his sides. "Thanks. I'll be taking what you know of Camden's kidnapping now."

"In due time."

Nita turned on him, making a fist in Victor's robes just under his chin, "Now."

"Easy, little Bell." He said with a smile, cupping her face in his hands again, "I said I shall make no promise. I never do."

"Victor." Hugh's voice held a note of warning.

Nita pulled away from him, shoving him with her hands at the same time. "Enough. I'm leaving. I expect you to send me everything you have. Or to tell me right now."

Zee reached for her, placing his hand on her elbow, "Nita, I have it for you. Victor just likes to tease those who rise to the occasion."

She bit the inside of her cheek to keep from spitting in Victor's face.

"Come in. The file is in there. I made copies of everything." Zee tugged her gently toward the door. Toward Jasper.

She stared at him. Jasper. His hands were still in fists at his sides. Trembling. His eyes were wild as he looked her over. "I'm sorry."

"Part of the ritual. Right?"

She didn't think so.

"Yes, of course." Zee murmured with a small smile. "Come inside."

They sat around a small table just outside the kitchen. Zee passed over a file as thick as three of her fingers. She flipped through some of it, passing a few pages to Jasper, who sat so close beside her, she could feel the heat of his body through her robes.

Ginger brought a tray in and set it down on the table. She poured them each a cup of fragrant tea. A light mint with a hint of rose. Then she left.

"Now that you are family, we can give you what you need. But please, leave the searching to Hugh, Kent and Victor. They excel in such matters. You may also see a young woman, Terri, about investigating too. She's a cop."

Nita looked at Zee, "An earth witch can uncover exclusive knowledge from the environment."

"Understand." Zee looked up at something behind her.

Her neck hairs shifted, ready to stand on end. Then a hand came down on her. Jasper tensed beside her.

"If we need you, we will send for you." Victor stated, squeezing her shoulder.

She wondered if all coven leaders were as grabby as Victor. It had to be just him. Otherwise, no one would ever join a coven without tactics like they pulled on her.

Coven. She was part of the coven now. Regret settled its heavy cowl over her. Maybe once she got what she needed, Camden, she could leave like her grandmother did. Quick, in and out. Like a robbery.

"We'll talk about you taking classes and getting what you need once this mess with the missing is completed." Victor added, patting her shoulder before leaving the room.

"That will be nice." Nita said to Zee. She could use further training. Her grandmother and the grimoires were her only teachers. Maybe less of a quick out than she initially planned.

After taking the file and running away from the coven, Jasper finally asked while driving, "Why did he kiss you?"

"I don't know," Nita muttered, trying to ignore all the cars on the road by reading more of the file the coven gave her. "How did they spell you?" She couldn't lift her gaze to him, for fear of watching all the traffic.

Jasper's fingers flexed on the wheel. "I dunno. I couldn't breathe. Passed out, I think. Next thing I knew, I was sitting on the couch and that jerk was talkin' to me."

Maybe they drove his truck for him when they took them.

"They take the mark off you?" Nita smoothed a paper after realizing she was crumpling the edge in a death grip.

"Yeah."

Nita tried to focus on anything but all the noise. The lack of plants. How tight the truck was. "Where was it this time?"

"The back of my head."

She saw out of the corner of her eye him touch the back of his head, the thickest part of his hair, just under the crown of his head. "You remember them putting it on you?"

"No, not really."

"Must have been when you were out. That would be Kent, I guess. Taking the air from your lungs." She dragged in a deep breath, telling her body she was fine. No need for additional adrenaline pumping. "These witches are powerful. Half of them in the inner circle, the ones with titles, are young though. I assumed most of them would be older."

"Like your grandmother."

"She left," Nita reflected briefly. Her reason for leaving must have been more than just not liking the changes. There's more to it.

"She didn't like Victor being put in charge? I don't." Jasper held venom in his voice.

She said with a slight smirk, "Me neither. He reminds me of a car salesman." Worse.

"Why did you join?" She could feel his gaze on her as he asked.

"To get this." She tapped the file in her lap. Nita regretted looking up and seeing the taillights surrounding them. She groaned, closing her eyes as she curled into a tighter ball in the front seat. "Any idea what happened to the dogs and Belsauros?"

"They better not have done anything, 'cept take 'em home!" Jasper clutched the steering wheel. He glanced at her, "Would you feel better in the back seat?"

"No!" she caught the scream in her throat.

"Okay. Okay. Breathe, baby." He breathed in a deep breath and let it out slowly. "Listen to my breathing and follow it, okay? You're okay. You're good. You're safe." He took in more steady, deep breaths.

Nita tried to follow with her own. Her heart thundered in her ears and she swore the acidic scent of smoke filled her nose. She heard the screech of metal against metal.

"Open your eyes, Nita. Look at my hand on the file, please. See? We're fine. We're safe. You're safe." Jasper's voice was soothing, a low, calm baritone he took on when she was being unreasonable. No, when he wanted to calm her down from a panic attack.

Nita inhaled again, gazed at his untouched hand, and noted the thunder in her ears diminish ever so slightly. "Keep talking."

Jasper nodded, "Alright. You look great in that green shade. You know, the dark shade. Consider trying that hair color next time. What do you think?"

She caught his smile, focused on his words. Placing her hand over his, she focused on his warmth, too. "Maybe."

"Wade suggested you go all red." Jasper chuckled, "Something about all the redheads are magic."

Nita snorted at that, "Not just redheads."

"That's what I said." Jasper flipped his hand over, tangling his fingers in hers and giving them a gentle squeeze as he kept talking.

It was the most Nita remembered Jasper talking at once. A constant stream of words, thoughts, memories, and stories. He plugged in a few old jokes that made her smile. Soon, whether it was his comforting sound and presence or if he held some magic in his tone, her body slowed. She eased into a state of alertness, but calm.

No longer did she scent the smoke of burning foam and fabric, or the stench of melting metals. She didn't hear in her mind the screech of the car bending and glass shattering. She didn't feel the whoosh of air pushing her to safety and cradling her in the night as the power lines zapped and whipped over her head.

"Better?" He asked, once they were free of most of the traffic of the large city and its suburbs.

She checked herself, pleased she made it through without leaping from the truck. "Yeah, thanks."

"That's what I'm here for."

Chapter Sixteen

For the next few days, Nita struggled with catching up on her duties. Gretta's treatment was coming along well. She was waiting for another supplement to arrive from one of her suppliers overseas before she could complete a powder she could use for a tea or milk. Nothing in her greenhouse or on her mountain was of use.

Jasper convinced her to go into town and purchase a new cell phone.

The house didn't like the new thing. It was bright, had too many apps, and the dwelling liked to zap it of its battery life rather than charge it. Nita hoped it would soon find something else to torture. Eventually. Maybe on another trip in she could charge it without worrying.

Her load to the Greene's was only three quarters of their order. While unloaded, she apologized to Mr. Greene repeatedly. "I'll make up for it next week. I promise."

"Don't worry about it, girl. You got enough goin' on in that life of yourn." Mr Green tucked his hands behind the bib in his denim overalls. "Yer lookin' a little green. 'N I'm not talkin' about yer hair. Ye alright?"

She nodded, puffing a strand of said green hair out of her eyes that had escaped her braid. "Yeah, I'm good."

"Ya know if'n ya need help with the farm, I gotta couple of boys that could take on some extra work." He said thoughtfully, moving his folded hands under the overalls so it looked like a heartbeat coming out of his chest.

Nita shook her head, "Oh no, that's unnecessary, sir."

He puffed a breath, "Suit yerself. If'n ya get sick from worryin' and runnin' around doing all the work that your brother did on top of yours, then it'll be just that much more painful." He leaned toward her slightly, placing a hand on the edge of the cart she loaded, "Trust me, girl.

Take it from an old man that ran himself into the ground at your age, take the help when it's offered."

"I ken, Mr. Greene. I got some help. Jasper and Christy. I'll be fine."

"Okay then." He nodded, turning and making his way back up to the intake room. "Ya still lemme know, wontcha?"

A smile bloomed, "I will." The elder worried more about her than she did herself. She glanced down at Belsauros climbing into the bottom of the cart with his ear of corn half eaten. Nita let him settle before pushing it to where it needed to go. She double checked her supplies that the Greene's used to package her produce and found them set for a while. At least she didn't have to worry about that.

Entering the diner, Mrs. Greene set a slice of a new cake in front of her. "Try this."

Nita raised a brow, "What is it?" She knew before Mrs. Greene answered after smelling it. Orange cream with cranberries and a citrus buttercream. She could already sense her sugar spiking.

"New recipe one of the girls found on a recipe site. Forget which one. Thought it might improve my old orange cream." Mrs. Greene grinned as she explained.

She rolled her eyes, "Your recipe don't need improvement. But I'll try it." Nita took a bite and shook her head, "This is good, but I like the old one best," she said after swallowing the mouthful, "It had more cream and this is like sweetness overload."

Mrs. Greene chuckled, "Alright dear, I'll take that into consideration." She paused, gripping the towel she tugged off her shoulder in both hands. "Any news?"

"No, not really." Nita replied duly with another shake of her head.

"I'm sorry, girl. I pray every night that he's well and comes back to us soon."

"Thanks. Me too." Nita answered with a small nod at the older woman.

"If only your grandma were alive," Mrs. Greene heaved a sigh, "She'd know exactly what to do and where to find him. Bring him back by the ear."

Nita couldn't help but smile at the mental image her words conjured, "Yeah, she would."

"You need anythin'? Some food to take home for a couple of suppers?"

"I'm alright. Thank you, though."

Mrs. Greene patted her hand, "You just let me hear. You can stay with us too, if you need to not be alone in that old house of yours. Or supper, or breakfast. Anythin'. We're here for ya."

"Thanks." Nita said again, feeling the love bloom in her chest, but at the same time a shadow of shame flickered too. She hated being pitied or seen as needy. They couldn't help it. The good people of the town. Big hearts meant big help. Others needed the bit of gossip they could glean from such gatherings as pretending to give could provide. The Greenes were part of the latter, the good-hearted with closed lips.

She finished the cake, paid her tab, and headed back home. Bel chirped contentedly beside her, sitting like a human in the passenger seat as he groomed his jiggling belly. At the stoplight, she studied him for a moment.

"How do I put a raccoon on a diet?"

His contentment stopped.

She grinned as he started waving his paws around, growling and hissing at her. Her phone rang, and she picked it up. Imagine, a few more years and she'd be able to get a signal anywhere. Not recognizing the number, she answered, "Bell's Herbs and Spices."

"Nita, my darling, it is nice to hear your voice."

She pulled the phone away from her ear a bit to make a face at the crooning notes. Was he trying to be

Sinatra or Dean? He was missing something. Charm, perhaps? "Same." She tried for neutrality, "What's up?"

His chuckle sent ice covered fingertips dancing down her spine, "Glad you've missed me too. I'm going to be in your neck of the woods next week and wondered if you would like to join me on the hunt."

"Hunting for Camden and the others?"

Victor Martin's voice wasn't as purr-like as he imagined she thought, as he said, "Of course, darling, I've already found you, so I have no need to hunt for anything else."

Another dancing set of fingernails down her spine, "Yeah, I'd like that."

"Perfect. I'll be there on Sunday, darling. Care to join me for dinner?"

She nearly gagged, "Jasper and I have a date."

"Ah, still toying with the help, I see. Very well. I'll see you Monday morning. Meet me at the Greene's little produce place, yes?" His tone darkened with each word.

Nita tried to stay calm as she swallowed down the bile his voice summoned. What was it with him? "Alright. When?"

"Dawn, of course."

"I'll see you then."

"I look forward to it, love. Until then... think of me."

Before she could retort, the phone went silent. "Can I kill him? Ima kill him." She nodded, tossing the phone into a wired together plastic cup holder dangling from her dash. Bel sounded his warning note, and she sighed. "I know. Killing the leader will be tricky. I think I can do it. Just so long as I keep my distance from his soul sucking powers."

Bel huffed.

"Yeah, I hear ya." Nita muttered, "I guess I better keep him around until we find Camden."

Sunday night rolled around far too quickly for Nita's taste. She stood in front of the old oven, watching the timer click away the minutes. Baked chicken was to be served for her pretend date night. Only her date was late.

Which was fine. Better actually. The ancient bratty house had fought her with the stove for a few minutes before it finally gave in and started preheating.

Jasper barrelled into the door, his face pale, making his dark eyes hauntingly black.

"What's wrong?"

He swallowed, placing shaking hands on the counter beside the stove. "I... let me get my wits about me."

She waited, her heart tearing into a faster beat with each breath she took and each scenario that played through her mind. Had they found Camden? Had they found one of the others? Was another one missing? Someone that was close to them? Was Camden... hurt?

Jasper forced out in a pain filled tone, "I saw him."

"Who?"

"Cam." Jasper's voice was a rasp. "He was... he put someone in a truck. Didn't even turn around when I yelled for him. It was like he was... like he was a puppet or somethin'."

"What?" Nita mouthed the word, not sure if she spoke it or not over the thundering silence in her ears. When had her heart stopped?

He turned on her, gripping her arms. His fingers dug in slightly, just enough to hold her still, but not hurt. "Cam... he kidnapped someone. I saw it."

"No, he didn't. That had to be someone... anyone... someone else." She tried to pull away from him, half in the need to just have some space. To breathe. The other half to run away from this thing that told lies about her brother.

"It was him. Nita. It was him. I know him better than I know myself. It was Cam." Jasper's fingers dug in further, "But it was like he was different. He was skinnier. Pale."

The fingerprints settled in her muscles and she tugged harder to get away from him. "No. You saw wrong. He was trying to run away. The other person was controlling him." She gritted her teeth before jerking her arms free, "He's been kidnapped! Of course, he's pale and skinny!" She stopped, staring at the man in front of her. "What kind of truck?"

"Gray, a Ford 150. I got a partial plate." His hands shook in front of him, and he stared at them like he couldn't believe they were not holding her anymore.

She swallowed, hoping to drown out the fluttering and sick feelings roiling in her body. "Did you tell the cops already?"

"Yeah, I-one of them heard me yelling and came running. So I gave him my report thing." He shook his head, "Nita... he's alive. He's moving." Jasper smiled a little, "But he's still... he's still caught."

"He wasn't kidnapping another person!" Nita felt the outrage, the hurt washed over her and beat out the panic, for a too brief moment.

Jasper shook his head, "It looked like he was."

"Did you tell the cop that?"

Jasper spread his hands, eyes wide and on hers. "Yeah... well, I had to."

"What?!" Nita jumped as the timer screeched. She cursed and kicked the oven, whirling back on Jasper, "He's not a kidnapper!"

"I know that! Maybe... maybe he's forced."

"He wouldn't." Nita turned the oven off. Tendrils curled under her heart. The man that usually caused that sickening sensation wasn't here, though. Jasper was. She eyed him for a moment. "Eat. I'm going out."

The screen door slammed behind her a few times as she ran out of the house. She didn't even pause to pick up Bel. Jasper called out after her, but she was already in her truck and cranking the old thing awake. Dirt flew under her tires, the shocks squealing in protest as she slid through the curves of her long driveway.

Rubber bounced and then caught on the old pavement once she hit the main road toward town. There was only one place he would stay in town. Someone with that much power and slimy charm. That is, if he was there and not standing in her driveway. Could Spirit wielders do that?

She cursed herself for not studying other powers. She cursed herself further for not grabbing Bel. As a last curse, she cursed herself for not making her grandmother explain what had gone wrong with the coven.

Nita slowed as blue lights flashed off the treetops. She rounded a curve and was met with two cops cars sitting in the road, barely enough room for a vehicle to go in between them. A cop in a yellow vest waved her down and came to her driver side window. "What's going on?"

"A person of interest has been... Is your last name Bell?" The cop began in a bored tone, but then awareness entered as he recognized her.

"Yeah."

"Cap'tn's been tryin' to reach ya, ma'am. Can I escort you-"

"No need, I'm heading into town." Nita felt her lip begin to tremble. It was true. Cam had been spotted.

He studied her, "You alright to drive?"

"Yeah. I'm fine." She didn't believer her words, but somehow he did.

Sam Wicker

He nodded and waved at his partner, who dragged a barrier away, making more room for her old truck to pass through.

She cursed herself again for forgetting her phone. The cops probably wanted to discuss why Camden was seen, or something like that. She'd gather the truth from them. Hopefully.

Unless Jasper convinced them that Camden was a kidnapper and not kidnapped.

She pulled in front of the small police station. Parking between two black and white cruisers with gold lettering. Bulldog colors, because they thought that was the only school that mattered in the county. Nevermind there were three other high schools and a handful more middle and elementary.

She bit back the negativity and strode into the station. A surly gentleman with a graying handlebar mustache and black-rimmed glasses greeted her with a grunt. "Ms. Bell are ya?" He asked after she signed in on a clipboard he slid to her through his thick glass pane window.

"Yes, sir."

"Through the door, Officer Payne will be the one talkin' to ya. Head to the right and he'll meet ya." He waved in the general direction to the right.

The door buzzed after an audible click at his side. She pushed it open, and he bellowed for Payne.

"Jaysus man, I'm right here. We have pages over phones for a reason." A man with brown hair clipped close to his scalp stood from behind a metal desk with a computer and files stacked on a file organizer. Wrinkles bracketing his mouth and brown eyes were the only tell of his age. A hard, damaged soul spoke to her from his gaze. "Ms. Bell?"

"Nita, yes." She took his hand and shared in a firm handshake. "Did you find him?"

"He was sighted." He glanced around. "You alright with talking out here or would you like to go into a room?"

She lifted a shoulder, "Either's fine." With the way her adrenaline kept fluctuating between anger and flight, it didn't matter where she was in this building. She blamed it on her ancestors making 'shine on how nervous she was around badges.

He nodded and motioned for her to sit in the plastic chair beside his desk. Officer Payne sat down in his, the spring squeaking a little as he turned to his desk and tapped a few keys on his keyboard. "I'm gonna record this. Just so we both have a record of the conversation."

Nita swallowed, "Sounds good."

"Ms. Bell, Nita, at seven pm on May twenty-sixth with Officer Payne, case number 567843, missing persons, Camden Bell. You are Mr. Bell's sister, younger, correct?"

"Yes."

"Still no one else to contact on this case other than a Jasper Price, correct?"

"If you cannot reach me, yes."

"Understood. Ms. Bell...er...Nita, do you know your brother was seen by Jasper Price in town today?"

"He told me. Just a little while ago."

He nodded, leaning back in his chair, "Do you have any idea why he would come into town, while allegedly kidnapping another, instead of going home to you?"

She didn't like that tone, nor the question. "He is kidnapped. No, I don't know why he would be here. Someone, his kidnapper, probably brought him here."

"Has Camden been in any relationships lately?"

Nita clamped down on the retort and answered the question instead, "No."

"Would you know if he was seeing someone?"

"Yes, of course."

Officer Payne nodded, making a note on a sticky pad with lines on it she couldn't read. Chickens wrote better letters than that. "Have you thought of anyone that might want to harm him or keep him from work, home, and you since you last spoke with us?"

"No."

"Mr. Price saw something interesting. Would you like to see it?"

She blinked at him; they had a recording of today. "Yes."

He touched the computer screen, moving it so that she could see it better. Then, switched screens to a video player and hit the large play button in the middle. She recognized the street in front of Dickey's hardware, and Jasper's truck.

"Pay attention to this right here." He pointed to a truck at the edge of the screen.

"It's blurry."

"Correct. We've been trying to narrow down and search for plates that could match what we can come up with. There's only so much zooming in you can do on these things. Mr. Price provided us with a partial, and that's good." The last sentence was spoken in a reassuring tone, but it didn't meet his hazel eyes.

She nodded. Pity technology wasn't like on the television shows Camden entertained now and then. Otherwise, they'd already have the truck, and Camden would be found. She saw a man slide out of the driver's side. Camden's height.

Biting her lip, she watched as he waited, loitered around the tailgate of the truck for a moment before grabbing a teen by the scruff of the neck and slamming their head into the truck bed. She gasped, clutching the edge of Officer Payne's desk. The teen slumped into Camden, who slung him, maybe her, into the truck cab.

Jasper came into the screen, bags dangling from his hands before he tossed them into the back of his truck in his toolbox. He froze after slamming it shut. The muscles on his neck bulged as he bellowed and then he was sprinting toward her brother.

Camden didn't even look at his best friend. Jasper, who was like a brother to him, wasn't worth a glance. He just got in the truck with the teen and sped off.

Nita sniffed, staring at Officer Payne's hand as he held it out for her. That's when she felt the hot stream down her cheek. She grabbed the tissues, dabbing at the tears. "Is there anything that you can use? Any idea..."

He nodded, "We have the make and model of the truck. Unfortunately, Dickey's is the only store that has a decent camera. The little thrift shop here," he pointed to the store two doors down from Dickey's that would have the best angle, "is blocked by this tree here. They just haven't taken the time to move it." He clicked on another pane and showed her the footage of it. She could barely make out a tire and the white of the door behind the rough bark of the maple.

"Because there's so many people missing now, Atlanta has taken notice. The feds. They'll be here tomorrow or the next day." Officer Payne explained, a dark annoyance tilting his voice.

She swallowed, "That's good, right?"

He gave her a blank look, "Well, I hope so." He studied her for a moment, "Did you recognize the victim?"

Nita shook her head.

He frowned, "I cannot tell you who. Not yet. We've informed the family, but they haven't decided whether they want to go public with it. But I have to ask you this... does Camden have anything against anyone enough that he would do this?"

"No."

"Now, Ms. Bell, think for a moment."

"He's not like that!" Nita pressed her fists into her thighs, "Yeah, sure, he's gotten into a few fights. After them, though, he's more likely to take them out for drinks and fishing later than get into another fight with them. He has few enemies and none of them are that young."

"Any of his enemies have siblings around that age?"

She frowned, "Are you really saying that he wasn't forced to do that? That he would want to hurt a kid on his own?" She shook her head, "He wouldn't. Someone's forcing him. Someone's threatening him and he had to do it to survive or... protect me."

"Protect you by kidnapping someone? Do you know how this looks?"

The adrenaline pumping through her died down. Its disappearance had her slumping in the chair, "It looks bad."

"It looks like he hasn't been kidnapped. Like he's the one doing the kidnapping. He's dangerous."

"He is not!"

Officer Payne's face hardened along with his words, "I am going to inform you of what is going to happen tomorrow. Tomorrow you will have a cop or two watching your place, you, Jasper Price, and the businesses that Camden and you frequent. If we see you do anything suspicious, like try to contact him, we'll bring you in."

Nita shook her head, "We're not the bad guys here."

"I hope not."

She stared into the soulless eyes of the officer. A million things going through her mind that she wanted to say to him. One voice in her thoughts kept them from spilling out of her lips. The calm, firm voice of her grandmother.

"Head down girl, smile, nod, and go on. Do as they say, and it won't hurt for long. Bite that tongue, girl. One day, they'll ken. One day, they'll crawl like they made us

crawl. One day, you can say all those things and then some because they'll be askin' for you."

"Thank you, Officer Payne. Anything else?"

"Do you recognize the truck?" He asked as he flipped back to the blurry screen.

"No."

"Has Camden ever done this before?"

"No."

He paused, staring her down again, "That's all for now, Ms. Bell."

She nodded, "Thanks." She stood, as did he. He shook her hand again and walked her out. She gave a nod to the intake officer before making her way back outside and into her truck. She sat for a moment, collecting her thoughts.

Exhaustion creeped into her bones, and she tried to force it off. She wasn't done yet. For the life of her, she couldn't shake the dread of being beaten. She tried for anger again.

"How dare they suspect Camden." She growled to herself. The adrenaline didn't come back. She sighed and backed out, debated on slamming into a cruiser, decided she didn't need jail time, and went to the bed-and-breakfast just inside the city limits.

This house was the closest in age to her own in town. Built by one of the founding families, it stood like a white monument with a bright red front door and black shutters on every window except for the bays. Two gigantic oaks stretched stoic in the front yard, nearly as old as the dwelling. In the early 1900s it had been turned into a bed-and-breakfast, and had lasted as such ever since. The family still owned it, the Forsyths.

She climbed out of her truck and sensed him. He was definitely here. Was it because of the coven ritual that she became so in tune to him?

Something was off. Nita shouldn't be in harmony with anyone other than her family and friends. She couldn't tell if they were in a building or not. But the Martin witch was different. It was like his essence oozed out of the windows, like the soft light from the fancy chandelier in the foyer.

Standing in the shadow of one of the old oaks, she placed a hand on the rough bark of its trunk. Its knowledge and strength soothed her. It was the trees. They were telling her what was going on. It wasn't as if there was some special bond between her and a spirit magic user.

The memory of the kiss Victor Martin stole from her reared its head. Nita touched her lips with her free hand, fingertips gently pressing in semblance at what his lips had done to them. Ice filled her heart, but heat filled her belly.

Pushing away from the tree, she marched to the front door and pulled it open. A tinkling bell startled her into letting it close on its own behind her. Luckily, it was on one of those fancy hinges and it just clicked shut instead of slamming. The latest Forsyth in control of the place rounded a corner, wiping his hands on a dishtowel. A smile, wide, showing off crooked bicuspids, but not genuine enough to put a shine in his green eyes, preceded a curt greeting.

"I'm here to see Victor Martin."

"Is he expecting you, honey?" His voice was nearly as sweet as the last word.

She nodded, "Yes."

"Ah, yes, I see the note here. Silly me, I forgot he said he was going to have a guest. Nita is it?"

"That's me." She said after a hard swallow.

Something began screeching in the kitchen, "Ah... please, go on up. He's in room number nine. Up the stairs to the second floor and take a left down that hall. It will be on the right, at the end. If you'll excuse me. So sorry."

Nita stared after him as he bustled out of the foyer and smiled at the smell of freshly baked peaches. She wondered if she would be invited to dinner since she was here with one of their guests. The stairs were made of dark wood, with a rich navy blue carpet centered in them and bordered with silver thread. Everything gleamed. Even the spokes of the staircase banister.

The directions he gave her were exact. She spent some time peering at the aged portraits hanging on the walls. Some were of Forsyths, while others were delicate watercolor landscapes or paintings of florals. In a section of the left wall, was how Murphy was at its birth. Or near enough. The town had dirt tracks for roads, large brick and marble buildings menaced over their log and plank counterparts. The first of the courthouses was being built in the drawing. If her memory served her correctly, it burned down not ten years after its completion.

Two more would go up in its place before the famous blue marble one that still stood.

What fascinated her the most was the bullpen. An area in the middle, a square of sorts, where plenty held trades and sales, among other nastier things. It was a large stone pillar with three iron rings down each of the six sides for the livestock to be tied to during the sales.

One of her ancestors was crudely depicted in that drawing, as there were several natives in it with feathers in their long, wild tresses.

With a snort, she turned away and knocked on the polished wood with a bronze nine on it.

She heard a muffled, "Just a moment." From within and footsteps coming from the back of the room.

The door opened, and she let her eyes roam.

Dark whirls circled three runes, Ansuz, Tiwaz, and Eihwaz, curved over and around his sharp collar bones. Sowulo with an intricate design, rested over the center of his sternum and Wunjo peeked from under the top of his low slung black dress pants.

"You're early, darling. Glad to see I'm not the only one eager for us." He said after leaning a bit against the jamb.

She blinked, looking into those eerie blue eyes of his. She felt her cheeks and neck heat, "I just want to find my brother."

"Of course. As do I." He intoned, his dimples winking at her with a smile. "Please, come in." He opened the door wide and took a small step back on bare feet.

"I'll wait for you out here."

"Don't be silly." He shook his head and motioned for her to come on in. "I'll only be a moment and you can look over another file or two whilst I finish."

Files. Knowledge. It dragged her into the room and she glanced around it. The click of the door shutting behind her had the hair on the back of her neck stand on end. Damn him. Not a file in sight.

Warm breath made a few strands tickle the shell of her ear before he said, "I'm glad you came, darling."

More tendrils rose as something tugged on a strand and she turned just enough to see him wrapping one around his finger. He brought it to his lips, kissed it, and released. He smiled.

She wasn't sure what to do with that. She approached a table that was set against a window covered in lace curtains. "The file?"

"Always with the business, never the pleasure." He muttered before moving in behind her and tugging a file out of a black case sitting on a chair, along with a long overcoat. He handed it to her.

"As it should be until my brother is returned to me." She stated as she took the file from him and looked at the shield emblazoned on the front. "You have an actual police report?"

"Several. That one is yours."

"Mine?"

"Yes, you are a suspect." His smile reached his eyes, making them shine with mischievous light. Part of that aura he had when she first met him that night ebbed, and he seemed larger than the room they were in. Quite a feat, considering it was nearly as large as her kitchen and living room put together. He loomed over her, "Are you part of this plot?"

"No."

"Am I just to take your word for it, my darling Bell?"

Her anger bubbled, and she stepped into him. Damn the aura of foreboding and every bone in her body telling her to get her feet on land. "I'm not you're darlin', and I'm not part of this kidnapping thing."

"Maybe not, but you are a criminal." He didn't back down. Just seemed to loom ever closer.

"How so?"

The jovial look on his face faltered, his eyes narrowing upon her. "You did a rather dangerous spell, without the coven or any other witch to aid you. Then you used a civilian to help you replenish yourself."

Nita scoffed, "I wasn't in it then. What was I to do?"

"Fair enough. But there's one other thing." Some of the bright mischief returned to his blue gaze.

She rolled her eyes, her jaw tight, "What?"

"You leave me begging, wanting you. I desire you more than water, more than air. Yet you leave me desolate. Is that not a crime?"

She laughed in his face. "Don't be ridiculous. Go back to Atlanta and have an orgy with your little coven groupies, Martin."

He frowned, the aura dissipating as quickly as it came. "Groupies? Orgy?"

Nita's brow quirked. "Yes. And yes. How did you know about my spell?"

Victor curled his lips up and spread his hands, "Zee felt a prodding of magic like he'd never sensed before saying the source was up here. Also, Ginger picked up on it. She reads damage like that. Like you can, the age rings of a tree, as she puts it."

She shrugged and returned to the file. So much for the healing hands of friends if spells like that left markers on her.

He stood still for a moment longer, before retreating to what she learned to be a bathroom after she heard the tell-tale signs of brushing teeth. The file in her hands was not, in fact, hers. It was Camden's file.

In it were copies of the photos they were given of Camden, his visual details all typed neatly, and then the interviews, including all of hers, that the local police had conducted. They had been pretty thorough, asking most of the townspeople and some of the visitors if they had seen Cam. Those that said yes, they interviewed. Standard questions.

Following was a graph. A red bar marking missing moments of what they pieced sequentially of Camden's day. Two of them, spanning about an hour each. The next was a timeline of the week before the day he had been missing. More red bars. Mostly at night, where there was a note written above of 'assumed sleeping'.

Seeing his days laid out like this helped her place everything in her own mind. It clicked together like pieces of a puzzle's edge.

Next was a map of the county; the areas the police had canvased. Her heart dropped at seeing the river in town, the Hiawassee, highlighted and the dates it had been dragged. They had explored Murphy and a perimeter of a mile out. The same with her house and land. Darker spots denoted the overlap with the searches for Randy and the others.

She glared, flipping to the next section. Here were lists of suspects and the reasons why. Also, random thoughts of the officers working the cases, hunches.

Jasper was at the top of the list. She was second. The names Kent Allen and Victor Martin were next.

Her heart turned cold.

What had they done to denote suspicion?

She read the notes beside them. Both coven members had been in the town during the times of the disappearances of Randy, Camden, and Mr. Wright. A hand came down on her shoulder and she nearly jumped out of her skin.

"Easy, darling." He purred with a small smile.

He had a shirt on now, at least. The last of his undone buttons showed her flashes of the tattoos on his collar bones. A tie hung loose around his neck and he sat on the little couch thing, it had a proper name she knew, but she couldn't think of it. He peered up at her, a pair of ebony socks in one hand. "You alright?"

She nodded, not trusting her voice.

"Nice to know that a well-pressed shirt makes you speechless." He said with a slight note of bitterness as he took up the task of putting on his socks and glistening shoes.

Nita glanced at the open closet, looking at anything but him. And counted enough clothes to last him a month. "Staying long?"

"Yes. I am. I have to monitor our newest member. Guide her. A bit of a wild card. No one's sure what she's liable to do next."

"Must be a pain."

"Nah, she's easy on the eyes, which makes this job far less difficult than it could be. Plus, she's of a family I've wanted in my acquaintance, and pulled into the coven for quite some time."

Sam Wicker

He talked as if he was centuries old, instead of just a year or two older than her.

He finished getting ready. "Let's eat. Then we shall begin our own search." He took the file from her and tucked it back into the case before taking her hand in his and guiding her out the door.

Chapter Seventeen

The rest of that night was a haze. Nita felt she had fought off a bear and lost by the time she crawled into her bed beside Jasper. She was almost in blissful slumber when he curled around her. Her body warmed as he enveloped her. His soft snores tickled her shoulder as sleep claimed her.

The next morning, she set about her usual routine. Jasper gone. A carafe full of coffee, still hot in the maker, and a lingering scent of eggs and sawdust let her know he'd wanted her to sleep. Not mad. Just sleep. Right?

She put her phone to her ear and the daunting task of calling up coven members chilled her to the bone. She started with the obvious, the inner circle, those closest to Victor and Kent. "Hello, Mr. Haskins, sir, it's Nita- oh, yeah, I'm fine. No, no, there isn't any danger. Yes, I understand. I was contacting you to ask a few questions." She finally got in a word edgewise, the chill rising to the warmth of anger after his barrage to ensure her safety. "So, when my brother went missing, how did ya'll find out, all the way down there since I wasn't part of the coven?"

"We keep tabs on all family members of witches, whether or not they are coven."

"Well, that's a daunting task." Nita said with raised brows. That meant thousands of people were tracked.

"Indeed."

"You think they're all connected, don't you?" When he answered with a grunt and nothing more, Nita continued, "It's nice that you can send such high officials up here at the drop of a hat. Has Allen and Martin been up here around each of the missing cases here?"

"Of course they have. They have the safety and best interests of all witches at heart."

That sounded rehearsed. "You're pretty much the protector and stuff, right? Why don't you come up here?"

"I stay here to coordinate with officials and our coven. I'm getting a bit old to go traipsing about the mountains, girl. What's the meaning of you calling me and asking me these things?" His gruff voice was filled to the brim with suspicion.

"Curious is all. I dunno how the you, we work. Martin says I've stepped over lines and on toes while trying to find out clues." She wanted to say she didn't mean to, but she couldn't bring herself to say the lie.

"Let the big boys handle it."

With that, he ended the call. Her hand tightened on the phone as she stared at his name on the screen. It wouldn't last through her throwing it. Not like her old one. The rest of her calls, if they even answered her, followed much the same. All she gathered was that both Allen and Martin were in the mountains. At the same timeframe of each disappearance, no other coven members were allowed. When a search party was brought up, Martin denied it, saying he and Allen could handle it.

The hair at the base of her neck was perpetually on end. She slid the new phone into her back pocket and used her breathing techniques to calm herself. Rain was on the air. Digging her toes and heels into the rich earth, she let it drag all the weariness away. As she soaked up its empowering strength, Nita sung an old hymn her grandmother passed down for calmness. Martin and Allen, both probably, were part of this. If they weren't the ones responsible.

She wondered if she could follow them.

Remembering the tie she vibed around Martin, she figured that would be a bad idea. Someone like Christy, on the other hand... no. She couldn't put her friend in danger. Frowning, she trailed a fingertip over a morning glory leaf, then the vine up to the stared face of the blue flower.

"If only they hadn't invented pavement or cement." She whispered to the plant. While she could tell little from cement, pavement was far more difficult to talk to. It was ageless, dead, and rotted. Putting her bare feet on it made her feel filthy and exhausted.

Otherwise, they would have been easy to track with a simple spell. She kept one on Belsauros in case he ever got carried away by something larger. Like Jasper's dogs.

She froze, a thought tackling her mind.

The emotion. The tie. The knowing of him. She pressed her fingertips to her lips and bolted inside her house. Belsauros screeched as she nearly barreled him over to gain the stairs and race up to the bathroom. She leaned close to the mirror, flipping every yellow bulbed light on in the room she could, and looked over her lips. She pulled them out, looking at her gums, teeth, the inside of her mouth. Frowning, she looked under her tongue next.

Nothing.

She dug through the drawers until she found the little dental mirror and used it to study the hard-to-reach places, and the roof of her mouth. Nothing still.

He'd touched her hair. Her hand shot toward Jasper's clippers and she stilled before grasping it. "Let's not get excited." Nita took in a long, deep breath and let it out slowly. Belsauros chattered at her grumpily from the doorway. She turned, watching him for a moment, then scooped him up. She deposited him on the bed and lay down on her stomach.

"Look for marks. Here." She ran her fingers through her hair.

Bel grumbled as he worked. Using his little paws to delicately comb over every inch of her scalp and the back of her neck. He even looked through the length of her tresses. How a spell could be strong enough to give that level of emotion whilst being drawn on shifting hair she couldn't fathom. But she wasn't about to leave a stone unturned.

Her shirt fell to the floor as she padded across the hall to study every inch of her back in the mirror. Nothing was there either. Had he touched her ass? She looked over her lips again as she brought up every interaction with him.

"Dammit," she muttered, telling herself, "You were out, dumbass."

The raccoon's grumblings were louder as he had to look over her privates that she couldn't see after she looked over her legs, her feet, and in between her toes. She scanned between her fingers, and under her fingernails. Her eyelids were a challenge, but she managed.

"Well…" Jasper cleared his throat, leaning against the doorframe, "Hi."

She automatically covered herself, then rolled her eyes.

He grinned, "While this has been my dream to be welcomed by you dressed in nothin' I'm gatherin' there is another purpose to your nakedness. Right?"

"I wanted to check for spells. In case." Sawdust, and rain on wet earth wafted toward her from him.

"Find any?"

"No."

"That's good."

"Yeah."

"Yeah."

They stood, locked in a gaze, until he cleared his throat, "Look, I'm sorry I… Camden wouldn't go after people. Hurt people. Take them from their families without being… spelled or somethin'. I just," he raked a hand through his damp hair, his eyes drifting down to somewhere beside his feet, "Hell, Nita, I'm overwhelmed with all this."

Her eyes narrowed, her heart spiking between one emotion to the other, "Overwhelmed."

"Yeah. He's missing. It's like I lost my right arm. There's... there's..." he used the same hand he had mussed his hair with to motion to the air between them, "And there's this coven thing. I dunno if I'm comin' or goin' half the time."

"The coven has nothin' to do with you. And if I'm distractin' you, by all means, this," she motioned to the air between them like he had, "can stop."

"What the... hell no! That's not what I meant." His eyes had flown back up to hers, wide, erratic. "Life's a bit of a mess right now. That's all I meant. It was an apology not to pick another fight, woman!"

If she were a raccoon, her hackles would raise, "Nita. Not woman. Nita."

Jasper flashed his teeth like he was about to sink them into a threat, her. "Dammit. Do you just want to take a go then? Alright. Come on." He dropped his tool belt with a heavy thump and rattle of metal. Jasper held both arms out while stepping into the hall.

Belsauros growled, his little head turning to look up at the ceiling while he chattered low. He waddled off, going down the hall to the stairs. If he'd been human, Nita figured the fur ball would have been cursing them under his breath.

She pulled her underwear and shorts back on. Unfortunately, her shirt was in the room behind him. The way he waved her toward him tugged into fire, "Why were you so chummy with them?"

"I was under a damn spell!" Jasper huffed, hands still out like a martyr.

"Maybe you still are."

"Then search!" He ripped his wet clinging shirts off over his head and they fell over his tool belt. He held his arms back out. Circling slowly. "See anythin'?"

She didn't. Nothing but the gleam of a day's sweat and stray pieces of sawdust. As soon as he faced her again, she crossed her arms over her chest. She watched as his eyes dipped to her now hugged breasts. The darkness of anger deepened with something else.

"You were apologizing?"

Jasper stopped, gaze flicking back up to her eyes and narrowing. "I was."

"Continue."

"No. No, I'm not gonna." He spread his feet to shoulder width even as he crossed his own arms.

"Why?"

"It's not my fault that you don't trust me." His voice was low, nearly growling. "I haven't done anythin' to deserve doubt."

"You tossed me in mud holes after telling me that you'd help me cross them. You put twigs in my hair while at parties. You acted like you were gonna kiss me, but you didn't. Should I go on?" Nita spat out, her spine rigid.

"We were kids!"

"Some of those were only two years ago!"

Jasper blinked at her, "It's playin'. It's not like this." He shook his head, shoulders sagging a little, "It's like you think I pushed Camden to run away or something."

"I don't know what to believe. I'm a little overwhelmed here, too." Nita felt the rage within disappear like smoke on a brisk wind.

He sighed, "I know."

What she told herself not to say dragged its way up her throat. "You were the last to see him. You were the last to be with him for a while because of y'alls' trip to Yellowstone."

"I know." His gaze turned hot again, "You're not a damn cop and I'm no stranger. Hell, we've known each other since we were knee high!"

"Yeah, and I've known Camden since birth and he left me." Her voice cracked, and she hated herself for it. *One emotion or the other, Nita, that'd be grand.* "Maybe willingly, and that's what haunts me the most."

That done him in. His arms uncrossed, "I'm sorry, Bellbean."

He made no other move. Just stared at her.

He didn't seem right, standing alone, looking about like he was about to cry for her. So she strode to him, pressing a kiss to his lips. His arms came around her. She pulled back, "Your apologies suck."

"Yeah, well, your head's like a rock, so they gotta be long and explained well."

She pinched his nipple.

"Ow! Hell!" He cupped his breast and glared at her. Then he had her against the wall. His hands squeezing her breasts as his groin pressed into hers and she wished for the denim between them to be gone already.

He read her mind, because he made quick work of both, not even stepping out of his when he hauled her up. Her shoulder blades dug into the doorframe. His cock rammed into her and she gasped, reaching up to hold on to the door header by her fingertips.

She'd barely wrapped her legs around his hips when the second thrust hit with a wet slap. Her hand slid over his flesh before she found a grip on his biceps. Every muscle in his body was tense.

"Doin' more than kissin' now."

He made her groan with his smirk before he rammed again, tearing another gasp from her. This time he kept up a hard, slapping rhythm. Nita didn't have the presence to prepare for the crescendo. Overwhelmed by pleasure, she could only cling.

Chapter Eighteen

Jasper wasn't in her bed that morning. The sun was already up over the mountains, soft morning light filtering through the cheap green drapes she'd bought to replace her frilly childhood ones. With a groan, she stretched her sore muscles before getting out of the bed.

A post-it on her door caught her eye.

"Thought I'd let you sleep in. Yogurt needs to be stomached. I'll be back tonight, don't cook, I'll bring us supper. Working in town today at Dickey's. Love, Jasper."

His handwriting was so cramped she had to decipher his words as if she was reading runes.

She ate the rest of the yogurt; it was going out of date in two days, anyway. She didn't like it much, unless it was loaded down with fruit and granola. The same way her grandmother liked it.

After making more phone calls and subscribing to the coven newspaper, she felt a slight relaxation in her shoulders. As much as they could be with Camden still missing. With the last month's issues in her hands, she sat down on the front step of her back porch and skimmed through them. She'd found them in the back of the file they had given her in Atlanta. Why not try to relax? Or not.

The goal was to locate anything that could inform her about the movements of the coven leader and his second-in-command.

Not a lick of disappointment to be had. Victor Martin was the Newspaper's dominant story. He was in every issue. Whether it be a puff piece about him taking another child under his wing to feed or enroll in school, or a piece about his favorite place to eat. He liked Italian, apparently.

After going through half the stack, she paused on the classifieds. A bold title catching her eye, 'Save The Witch Realm'. Since when was there a witch realm? Were realms even real? She read to find out more.

They have subjected us to persecution for our practices and mere existence, even before Salem. No more. Help us. Help us save ourselves from the lowly humans that would rather burn us than allow us to help them move into the next centuries. Let us come together and create our own world of love, peace, and freedom to live as we choose in the Mystic Realm.

A number followed the piece along with a single word. Vic.

As in Victor? She started back at the beginning of the month to skim through the classifieds. The ads were there. The same number, the same name, but the message changed every few days. Some called for powerful witches to join forces to create a protective realm for all. Others cajoled for time and patience, that a saving grace was on its way.

She imagined him saying the words. It worked. She could hear his voice uttering such things, and believed that he would.

She'd read something about creating realms in one of her grandmother's books, hadn't she? She stood, taking the pile of papers in with her and putting them on the table as she thought. Were the realm and the disappearances tied? Was it Victor?

Her gut hit a true tone, and she knew she was getting close to something. Something dangerous. She probably had no business digging into this.

"Hey!"

She jumped out of her skin and whirled. Christy stood just inside the door, a tray of coffees in her hand and a bag with Greene's Diner logo on it. "Hi."

"Oh, don't just 'hi' me, what were you lost in?" Christy muttered with a glare as she put the tray down on the table. She raised a brow at the newspapers. "I've never seen these before, are they… they're coven papers?"

Nita nodded.

"Wait. So how did you get a hold of them?"

Oh, Christy was going to kill her for not giving her details. "I'm part of the coven now."

Christy's eyes grew as wide as the domes on top of the blended coffees. "What?"

"Yeah. I thought it might help me find Camden. You know, having more than one searching for him." She said as nonchalantly as she could manage.

Her best friend sat slowly, still staring at the papers. "But, your granny hated them. Didn't she?"

"Yeah, I wanted to figure that out, too."

"Nit. This is… are you sure?"

Too late to back out now. "No, but here I am." She sat down across from Christy and opened the bag. A glistening pair of jellied donuts begged to be devoured. She grabbed one and raised her brows as her bestie mechanically took her own. "Look, I'm careful."

She snorted, "No, no you're not. Not now." Christy said around a mouthful of donut. "Ever since Cam went missing, you've been off the rails."

"What do you mean?"

Christy gave her a look. "This is the first time I've ever seen something on your land a little wilty. I hardly hear from you. You joined the coven. You did a spell that nearly killed you, on your own, telling no one that you were doing it. What more do I need to list off?"

Nita groaned because she knew Christy was right. Ever since Camden left, it took her twice as long to complete her usual tasks. "Wait, what's wilting?"

"End of the garden, north side. We've had a lot of sun lately."

Her powers flittered out, feeling the dryness in that area. The ache of the plants in her care. Tears burned the back of her eyes.

"Hey, it's okay." Christy murmured, reaching out to lay her hand flat on the newspapers between them.

"You're going through too much. You're doing better than I thought."

Her brow twitched as she put her hand on top of Christy's and gave it a squeeze, "What had you expected?"

"Lots of you curled in grass or in the middle of your garden for days on end. Hell, once I even imagined you growing into a tree with a note saying that you wouldn't go back to being human until Camden came home." Christy explained with a dramatic wave of her donut.

Nita admitted with some amusement bubbling, "Maybe I should do that."

"Please don't. I'm barely hanging on to my sanity. If you do that, you have to make me one, too." She paused for a moment before adding, "The Greenes are worried about you. Say that you look more and more skinny and with bags under your eyes than ever before. I see that they're right."

Nita lifted a shoulder, "I'm still eating, I promise."

They talked, getting caught up on each other's lives that they had missed in the past handful of days. Christy kept broaching the subject of the coven, but Nita wasn't ready to reopen that nest of wasps just yet.

"I'm just using them for information. Some of them have connections to the police department and get copies of their reports. After Camden's safe, I'll get back out."

Christy squirmed, "Well, is that wise? Can you?"

She nodded, "Yeah, it'll be fine."

Her best friend still looked skeptical, but she dropped it. When Christy left, the emptiness of the house gnawed at her like a dog on a bone. After tending to her garden, and having a nice, long cry over them; she visited the old Ironwood. And lost herself.

The sound of Jasper's truck coming down the drive lifted her and Belsauros from the meditative state at the trunk of the ancient tree. She breathed in the scents of wet moss, damp leaf litter, and the bark of the ageless around her. Her energies were solid. Renewed, she stood and made her way back to the house.

The tickling at the bottom of her heart started again. She frowned, looking in through the screen door to watch Jasper. He was leaning over the table. The white plastic bag stuffed with little foam boxes sat, seemingly forgotten, on the corner of the counter behind him.

As she watched, the tickling grew stronger. She could hear him humming. As soon as it clicked in her mind what was going on, what he was doing, he whirled and met her gaze. The sensation stopped.

"No," she stepped back, fingertips pressed to her sternum, where the tickle had been.

"Bellbean..." He murmured, stepping toward her.

She backed off the porch as he advanced on the screen door. Confused, Bel chattered quietly as he looked back and forth between them, standing on the steps. "Stay. Stay away."

It wasn't possible. He'd never used magic before. Not once.

"Please, let me explain."

He'd used his dogs before. So why could he...

"Panic."

The answer shot out at her like an arrow from his lips and shattered her mind. "To hell with you. Find Camden!"

"I've tried." He croaked, his face going paler with each breath. With each step, she took away from him.

"Get! Get off my land!" She bellowed, fists clenched at her sides. There was always something off about their relationship. She had a feeling about it. It was why they had such stupid fights. Why her heart wouldn't settle, but keep fluttering to one excuse or another. This underlying thing... a lie. A huge secret.

It reared up between them with growls and shredding claws, destroying what they were trying to build.

"Nita, please. Just listen to me."

"I've been listening. Always. Never… you never told me." She cursed the hot tears pouring down her cheeks. "Leave."

Jasper stared at her, shoulders curling in on him. "I don't want you to be alone. I'll sleep in the guest bedroom."

She shook her head, "No."

He strode toward her.

Nita hissed, throwing her arm wide, and a furrow fell in the ground between them. The spell she broke off him was more powerful than she thought, as he was an energy witch. It could be the reason Jasper hadn't been able to find Camden at first. What was the excuse now?

Nita hissed through her teeth, filling her lungs with rain rich air. "Why can't you find him?"

Jasper was staring at the furrow, slowly, he looked up to her. "I can't sense his energy. Not even that day in town when I laid eyes on him."

"How long have you been practicing?"

His swallow was hard, she studied his Adam's apple bob. "Since I could. I didn't really have anyone to teach me. So it's just been… fumbling until-" He broke off, his lips forming a thin line.

"Until the coven?" Something dreadful seemed to crawl all over her with the question.

He dropped his gaze, "Yeah."

"When?"

"Eighteen."

The jobs out of town he took. And the carpentry school. The ease he spoke with Martin. The act at the old Wright home had been impressive now that she looked back on it.

"Have you been talking to Martin all this time?"
He nodded.

"Get!" Her voice was a bark as the wave of dirt toppled Jasper over, sending him tumbling toward his vehicle. The scent of freshly disturbed earth filled the yard.

"Nita, be wary of him. Still! There's something-" his voice cut off as the grass slashed toward him and the earth shook threateningly.

She watched him crab walk backwards before scrambling to his feet. He opened his truck door, standing on the inside with his arms braced on the door and the hood. He was pale, like the moon.

"I'm sorry."

Those two paltry words fell as weights in her stomach. "Me too." She muttered, turning her back to him and gathering Bel in her arms.

Chapter Nineteen

She dumped the Chinese into Bel's bowl. At the table, slumped in her seat, she faded. Allowing herself a moment to feel and be still. The rejuvenation she had gathered from the old ironwood had dissipated. Her flesh burned like a sunburn while her insides were being scraped raw.

Nita had nothing more.

Before she recognized it was her phone ringing, her hand had swiped the green button and was holding it up to her ear, "Hello?"

"I think I've found something. Meet me at the address I'm sending you now."

She hung up on him, but looked at the address, anyway. Had that been Jasper's voice or Victor's? It didn't matter. She stood, "Bel, come on."

He hadn't touched the food.

The oddness of Bel not eating gently struck her. She thought much of it. Often when she was empty, he was too. Maybe he was as numb as she was at the moment and a meal was the last thing on her familiar's mind.

The address wasn't that far away. Her truck rambled into the parking lot at an old factory on the outskirts of town. Years ago, the company had moved its operations to Mexico, and nothing had ever filled the crumbling textile building. The worst of the sinkholes dodged in the golden glow of the fading sunlight, she parked near Victor Martin's sleek car.

With no one around, she walked toward the building in the fading light.

The door stood ajar, so she entered the moldy interior.

Something shot up through her shoes and into her legs, throughout her body. Bel hissed at her side, then screamed in pain. Before her gaze went black, she saw a shadow standing down the hall.

Her head was on fire.

Hollow on the inside, and flames on her brain, the rest of her was ice. Especially her hands and toes. Her tongue stuck to what tasted like burlap, and the same cloth tore into the corners of her lips and into her cheeks. Slowly, she noted an orange glow behind her eyelids.

Opening them, she looked out across the cracked concrete flooring of the old factory. From a small black wired cage, two bright eyes stared right back at her, accompanied by a bundle of fur. At least he was alive. They blinked together, and a moment of relief washed over her at the sign she had trained him to do if he was unharmed. A tiny, single paw, wave.

She turned her head slightly, chin dragging a pebble of concrete along before she could lift off it. Nita wanted to reach for it, but her arms twanged in pain and pin needles. She fingered the nylon wrapped around her wrists with pricking fingers and growled her annoyance. She wriggled her feet, noting the tight bands around her ankles too. Someone was taking enough precautions. For a normal human.

Flames flickered atop scattered metal barrels, illuminating the room.

From her prone position, Nita swept her gaze, she finally spotted the shadow. Same build and shape as the one that had been in the hall. Blinking, she tried to get a clear look at the man. For it had a man's build. Shape.

"Ah, you're awake again. I never remember how powerful those little electric spells of Vash's are until I see them in action. She must really not like you."

The feeling was mutual.

After failing to work some moisture into her mouth to peel her tongue away from the cloth, Nita glared at him. His voice had trailed off. He stared into a barrel like a fire user instead of a spirit wielder.

She tried a hum, keeping it light, a whisper as best as she could. Nita reached for the earth, the dirt and sand in the concrete and the quiet underneath. She searched for any small plant that wound its way into the building.

It was very little, but she had something.

"Your tone is magnificent, my Bell."

She had to rework his words over in her mind to decipher his mutter. Was he listening to her? The popping fires made it impossible to hear every other word. Barely understand herself.

"Save your strength. In a few moments, we'll begin."

Footfalls echoed into the room from what she assumed was a hallway. Allen entered through a wide double door in the wall farthest from them. Others followed behind him, most from the inner circle, with a few unfamiliar faces.

Once they saw her tied up, a few came to a standstill.

"I thought she said you convinced her!" Ginger cried, after overcoming her momentary freeze. She rushed over to Nita, crouched, and untied her hands.

Nita grimaced at the pops in Ginger's knees as she moved around her. She kept her eyes on Haskins and Zee, the two who had also stopped with Ginger. At least some of the coven weren't terrible kidnappers.

Half expecting he would tell Ginger to stop, Nita prepared to break herself the rest of the way out. Ginger had her wrists free, and Nita rubbed them, hissing at the pinpricks of pain as blood circulated freely to her fingertips again. The nylon ropes loosened, then slid free of her ankles and she sat up.

Ginger caught her eyes, "I'm sorry."

Nita pulled the gag from her mouth, her voice hoarse, "Why am I here?"

The old woman dropped her gaze, standing. Meandering around the barrels, she distanced herself from Martin and Nita, while still remaining in the room. Nita started a low hum again, wishing for water.

Through the pull of her tone, she sensed something useful getting closer. She smiled to herself, hiding her face in her hands as she pretended to wipe herself down. Only, what she sensed coming wasn't the first to enter. A little forklift carried a large plastic container that some used as an extra water reservoir on their land. They placed it halfway between two barrels, near Ash.

As soon as that forklift left, another entered, carrying something that aided a certain element. All except fire. The earth getting closer finally made it. The large bin spilled out onto the concrete near her and Bel. She met her brother's dark eyes.

Purple half moons made deep shadows under his eyelashes, his cheeks sunk into his teeth, his thick, black hair hung lanky and untethered about his face, making him look even more skeletal. She scurried to her feet, bolting toward him, slip-tripping over the mound of dirt.

He shook his head slightly, his gaze boring into hers.

Nita froze. Her throat and eyes burning with tears of relief. Of not understanding.

Camden held up a single finger, then created a fist.

Wait in silence. Hold ground.

It was a silly thing he and Jasper would mimic as kids. Pretend they were military or cops. They'd spent hours looking up hand signals forces used to communicate. She familiarized herself with a few to prevent ambush or traps.

He backed away, disappearing out the opening he had entered through, and her heart ripped from her body to follow him. She swallowed, sinking down into the dirt as her knees tried to knock together. Several forklifts brought in more rich soil.

She slid down to rescue her raccoon, holding Bel in her lap on top of the mound.

Seventeen of them, only one of her. Her eyes trailed to the forklift operators. Some walking in after their job was done, and spotted Randy. Eighteen of them. Mr. Wright was not among them.

"Now then. Let's drink some water so that we can all be ready. No parched throats to start this beautiful collaboration!" As he spoke, his eyes never strayed from her. His hands clasped behind his back, his lips twisted to the left a bit. "Nita darling, if you would be so kind. Please leave that rabid thing in the dirt."

Bel and she hissed simultaneously, and out of the corner of her eye she saw a flash of teeth and her brother's shoulders pull back as his head raised. The people scurrying around with water bottles paused at her mound, then threw a bottle up to her.

He was ready.

For what, though?

Nita drank down all she could of the water at one go. Then asked with a wipe of her mouth on her wrist, "Why? What are you doing?"

"We. WE, my dear Bell, are going to end all our suffering."

Nita glanced around. As he spoke to her, the kidnapped ones were bracketing the witches. Camden and another that she didn't recognize, but something emanated earth from her, like home, neared her and planted themselves on each side of her pile of dirt.

Zee stood before her, his eyes filled with affection, and she recognized his deep love for the strange woman.

She glanced back at Martin, "Seems like many have suffered because of you. How do you propose to end suffering when you so freely give it?"

Martin seemed to recoil, the smile on his face fell, his jaw slackened. Then it was back, as if he never slipped, "We must sacrifice for the greater good."

"What sacrifices?" She motioned to her brother, "Why did you take them?"

"To ready them for what we're about to do."

She ground her teeth, and she spoke through them, "Which is?"

"We are creating our own realm, my dear. Bloodline members without magic still possess the talent, the tones, but cannot hear them. Tone deaf, if you will. I created a spell where they are no longer incapable of using their tones. And they, as magical purities, are the base for our new realm."

None of that made sense. She was unaware of the possibility of someone without magical abilities being transformed into having access to it. To use their tones to reach the magical cores and streams around the world.

He kept on.

His voice droned in her ears, and she looked at Camden out of the corner of her eye. He was watching her. He made a fist at his side. Still hold.

"... now that we have a Bell, technically two, we have the central, most powerful tone we need to create a world for us! For witches only! No more persecution. No more hiding! We can live freely! Envision the potential for creation if we were unleashed!"

"Another planet, apparently," Nita muttered, crossing her arms over her chest. She still experienced a sensation of coldness from all his talk, after lying on the unforgiving concrete for an unknown duration.

He laughed, "Yes! Although, after we're through, there won't be a need." He held out a hand to her, "Come. Join me. Don't you want to live freely? To help those that will truly appreciate your gifts? To not hide in your home, on your land forever?"

"Nah. I'm good. Thanks though." Nita shook her head.

Zee made a strangling noise in his throat, casting a wide-eyed glance at her.

She sensed it then, that power. A swirl of dirt erupted up with her as she was hauled off her feet and tossed to Victor. Nita couldn't hear him humming or singing. Allen used his magic in silence, apparently? She would have to figure that out later.

At present, Victor held her in a tango-like embrace, and her skin seemed ready to crawl away.

"You have a perfectly fine earth witch in Zee, why do you need me?"

"I need a Bell. The tones you are born with are perfect. Perfect harmony. Perfect accompaniment. Your bloodline ties all the tones together, weaves them until the most beautiful and pure magic lifts into existence." His voice echoed through the darkness, curling into the shadows and erupting back to her.

"Hate to tell you this after all your careful planning, but my tones only work when I'm willin'. And I ain't willin'."

"Oh?" Victor's grip on her tightened two-fold.

She saw newcomers making their way into the room just over his shoulder. Two were frog walked in front of three others. The blonde curls of one and the build of the other made Nita's heart sink to her stomach. Her brother's low battle cry behind her sounded weak.

The thugs made Christy and Jasper fall on their knees behind and to the side of Camden.

"Whatever it is, Nit, don't do it!" Christy spat, then grunted as her captor backhanded her.

"Touch her again and I'll bring the whole building down on us." Nita screeched, throwing her weight to one side and the other, but his grip was iron.

"You can't do that on your own," Victor murmured in her ear.

"Wanna bet?" Nita smiled in his face, "Try me."

"They'll be dead before you finish. They'll die if you don't work with us. With me." Victor cupped her cheek.

She tore away from him, only to be bound by some invisible, cutting force. Her arms pinned to her sides. Her feet kicked to regain the concrete underneath them as she rose.

Victor took her in his arms again, smiling sweetly, "Think of the lives you will save. Upcoming generations of witches won't face threats or secrecy. Think of that. Won't you give them a chance? Won't you give those that live now a choice?"

"I don't have a choice here."

"You do, in a way." Vash growled from across the room. "Death and those of all you care for, or join us in this."

Her ultimate intention was to use a boulder to crush that woman. Or maybe choke her with some vines. Fill every one of her holes with dirt. Something.

"That's like asking an either or question and the answer you get is 'yes'." Nita rolled her eyes at Vashiana. Then she glanced back at her brother.

Camden widened his eyes.

Just what was that supposed to mean?

She glared at him.

He jerked his chin.

That narrowed it down to two options. Either stop provoking and stalling or begin working. So she canted her head to the side. She wanted to strangle him, as he just shrugged.

Jasper looked between the two of them. She witnessed his shoulders lift and then fall. Had he just sighed at them? Bastard.

"Let's get started, shall we? We've wasted enough time." Victor grabbed Nita's hand and continued speaking, "Follow my lead."

The team of witches began their tones. Deep within their bodies and then flowing out. The tones were everywhere at first, then they began to mingle and weave together.

Her magic stretched for theirs. The world around her melted into a melody. Nothing existed but the spell.

Swept away in the moment, Nita began her tone. It caressed theirs, pulling it down or up, molding it into perfection. Magic flowed freely. The witches of the room created their own pool. All elements. All powers and tones united as one.

"That's it." Victor sang with a wide grin.

Wait. No. No.

Nita tried to pull back. The magic swept her further in. It was wrong. This had to be wrong. The magic must know this was wrong.

She turned, using all her weight to smash her fist into Victor. Finally, her tone broke, dragging the others away from perfection. Victor's stopped altogether as he roared.

Plan? None.

Nita stepped back, the magic pulling her one way and her desire to flee pulling her another. The image of two wolves inside her flashed as she attempted to fend off Victor's hands. The pool of magic that had gathered shimmered visibly. Even those that had no power watched it.

Some were still singing.

The pool toppled her inside like a lake monster grabbing its next meal. Magic swarmed her, needing the base, the anchor she provided. She couldn't breathe. Wildly, she tore at the magic, ripping it away from her only to be swallowed by it again.

There was no coming up for air. Air was there, ripping the rest of it from her lungs. Her throat felt like it was going to close. Her vision tunneled. She turned her eyes, trying to speak, to sing, to do anything as she looked for something. Zee. Sweat popped out on his brow and ran like rivulets down his temples and into his eyes.

His tone was off. His anchor was weak.

A hand sank into her flesh.

No. It grabbed her. It felt like it sank into her. It pulled. She was ripping in two.

Then that tone. That eerie tone erupted from outside the circle of coven members toward the elements. Underneath, her heart tickled.

She knew.

The hand ripped at her again and she looked to see Camden's hands on her arm, hauling her toward him. His magic was weak, but his tone. His tone was such a soothing presence. She reached out to him and she was out of the pool. Onto the floor she splat, Camden too weak to catch her.

"Finish!" Victor roared.

Nita was too busy filling her lungs and making sure her throat worked to be bothered by him.

Until Camden jerked, eyes wide, and his face grew ghostly pale.

"Finish!" Victor cried again.

Nita wanted to weep. She noticed how Victor had control over her brother amidst the magic. His spirit was desperately fighting the abuse, but losing. Until Camden softened. His body relaxed into a sitting pose. A smile spread over his lips as his color returned. The hold on his spirit dissipated like a light mist in sunlight.

Jasper was there. Camden grinned more and the earth behind them shook. Others were engaged in some activity. Moving around a lot. Some of their elements doing odd things.

The tones broke off one by one.

"No!" Victor screamed, "Focus!"

With her raw throat, there would not be a decent tone coming from her, anyway. No anchor. No Bell to keep the others in tune.

The witches were taken away from their duty. Distracted by the kidnapped, or knocked out one by one.

Nita scrambled to her feet, managing a four-legged to three-legged run at Victor and tackling him down. She straddled him, drawing back her fist as she used her weight again. Her fist slammed into the concrete beside his head as he dodged. Each bone snapped. Her wrist and arm jarred. She screamed out the pain. It lanced up her arm in regular intervals. She rubbed her fist, its fingers hanging oddly, and she swallowed back a sob.

Victor's hands clamped around head, covering her mouth, fingers pressing into her cheekbones and jaw. He ripped her off him, slamming her to the concrete. He snarled in her face, "I'll shatter you if you don't work, little Bell."

She hugged her broken hand to her sternum. Thrashing her legs wildly, she unbalanced him. A knee to his ribcage had him toppling off her to his side. Scrambling away, she kicked his chest with both feet as if trying to run on him. Then her foot contacted his face, and she perceived the crack underneath before a spurt of blood erupted under her boot.

"I just shattered your nose. You won't work either, fucker." She slammed the hell of her boot into his face.

Air whooshed out of her lungs. Nothing tightened around her until every bone in her body felt like it was about to break into a million tiny pieces. Something flashed beside her and she could breathe again. Move again.

Jasper was on top of Allen, punching and kicking.

Nita shook her head. For such powerful witches, they couldn't stand a fist to them.

All around her were bodies. Twisting. Pummeling. Thrashing.

Camden. He grinned at her, wiping a dab of blood out from under his nose. The next instant, she sobbed at how boney he had become. Somehow, she got to him. Her arms trembled as she wrapped around him. His heartbeat was strong against her arms and cheek.

"How?"

"Part of his conditioning of us was awakening some magic. I remembered some lessons that Grandma gave you. Made do. Some others could remember little things here and there, too. Kinda taught each other as best we could." Camden's voice was weak, raw, like he'd been swallowing nails.

They held each other for a while. Letting the witch world of District Two crumble around them.

"We have company."

Nita looked toward the door at Zee's raspy voice. She smiled as Megs sauntered in, fireballs in her hands and singing like a canary. Many more followed her in. She recognized the whole Stalcup clan and the Littles.

"How did they know?" Nita asked, her eyes wide as the so-called calvary arrived.

Megs hugged her brother tightly after incinerating another member.

"Had Randy call. You know this old place still has a landline?" Camden joked, giving her a wink.

Within moments, the coven stilled. Not a single tone heard.

Nita looked around. Panic clawing up her throat. "Where is he?!"

Chapter Twenty

After a search of the premises, Nita noticed his car was gone once she hit the pavement from the musty factory. She slumped against the crumbling brick wall. Cursing their luck.

At least they had the rest of the coven leaders. Just not the smarmy Victor Martin. The worst of them all.

She headed back inside, hugging her shattered hand to her chest. Nita watched in horror at a battle she didn't think would take so long. It took three of them to force the beast, Vashiana, down. Vash sneered in her direction. Nita kicked her in the face, creating a matching set of blood spurts on her boots. She wanted to do more, but Zee shook his head. Another time.

What was Victor capable of by himself? The thought crossed her mind as she reined herself in, picking at Vash's blood on her boot with a stick.

She didn't want to think about the answers that jumped around her thoughts. Kidnap others. Worm his way into another district's coven. Come back in a few minutes to finish the job with his army of supporters. She returned to the main room. Her bones were like a fine china plate. Ready to crack at any touch. Her fingers and wrist were useless. Bel was going to have to perform double duty until her broken bones healed.

Ginger was healing some others under the watchful eyes of Megs and Randy.

Nita nodded at Megs and tried a smile. The fire witch matched her nod with one of her own and another weak smile.

She went back to Camden's side, sitting beside him on the now leveled dirt. Upon further observation, she saw that he had used it to sandblast a few coven members. She didn't remember that lesson. Nita wished she could take her boots off and wriggle her toes in the loose earth. "You should get looked at."

"Speak for yourself. Your hand looks like Draculas from the old black and white movie." Camden said in a weak voice as he leaned heavily against her.

Nita snorted, "Glad to have you back."

The Littles, Stalcups and Megs' family said they would clean up and take care of the leaders and their lackeys. Nita listened to Zee apologize over and over again. Ginger on the other hand, just worked on healing the harmed without saying much about her participation in the mess.

She wondered what would happen to the coven. Would they choose a leader from outside, or from within? She should really study up on coven ways. Then again, she was out now. No more coven. She got what she wanted from them.

Camden yawned, "I can't wait to go home."

Nita smiled, her heart grew a size or two larger. Then something tickled just under it. She looked up and met Jasper's gaze.

"Forgive me enough to let me be family again?" He asked after a few sheepish shuffles of his feet.

Camden huffed, "Always family."

Jasper shook his head, "I need it from Bel-Nita."

Camden's eyes on her seared. She lifted a shoulder, "You're my brother's best friend."

The way his face fell should have pulled her heartstrings. But at that moment, it was already too broken. She had nothing else to shatter.

Turning to Camden, she wrapped her arms around her brother, letting her heart heal. He was safe. In her care. The mental nagging about needing to find Victor, she shoved to the back. Her family was her focus now. Her center.

"Let's go home." She nodded, about to put her hand down to push herself up, then she remembered as moving it from his shoulder caused shoots of pain up and down her arm. Grunting, she pushed up with her other one, ignoring Jasper's offer of assistance. She wrapped her good arm around Camden's middle.

The siblings leaned on one another, picking their way off the flat-top mound and toward the outside. Dew smelled better on grass than on concrete and pavement. But it was still a welcome familiarity and was far better than the mildew of the factory. Jasper's scuffling shuffle followed them, echoing in the corridors and making her ears itch once they were out.

Camden leaned, steering them toward the passenger door of her truck. "You can't drive with that in this old thing."

"I can."

"Not going to happen." Jasper stated, opening the driver's side and jumping in like the graceful ass he was.

Camden opened their door, and no one made a move. She raised a brow at him, and he motioned for her to get in. She balked, ice gripping her heart.

"You can't open the door, anyway," stated the driver, swiping at his torn bottom lip with a thumb before wiping the blood off on his shirt.

She looked at the truck bed, filled with empty plant crates and hauled herself up into the seat and slid over.

Jasper reached over her, buckling her in without a word before his hands returned to the wheel.

"Either of ya gonna fill me in on what happened between you two?" Cam asked over the screech of the truck door as he slammed it closed.

Nita sucked in a breath, stealing a glance. Witnessing the ticking jaw and how his hands shook when he turned the ignition, she snorted. "We fucked, that's it."

Camden positioned himself against the door and seat, allowing him a clearer view of both of them. His dark gaze flicking from one to the other of them. "Told you she'd be pissed you kept it from her."

"It wasn't like I meant to!"

"You knew?!" Nita glared at her brother, then rolled her eyes, "Well, of course you did." She really wanted to fold her arms for a proper sulk, but she couldn't. The truck bounced and squeaked over the potholes. Jasper hitting each and every one. "Can't you see them?"

"I can, but there's so damn many I'm taking the ones that aren't so deep or big." Jasper retorted, finally pulling out onto the road.

"Messing up my shocks."

"What shocks?" Jasper shook his head.

From the corner of her eye, Nita noticed something and turned to see Camden with a big grin. "What?"

"I can't believe I'm gonna say this, but I missed it."

"Missed what?" Nita asked, but she already knew the answer. Bickering.

"My best bud and my little sister fighting like the married couple they'll eventually be."

Nita twisted, halted from putting a proper finger in his face by the seatbelt, "You said to stay away from him!"

"Yeah, look how well that turned out. Said that just so you might... I dunno. Start dating, finally. Hell, you never did anything else I said." Camden whimpered like a toddler, his head lolling back on the window. "I'm so tired."

Nita placed her good hand on his knee and gave it a squeeze. All thoughts of whatever he'd said before gone as she studied his pale face, the skin-and-bones appearance. "I'll fix you some broth, and then you can sleep. 'Kay?"

"Yeah."

A week later, Nita stared at the beautiful blooms. Pots holding them filled her kitchen table, the counters, and some were precariously in chairs. Each pot was the same. The flowers they held were as different as could be.

"This is getting ridiculous. How are we supposed to eat?!" Camden huffed, as he stopped at the bottom of the stairs. Bel was beside him, seeming to share the same thought.

"I dunno. Take-out?" Nita suggested weakly, feeling her temples throb with her pulse.

"You'll get mobbed in town."

Nita sighed, sitting on the floor beside the stove, the only bare surface in the kitchen. "Is he trying to make more work for me?"

Her brother picked his way over to kneel and place a hand on her shoulder. "At least they can be planted. He could've sent over cut ones that'd die in a day or two." The dark circles under his eyes were softer. His skin wasn't as pale, slowly returning to its healthy tan after good meals and plenty of rest.

"I'd kill him."

"Yeah, he knows."

She eyed her brother, "You tell him to do this?"

Camden just gave her a cheshire grin and stood. "I'm taking the truck. Chicken okay?"

"Yeah."

Nita barely resisted the urge to follow him like a puppy. She hated seeing him go. Part of her feared he would never return. But she knew he would. Life had to get back to normal.

Once the old truck cranked and he cleared the driveway, Nita stared around her kitchen again. "This ain't normal." Bel chattered and growled his agreement, slapping a daffodil head out of his face.

In half an hour, by the time Camden got back with food, she'd hauled most of the flowers out to her greenhouse. It would have been a lot quicker if she'd allowed Ginger to heal her hand that day. The cast itched, and she wondered if she'd set the bones right before she wrapped it herself. She'd figure it out later.

They ate and together they started trying to figure out where each one would thrive on their property. They'd just finished planting the first fifteen when a vehicle turned in at the head of the driveway.

"I swear if it's another delivery..."

Camden chuckled, brushing his hands off before wiping the rest off on his jeans, "What will you do? Go find him and choke him? He might be into that kinda kink."

She refused to look at her brother, he'd be too satisfied. Nita walked around the greenhouse to the driveway. Jasper's truck stopped in front of her. Her blood boiled, the earth under her bare feet trembling in readiness.

"I'm sorry!" He said with his hands up after he slammed his truck door closed. "I did it online and ordered one of every live plant they had in stock by accident! I swear!"

"Sheeeit… what kind of messed up option is that for a florist website to have?!" Camden laughed.

"I'm still not going to forgive you."

"Aw come on, sis." Camden rolled his eyes, patted her shoulder, "You two've been driving me crazy all our lives with the flirting and ooglin' eyes. He's a witch. Perfect. You two can make all powerful spiritual earth benders."

"The dominant magic always wins." Nita reminded him.

"Earth?" Camden said with a lifted shoulder, amusement brightening his face.

Jasper smiled, "That's fine with me."

Nita rolled her eyes, "We're a loooong way from talkin' about kids, dumbasses." She felt like she was surrounded by idiots again. And it sent her heart to flying even as tears of happiness burned the back of her eyes. Nothing made her happier than Camden's smile and Jasper's chuckle. Even if she was still mad at him. A little.

The coven newspaper arrived the next month. Nothing in it mentioned the mess Victor had caused in the mountains. Not a single advert about a new world, either. Nita glanced over the highlights in the thin paper. No turmoil. Everything printed was normal in a way that scared her.

Why had they sent her a paper when she wasn't part of the coven anymore?

She flexed her fingertips around the cast and grimaced at the little shoots of pain still attached to any movement. For the past two weeks, she'd wondered if the doctor set her bones right after Jasper made her go.

"Hey."

Nita glanced up from scanning the final few pages of the newspaper, "Hey."

Jasper's lips twisted in a wry smile, "I got you something."

Despite being infrequent, his gifts seemed like an attempt to make amends for the past two months. She knew he had been enchanted by someone from the coven. Some of the old nagging feelings still got to her. He'd tire of her and leave. Someone new would come into town and take him from her. He'd lie to her or keep something important from her again. She wasn't sure which thoughts were worse.

He opened his hand, a silver chain dropped from his fingers, dangling a pendant in front of her eyes. A twisted trunk of silver wires with equally twisting branches, and jasper, green amethyst, and amazonite twinkled like gemstone leaves. "It's pretty." She held out her hand, and he deposited the pendant and the chain in her palm.

"Thought of you immediately." He paused before asking, "Want me to put it on you?"

Nita nodded and stood, giving him back the necklace as she pulled her mess of hair over her shoulder. Goosebumps rose over her flesh as he fastened the clasp, his knuckles brushing the back of her neck. Then his lips were on hers, and she melted into him. The metal and gems of the necklace made the skin prickle between her collarbones.

She knew, deep down, that this was right. She and Jasper were right for one another. Despite the negative thoughts and secrets, she couldn't deny her feelings. Still, she didn't believe she truly knew his feelings. And if she had the capacity to forgive him or trust him. Nita closed her eyes, his warmth wrapped around her. The solace that only he possessed comforted her, enveloping her like submerging into a warm bath.

Her phone rang, breaking the moment. Nita bit back a retort as Jasper cursed under his breath.

"Maybe I should've let you keep the brick." He muttered, letting her go so she could dig it out of her chair. "I've got to run up to see Gus and Wade, anyway. I'll bring back dinner, they want you to have some of whatever they're cooking tonight."

She gave him a quick peck and answered the phone without looking at the screen once he was in his truck. "Bell's Herbs and Spices."

As the new customer began a long explanation, Nita smiled. Normal. Things were finally back to normal.

Did you love The Bell Earth Witch? Then you should read I'm No Hero by Sam Wicker!

I'm No Hero is an epic fantasy romance about a reluctant heroine changing her family's status and bringing the gods to heel.

Read more at https://carderwickerwriting.com

About the Author

Sam Wicker is a small towner, married to a loving and the most supportive husband ever. They have a fur baby named Kona, a rescue, and the most adorable boxer-bulldog-cur mutt ever. Sam's always wanted to write stories full of romance, real people doing fantastical things, and animals that awe or make you go 'awww!' She hopes that her stories inspire those suffering from anxiety and gives them a place to escape to.

Be sure to follow her on Instagram, YouTube, and Twitch @WriterSamWicker

Website: https://carderwickerwriting.com

www.ingramcontent.com/pod-product-compliance
Lightning Source LLC
Chambersburg PA
CBHW061123310726
48974CB00002B/656